THIS IS US

HELEN MCGINN

First published in Great Britain in 2022 by Boldwood Books Ltd.

Copyright © Helen McGinn, 2022

Cover Design: Alice Moore Design

Cover Photography: Shutterstock

A CIP catalogue record for this book is available from the British Library.

Paperback ISBN 978-1-80280-603-8

Large Print ISBN 978-1-80280-599-4

Hardback ISBN 978-1-80280-598-7

Ebook ISBN 978-1-80280-596-3

Kindle ISBN 978-1-80280-597-0

Audio CD ISBN 978-1-80280-604-5

MP3 CD ISBN 978-1-80280-601-4

Digital audio download ISBN 978-1-80280-595-6

Boldwood Books Ltd
23 Bowerdean Street
London SW6 3TN

For my family

PROLOGUE

Stella powered her way along the length of the pool, her arms and legs moving rhythmically, her focus on taking a breath between strokes. The sound of water whooshed past her ears, temporarily shutting out the noise of the rest of the world.

Yet as much as she tried to swim away from the thoughts in her head, she couldn't escape them.

The way he had looked at her that awful night as they'd stood in the kitchen, facing each other across the marble island. Not with love, as he'd done for the last decade. This was different. In fact, it was indifference. He'd looked at her like he simply didn't care.

She barely recognised the woman in the scene playing in her mind, begging him to explain what was happening.

He'd just shrugged his shoulders, his eyes giving nothing away. 'I don't know. I just don't feel like I used to.' He'd paused. 'About you.'

The words had hit her with force, leaving her gasping for

'That's the problem.' His words had felt like daggers, each one breaking her skin. He'd sighed, picked up his bag from the floor and slung it over his shoulder. 'I have to go. I'm staying elsewhere tonight. I'll call you tomorrow.'

Stella was so stunned, she couldn't speak. She had heard the front door shut and looked around the room as if searching for clues. Her gaze had rested on the table, set for breakfast the next day. The silence was deafening.

Stella swam on, her broken heart pounding in her chest.

1

'Are you back in time to eat this evening?' Stella called out to her husband as she ushered the children towards the door.

'I'll cook tonight.'

Stella looked up to see Simon standing at the top of the stairs, tying his tie. 'Are you sure?' She pulled an oversized hoodie over her head before gathering her chestnut hair back from her face and tying it loosely with a hairband from her wrist.

'I'm out for lunch, remember. The one you've managed to wriggle out of.'

'I didn't wriggle out of it, it's just you're so much better with them than me and, to be honest, I find them so, well...'

'Boring? I know, but without investors like Annabel Collins and her insufferable husband, we won't have a business, so we don't have a choice, I'm afraid. Well, one of us doesn't.' He dropped down to tie a shoelace, smiling at her.

'I know, thank you. I owe you.' She blew him a kiss. Those kind of business lunches were not her thing. 'See you later, darling. Right, Max, have you got your lunch box?'

'Check.' Her son held his lunch box aloft, grinning.

Stella turned from her son to the twins, their matching blonde curls both defying the hairbands she'd hastily tried to tie them back with. 'How about you two?'

Millie stuffed books into her bag, while Isla stood impatiently by the door, holding hers.

'I've got mine,' said Isla. 'Come on, Millie, you're going to make us late. Again.' Isla rolled her eyes at her oblivious sister.

'Get a wriggle on, Millie.' Stella prodded Millie gently. 'I'll be in the car.'

'Shotgun,' Max cried, as he made his way out of the door.

'I don't know why you even bother saying that when you go in the front every morning,' said Millie as she tried to close her rucksack.

'Whatever, loser,' Max retorted.

'And why do you always get to go in the front anyway?' cried Isla.

'Because I'm the eldest, duh. Double figures.' Max held his hands up towards her showing all ten fingers and thumbs, smiling sarcastically at her.

'Still a moron, though,' Isla shot back.

'That's enough, you two. Come on please, I can't be late this morning.'

They walked down the path and out of the freshly painted white side gate onto the quiet London street. The house stood on a corner, a handsome three-storey Victorian building overlooking a large common already busy with runners, dog walkers and parents and children on the school run. The morning was crisp, the air cool on Stella's face. A February sun hung in the cloudless sky.

The short car journey was one of her favourite parts of the day because for those ten minutes the children had no choice but to answer her questions about school, friends or plans for the weekend. Even if she had to drag an answer out of them, Stella was determined to keep them talking. She remembered how the toddler years seemed to go on forever, but now Max was ten years old and the twins eight, time was passing at frightening speed.

Once they'd been dispatched at the school gate, Stella put on the radio. Hearing the familiar first few bars to one of her favourite karaoke songs, she smiled to herself as she turned up the volume. Glancing at the clock, she decided she had just enough time to go for her weekly swim before hitting the office and by the time she reached the chorus, Stella was singing at the top of her voice.

The team weren't due to sit down together until 10 a.m. for a general catch-up before a full day of meetings and tastings. Swimming was the only thing she did that could be classed as exercise, aside from walking the dog, which, to be fair, Simon did more than her, and she knew it would set her up for the day ahead.

She'd always loved swimming as a child and was one of the first in her class to swim a length underwater. Having spent years being picked last for netball matches, she'd never forgotten the thrill of discovering something she was good at doing.

When she swam, Stella's mind usually cleared, but on this particular morning, as she moved her long limbs through the water, there was something niggling her and no matter how much she tried, she couldn't shake it off. Simon's breeziness that morning hadn't sat right. Was it the way he'd offered to do the investor lunch alone? But that wasn't unusual. Perhaps it was the fact he'd offered to cook later? OK, so that didn't happen that often, she thought, but he was more than capable of throwing something together.

Then it hit her. The tie.

She'd never seen that tie before – pink and white checks.

Normally, he wore dark-coloured ties, always plain, never patterned. But this one had looked quite different, not like his usual choice at all.

Stella swam on, trying to focus on her day ahead, but the image of her husband at the top of the stairs tying that unfamiliar tie played over and over in her head. By the time she had finished her allotted twenty minutes in the fast lane, her heart was beating fast. Surely, there was a simple explanation, she told herself.

As she showered and dressed, Stella again tried to steer her thoughts back to the day's meetings. She knew there was a planning session for the book they'd been working on in the diary, followed by a photo shoot for an interview she'd given to one of the Sunday supplements. Normally, she'd be buzzing with excitement, planning outfits and answers in her head. But, instead, all she could think about was that damn tie.

* * *

The day she'd met Simon properly, in a soulless conference room at a supermarket head office, he'd arrived for their meeting before her. Stella remembered watching him as he'd unfurled his tall frame from his chair at the end of the table when she walked into the room. He'd extended his hand, smiling warmly. 'Hello, I'm Simon. Pleased to meet you.'

'Yes, I know who you are.' Stella took in his features as they proceeded to shake hands for what she felt was a little longer than necessary, his blue eyes fixed on hers. 'Stella.' She had smiled tightly. His hair was dark, his skin tanned and, from what she could make out from the sweeping glance she'd given him when he'd walked in, the body under his smart suit trim and toned.

At the time, Stella had been single – happily so – for a while, following a couple of long relationships that hadn't come to anything. She certainly wasn't looking for a new one, rather she was enjoying doing what she wanted, when she wanted. Which mostly involved seeing friends on a Friday and Saturday night before spending the rest of the weekend recovering in time to face the week ahead. The fact that she could go to the cinema any time she chose to or read a book all day at the weekend if she wanted to felt liberating.

But then Simon came along, so different from anyone she'd ever known before. A little older too, in his mid-thirties. For a start, he was far more mature than most of the boys she'd grown up with from school or met at university, most of whom were still basically giant children, much as she loved them.

Simon had been brought in to streamline the business, according to her boss, so although she'd seen him around the office, she'd spent much of her time trying to avoid him. But from that first proper meeting, he found increasingly tenuous reasons to arrange further ones with her and after half a dozen more, he'd asked her out for a drink after work.

Stella had spent longer than her usual few minutes picking out something to wear that particular morning. In the end, she'd gone for a loosely cut black crepe trouser suit with a black and white striped tee underneath, completing the look with box-fresh white trainers. She'd hoped to look casual but cool, but on glancing at herself in the mirror as she left, she suddenly felt self-conscious. Too late, she'd thought, as she added a slick of lipstick to her face and grabbed her bag on her way out.

They'd met in a hotel bar in the centre of town, not too flash but smart enough to feel like a treat. She guessed he'd brought a few people here before by the way he was greeted by the Italian barman, but made a conscious decision to try not to overthink it. Over the course of two dirty martinis, Simon had asked Stella about her family and she'd told him about growing up in Oxford with her sister, being raised by their father after her mother died unexpectedly young following a brief, cruel illness. 'Cancer,' said Stella, tears coming to her eyes. 'Sorry, must be the gin.' She pointed at her empty glass, smiling to show she was OK, really.

'Please don't apologise. I'm so sorry, that must have been very hard for you.'

Stella nodded. 'Well, I was only six years old, so I honestly don't remember that much about it. Caroline, my sister, was quite a bit older than me, so I think it was tougher for her.'

'Tough for both of you. And your father, is he still...?'

'Yes, he's very much alive. He lives in London with his wife, my stepmother, Susie. She's lovely.' Stella smiled at the thought of them. They really were her eternal cheerleaders. 'Anyway, how about you? Tell me about your family?'

Simon had signalled to the barman's attention, then turned back to Stella. 'My mother died when I was quite young too and I haven't seen my father for years. We sort of fell out quite a long time ago.' Simon looked at his empty glass on the bar. 'Unfortunately, he's a bit too fond of the bottle.'

Stella had reached for his hand. 'Oh, I'm so sorry. That's so sad. Have you tried...'

Simon shook his head a little. 'Yes, I have. But you can't really reason with an alcoholic.' He shrugged his shoulders and smiled a little.

'I'm sorry, I didn't realise...'

'Please don't worry, it's just how it is. But listen, enough of the sad stories for tonight, shall we talk about something else?'

There was so much more Stella wanted to ask him but now clearly wasn't the time. 'Of course.' Stella lifted her empty glass and looked him in the eye. 'Actually, I can't have another one of these or I'll be under the table. How about you walk me to the tube station instead?'

'Or how about we get a taxi back to mine?' Simon had held her gaze and she had felt herself blushing. *Stella, you're not a teenager*, she told herself. He laughed and for a moment she thought she must have said the words out loud.

'Um, that would be...' Before she could finish her sentence, he leaned across and kissed her gently on the mouth. The room seemed to tilt a little, though she couldn't be sure if that was down to Simon or the gin.

The next morning, she'd woken up in his bed, the flat morning light giving away the early hour. She'd turned over, relieved to see Simon still sleeping. The heavy cotton cover of the duvet had been shoved down, revealing the toned torso she'd imagined. She swept her eyes over him before creeping out of bed and heading downstairs in search of the kitchen.

The house – a house! – was like something out of a magazine from the Sunday newspapers, all stripped wooden floorboards and painted white throughout. The furniture was sparse but expensive, their discarded clothes across the sofa reminding her they hadn't even made it to the bed before making love for the first time the night before.

She picked up the empty pizza boxes from the table (she'd eaten pizza, naked!) and carried them into the kitchen, placing them neatly on the side before finding a glass in one of the kitchen cupboards and downing a glass of water as she waited for the kettle to boil.

Standing by the window, she had gazed out on to the back of the unfamiliar houses on the other side, the hour too early for any signs of life. A moment later, she felt arms around her waist, the warmth of Simon's body against her back.

'Well, I don't know how I'm going to keep a straight face in our next meeting now I know quite what you're capable of.' His voice was soft in her ear.

'You're not the only one,' she laughed. She turned to look at him, wishing she'd splashed water on her face before he'd come in.

'You look so beautiful.' He smiled, taking her face in his hands.

'Oh, please. I didn't even take my make-up off last night.' Stella put her own hands over her eyes.

He gently removed them. 'Actually, now you come to mention it, you do look a little off colour. I think perhaps it's better if you don't go in to work today.'

'But...' Stella had barely had a day off in her entire time at the company.

'And actually, I'm not feeling so good either.' He laughed gently, then kissed her.

'Yes, definitely peaky. In fact, I think I might need to lie down.' Stella couldn't quite believe what she was saying. This was not like her *at all*.

Returning home early the following morning, she'd sneaked in as quietly as she could, hoping not to wake her flatmate.

'Morning, you dirty stop-out,' called out a voice from behind a closed door.

'Morning, Bridget.' Stella had winced. She turned to hear the door open, her friend's face appearing with half-closed eyes. Bridget definitely wasn't a morning person, something Stella had known from the very first time they'd met when sharing a house as students, years before. They'd bonded over a love of really strong coffee and, in those days, a shared cigarette for breakfast, and had been best friends ever since.

'Honestly, one date and you stay over.' Bridget shook her head slowly.

'I know, couldn't help it. He's gorgeous.' Stella laughed.

'Seriously, you have no standards. Now, make yourself useful and put the coffee on,' said Bridget in a loud whisper.

'Why are you whispering?'

'No reason,' said Bridget, airily.

Just then, a man's voice called out from Bridget's bedroom. 'Did someone say coffee?'

Stella's eyes widened.

It was Bridget's turn to wince, before calling back over her shoulder: 'Don't push your luck. There's a very nice cafe on the corner.' She looked back at Stella and squeezed her eyes shut.

'Oh my god, did you bring back a total stranger last night?' Stella whispered before putting her hands over her mouth to stop the laugh that was threatening to burst out.

'Oh, shut up. You can't talk.' Bridget came out of her room, closing the door behind her, ushering Stella into their tiny kitchen.

'Mine wasn't a total stranger.' Stella raised an eyebrow at her flatmate.

'Practically! Anyway, whatever. Tell me about him then?' Bridget sat at the small table, watching Stella as she filled the coffee machine with water and reached for a couple of mugs.

'Well, you know I was worried he'd be a bit...' Stella searched for the word.

'Boring?'

'Did I say boring?' They'd discussed the impending drinks just a few nights before, Stella voicing her concerns that Simon and she would discover they had nothing but work in common. 'You're right, I think I did. I mean, he just seemed too good to be true, like there had to be a downside. No one's that good-looking without there being a downside, right?'

Bridget rolled her eyes, then laughed her loud, throaty laugh.

'I know what you mean, but honestly, despite being way more grown up than anyone I've ever had drinks with before... Seriously, we went to the most beautiful cocktail bar. Proper drinks, big fat olives. There was even a bloody piano player. We did talk about work a bit, but mostly we talked ourselves, about our lives. Well, mine, when I think about it.' Stella paused. 'He asked a lot of questions.'

'What about him?' Bridget signalled to Stella to pass her the glass of water Stella had just poured herself. 'Gasping.'

'Now you mention it, that's the funny thing. I asked him just as many questions, but he always seemed to turn the conversation back to me.'

'Maybe he was just being polite?'

'I know he's an only child, he moved down here from somewhere on the west coast of Scotland when he was a teenager apparently and he's worked in London ever since.'

'Accent?'

'Gentle lilt. Lovely, actually.'

'What else?' Bridget took a last gulp of water and put the empty glass on the table.

'His mother died when he was young, so we have that in common. Not that we talked about it much, he obviously didn't want to go into details. Doesn't see his father, who is an alcoholic apparently.' Stella felt sad at the thought. 'But he seems quite together about it all. Like I said, he seems, you know, sorted.'

'Must have been good if you didn't come home for thirty-six hours.' It was Bridget's turn to raise an eyebrow at Stella.

'Bridge!' Stella laughed, handing her friend a cup of steaming coffee before picking up her own and blowing on it gently. 'Very good, actually.' She smiled broadly.

'Excellent, then you may see him again.'

Their laughter brought the man from Bridget's bedroom to

the door. He stood there, in a crumpled shirt and boxer shorts, his hair tousled. He looked at them both expectantly, smiling nervously. There was an awkward silence.

Stella looked at Bridget, willing her to say something.

'Oh god, sorry. So rude. Stella, this is Roger,' blurted Bridget.

'Richard,' he corrected her.

'Richard!' Bridget repeated his name before looking back at Stella, her eyes wide.

'Hi, I'm Stella.' She waved from her seat.

He nodded. 'Right, I'd better be off.' He looked at their mugs of coffee longingly.

Bridget didn't move. 'OK, thank you, Richard. Thanks for a lovely evening.'

'Yes, absolutely, I'll be in touch.' He waved and went back to the bedroom.

Stella and Bridget sat at the table silently. A few moments later, the front door of their flat shut with a heavy thud.

'He seems nice,' said Stella.

'Stella, I got his name wrong.'

They looked at each other for a moment before dissolving into laughter once more.

Barely three months later, a tearful Bridget had stood on the steps of the front door to the flat they'd shared for years. They'd just loaded the last of Stella's belongings into the boot of Simon's car and Stella turned to hug her friend one last time before handing her the keys back.

'God, I'm going to miss you.' Bridget squeezed Stella tightly.

'Me too. But I'm not far, I'm literally round the corner. You're not getting rid of me that easily.' Stella hugged her friend back. 'We've got book club next week, remember?'

Book club was one of Stella's favourite things in the world. The group consisted of Stella, Bridget, Bridget's old school friend Sarah and Stella's cousin Lucy, who lived nearby. They'd formed a book club at Bridget's insistence when they'd all first moved to London, even though Stella had protested at the time that, surely, they were too young to be in a book club. As it turned out, they had only ever managed to finish one complete book between them, the first one. Still, they had got together every other month since to catch up, accompanied by crisps, wine and conversations that often left them helpless with laughter.

'Thank god for that, where are we meeting?'

Stella nudged Bridget because they always met in the same pub just off the King's Road. 'Funny. See you then. And don't be late.'

'I'm never late!' Bridget protested, though they both knew she was always the last to arrive.

Simon called over from the car. 'It's all in, ready when you are. No hurry.' He waved at them, smiling.

'You sure you know what you're doing?' Bridget whispered.

Stella looked at her friend. 'Not really, no. But it feels right. I really love him, Bridge.'

'Well then, you go and live with him and be happy. And I couldn't be happier for you.' Bridget kissed Stella on the cheek, then looked her squarely in the face. 'I love you.'

'Love you too, Bridge.'

Stella climbed into the car beside Simon and waved back at her friend from the open car window all the way down the street until they turned the corner at the end.

2

At first, Stella had felt like she was playing at being grown up, except this wasn't a Wendy house. It was an actual house, with paintings on the wall and cream furniture; there was even a wine fridge, of all things. Compared to her old flat, where the only 'art-work' consisted of photo collages of various family and friends, and the sofas were practically threadbare, this was quite the stylish change of scene.

Both of them were working harder than ever, Stella moving from one position to another at the supermarket's head office as she successfully climbed the corporate ladder. Meanwhile, Simon had left Stella's company for a different firm to do what he did best: streamlining with a smile.

Most weekends were spent at home, often in bed wrapped in one another's arms, with the occasional European city break thrown in for good measure. Their lives were busy, so much so Stella missed a few book club gatherings and had to face the wrath of Bridget for doing so.

'Come on, Bridge. You know I love our evenings more than anything,' Stella had said when calling to cancel yet again at the last minute. She'd said she was working late, not wanting to confess the real reason. Simon had in fact booked them a table at a restaurant that was near-impossible to get into and had begged Stella to change her plans.

'You missed the last one because of work,' said Bridget.

'I know. I'm a bad friend. I'm sorry, I promise I'll be at the next one. I miss you.' Stella had pushed down her feelings of guilt, hating the fact that she was resorting to a white lie. It really wasn't her style.

'OK, but if you miss the next one, I'm definitely going to hold a grudge and you know how brilliant I am at that.'

Stella couldn't help but laugh. 'Yes, I do. World-class, I know. I won't, I promise.'

That night, over a bottle of Barolo, Simon had brought up the one topic of conversation that had become something of a sticking point in their otherwise seemingly perfect relationship.

'So, I don't want to put any pressure on you, but we do need to talk about it sooner or later.' Simon swirled his glass and took a sip before putting the glass slowly back down on the table.

Stella had shifted in her seat. Simon often talked about them in the future tense as if it were the most normal thing in the world, as if them getting married was simply a given. And he talked about having children as if that wasn't up for discussion either. The first time he'd brought it up, she'd laughed it off, saying it was too early to even think about kids given they'd only met just a few months before. But it was a subject he came back to often.

Stella picked up her glass. 'You know how I feel about this. I hope to have kids one day, just not yet. I don't feel ready.' She shook her head. 'Anyway, we're not even married.' She took a long sip, holding his gaze.

'Not yet, no. But...' Simon had reached into his pocket and

pulled out a small burgundy velvet box, putting it on the table between them. He pushed it across the table towards her, smiling.

Stella gasped, almost choking on her wine. She looked at him, then back at the box. 'Is this...?'

'Open it.' Simon spoke softly.

She had hesitated before reaching across to pick it up. Slowly, she opened the box. Inside sat the most enormous diamond ring she'd ever seen. It looked like a priceless daisy, a yellow diamond in the middle, surrounded by lots of smaller ones, too many to even count. 'Oh my goodness.' The people at the tables on either side had turned towards them, looking but saying nothing. Stella just stared at the ring. 'Simon, it's beautiful,' she whispered.

'Well, don't just look at it, try it on.' He took her hand in his. 'Stella, I love you and I want us to be together. Please, will you marry me?'

Stella looked across the table at him. Even though she'd secretly hoped a proposal was coming at some point, it was still a shock. Her heart thumped in her chest.

'Yes,' she said, so quietly she wasn't even sure if she'd actually said it.

'I think that was a "yes"?' Simon leaned across the table and, taking the ring from the box, gently slipped it on her finger.

Stella looked at it on her hand, the weight of it feeling so unfamiliar. The stones sparkled in the candlelight.

'It belonged to my mother. She left it to me when she died, asking me to make sure I gave it to someone I really loved.'

'Simon, are you sure? I mean, it's only been...'

'Not long, I know. But, Stella, I know you're the person I want to marry.'

She had lifted her eyes to meet his. He had looked at her expectantly, smiling but with something else in his eyes. Was it fear she'd say no? She couldn't quite tell, but as if to reassure him, again, she said yes, only this time louder. Before she knew it, he was up from his side of the table and lifting her into his arms and kissing her on the mouth. He then wrapped his arms around her tightly, pulling her off the ground.

'Thank you... thank you.' He repeated the words into her hair as they hugged.

Applause had started at the tables either side before spreading across the room as people realised what was happening. There were cheers and a few whoops from other diners and, moments later, a waiter brought a tray with two glasses of champagne to the table.

'On the house,' he said, smiling at them both in turn.

'Thank you so much,' Stella said. She had felt light-headed, her heart still beating furiously. She sat back down in her chair.

The noise died down and people returned to their own conversations just as quickly as they'd left them.

'So, what do you think of the proposal?' Simon laughed.

'Well, you certainly caught me off guard.' Stella gazed at the ring on her finger again, wondering if this was all really happening. 'It was perfect. Thank you.'

'Thank you, my darling.' He squeezed her hand again, a broad smile across his face.

* * *

'You're WHAT?' Bridget's voice had shrieked down the phone.

'I know it's quick, but I promise you it feels right.' Stella tried to ignore the slight irritation at her friend's reaction. She'd hoped for an exclamation of joy, not incredulity.

'It's been about five minutes!'

'It's been six months.'

'Really?'

'OK, five.'

'You met him four months ago, Stella.'

'I love him, Bridge. And I know he loves me.'

'Well, as long as you're happy, I'm happy,' Bridget replied, rather unconvincingly in Stella's opinion.

'Yes, I am. I honestly, truly am. Can we get together to celebrate?'

'Now that is an excellent idea.' Bridget had sounded more excited at the thought of this than Stella's impending nuptials. 'I'll organise something asap with the others and let you know when.'

The following week, the four friends had sat around their usual table in the garden of their favourite pub, rosé with condensation on the enormous glasses in front of them. The late summer evening sun threw a golden light across their faces.

'So, let me get this right,' said Sarah, her enormous blue eyes fixed on Stella. Her sunglasses sat on top of her head, keeping her long blonde hair away from her face. As ever, her hands still bore spots of paint from her day job as a film set painter. She waved a finger across the table. 'You've known him for four months.'

'Five,' Bridget corrected her, winking at Stella.

'And you're getting married, when?' Sarah's finger continued to point.

'Well, we haven't chosen a date yet, but we're thinking the sooner, the better. Probably before Christmas.'

'Good luck with that.' The words shot out of Lucy's mouth and she looked as surprised as anyone. 'God, I'm sorry.' She reached across the table to touch Stella's arm. 'It's just that I'm already trying to book somewhere for our office Christmas bloody party and it's a nightmare, everywhere's booked up.' Lucy worked as an editor at a big publishing house and always seemed to be lumbered with organising any kind of office get-together. They all knew she secretly enjoyed it, despite her protestations.

'It'll be very small, to be honest. He doesn't have a big family, just his dad in fact. And I don't think he'll even be coming. They haven't spoken in years.' Stella felt sad at the thought of it. She'd tried to talk to Simon about his dad, suggesting that perhaps now was the time to mend bridges between them, but Simon had simply changed the subject each time. 'Actually,' she took a deep breath, 'we might even go and get married abroad, on a beach somewhere. Just us, between Christmas and New Year.' Stella picked up her glass and took a sip, her already much-admired engagement ring glinting in the light.

Bridget's eyes had practically popped out of her head. 'Are you serious? You always said you wanted a big wedding!'

Stella swallowed her wine with an audible gulp. 'Once, Bridge. I think I might have said that once, and if I remember correctly, we were pretty drunk when I said it.' Stella thought back to that very conversation. They'd been sitting on the grass outside their student halls, sharing a post-nightclub kebab. At the time, Stella had been madly in love with someone whose first name she couldn't even remember now. 'And anyway, you were busy planning to have babies with what's-his-name...'

'Clive.' Bridget tried to keep a straight face.

'That's it! Clive...' Stella laughed.

'Actually, I was planning how *not* to have babies.' Bridget had fallen for a mature student in her class and, at the time, thought him incredibly sophisticated. As it turned out, he was anything but. Also: married. Not that Bridget had known it back then. She steered the conversation quickly back to Stella, not wanting to open that particular can of worms. 'Anyway, back to you. A beach? Really?' Bridget couldn't hide her disappointment. Stella would be the first of her friends to get married and suddenly it looked like there might not even be a wedding to go to.

'Even if we go and get married somewhere, I promise we'll

have a party when we get back. I know that's what you're all really after.' Stella had grinned at her friends.

'I can't lie, I'd thought we were a shoo-in as bridesmaids.' Sarah sounded wistful.

'And I could have done the photographs for mates' rates,' Bridget chipped in. Bridget was much in demand as a wedding photographer, which amused her friends no end given her total aversion to having her own photograph taken. Whenever she was caught on camera, she always, always had her eyes closed.

'I know, I'm sorry. We want to do it quickly and it means we can do the whole wedding and honeymoon in one go.'

'How romantic.' Lucy's delivery was the verbal equivalent of an eye roll. 'What does Caroline think?' Knowing Stella's sister as she did, Lucy guessed Caroline would be just as disappointed with the whole small wedding idea.

'I haven't told her yet,' said Stella, taking another sip of her wine.

Sarah shot Lucy a look, then turned back to Stella. 'Whatever you decide, here's to you, my darling.' She raised her glass and smiled, looking to the others to join her.

'Absolutely, here's to you, Stella. To you and your happiness with... what's his name?' Bridget winked at her friend.

'Stop it.' Stella had laughed gently, nudging her friend's arm.

'To you and Simon, and a happy future together.' Sarah led the clinking of glasses and they all joined in congratulating Stella. If any of them weren't convinced by this whirlwind romance, none of them had wanted to be the one to let it show.

3

The beach wedding had taken place in between Christmas and New Year, just as Stella had said. In fact, plans had already been starting to take shape when the four of them met up in the pub that night, but Stella hadn't the heart – or guts, if she was honest with herself – to tell them. She knew they all thought it was too much, too soon, even if they didn't say it out loud.

But Stella felt as if she'd stepped into something that had always been waiting for her with Simon. He loved her, made her feel like anything was possible, that life was there for the taking. He was confident, caring and completely adored her. For the first time for as long as she could remember, Stella found herself daring to think ahead rather than worrying that something bad was around the corner. Most of all, she felt utterly loved and in love – and it was intoxicating.

When he had suggested they get married in Mustique, Stella had gasped at the idea, not least because she could only imagine what that might cost. They'd already discussed doing some work to the house, converting the basement into an office and putting another room in the loft. But before she could stop him, Simon had put down a deposit for a small one-bedroomed villa on the island a short walk from the beach.

They'd married at sunset, white sand between their toes. Stella was dressed in a simple pale gold silk bias-cut sleeveless dress and wore flowers in her hair. Simon wore a cream linen suit, a pale blue linen shirt and a smile that broke his face in two when he saw her. Tall palm trees swayed in the gentle breeze, the sound of the waves on the shore providing the most perfect backdrop to their simple ceremony. Afterwards, they had sat and feasted on fish sashimi and fresh lobster tails washed down with chilled Meursault before walking to the shoreline to feel the sea on their skin and look up at the stars. In the few days they had either side of the wedding, they fished, swam and snorkelled. The rest of the time was spent tangled in the cool white cotton sheets of their bed.

One evening, after a blissful dinner overlooking the bay, Stella had lay nestled into the crook of Simon's deeply tanned arm as they sat side by side on the swinging chair outside their villa by the beach.

'How about we stay here forever?' Simon had whispered into the top of her head.

'Actually, I've been thinking. I love my job, but I want to do something for myself one day. You know, start my own company.' Stella gazed out across the calm sea, the moonlight throwing silver beams across the surface.

'What do you want to do?'

'Well, that's the thing. I'm not entirely sure. I just know that I don't want to work for someone else forever.'

'Then that's what you'll do.' Simon ran his finger along her naked shoulder, his touch making her skin tingle.

'Yes, but I've got to come up with something first.'

'It'll come to you, don't you worry. But first, there's something else we need to work on.' He had turned to look at her.

'Simon, we're on our honeymoon. You're not thinking about kids already?' Stella tried to laugh it off.

'I just think the sooner, the better, you know? I don't want to be an old father.'

'We're hardly old! I'm not even thirty.'

'I know, but you know how it is. We'll get home, get stuck back into work and before we know it, another five years will have gone by. I just think there's no harm in at least thinking about it.' He had squeezed her arm gently, his other hand reaching across and slipping under her loose linen shirt before moving down to her breast.

Stella had looked up at him, searched for the words, but before she could speak, his mouth was on hers and her body responded without hesitation.

* * *

Three months later, Stella had watched as the blue line slowly appeared on the pregnancy test balanced precariously on the edge of the sink in front of her. With the presence of a little life inside her, she had felt both elated and terrified all at the same time.

Simon was beside himself with happiness at the news, going completely over the top and insisting that Stella put her feet up at every opportunity. She had to constantly remind him that she was pregnant, not a hundred and two.

She'd continued working as long as she could, grateful for the distraction from worrying about whether she'd have the first clue what to do when the baby did actually arrive. But from the moment she'd held Max in her arms for the first time, she knew they'd be all right. The birth had been quick; having had her waters broken and been told it would be at least six hours before anything happened, Max took everyone by surprise by appearing just a few hours later. So quickly in fact, Simon had missed the whole thing, having gone down to fetch something from the car.

As Stella had lay in the hospital bed, staring down into the enormous, unblinking blue eyes of her baby boy, she felt like she'd known him forever. 'Hello, you.' His little fingers had curled around hers and she felt as if the world had shifted on its axis, putting him at the centre of hers.

Simon and Stella had muddled through the first few months as parents to a new-born baby, neither really knowing what to do despite having an impressive pile of baby books by the side of the bed. Simon tried his best to help, but Max was far more interested in Stella. Or, more precisely, her breasts. At times, she felt more like a cow than a human, sitting at the kitchen table with a breast pump attached to each to produce enough milk to enable Simon to feed Max from the bottle for a few shifts.

After a week, Simon had gone back to work and Stella was left on her own in the house. None of her friends had babies yet, so she thought she'd better find some who did and promptly signed up to a local mother and baby group. It took her a few weeks to pluck up the courage to go, but eventually she managed to get herself and Max out of the house (which always seemed to take about an hour) and walked to the church hall down the road. There, she had found a room full of mothers who all seemed to know one another. No one so much as looked up when she walked in.

Sitting there on her own, holding her baby in her arms, Stella had felt a million miles away from her old life. The one where she sat in an office drinking coffee with frothy milk dressed in clean clothes with freshly highlighted hair and beautifully done, barely-there make-up. Instead, she was in the same maternity jeans she'd been wearing for months, her hair unwashed and piled on top of her head in a messy bun. She actually couldn't remember the last time she'd worn make-up.

She had looked around in the hope of making eye contact with a friendly face. In the meantime, Max had started to make it clear he wanted food – again – and so Stella tried to get Max into position so she could breastfeed him. But the brown plastic chairs were not helping, and before long, Max's wails filled the hall. Suddenly, Stella felt the eye contact, but this time it was unwanted. She hastily bundled Max back into the pram and made for the door, desperate to get away from the stuffiness of the room. She had walked quickly along the road back towards home, tears in her eyes. Max's crying continued, his red face screwed up in anger.

'I'm sorry, baby,' Stella whispered as big fat tears started to roll down her face. 'I'm so sorry, hang on and I'll get you sorted as soon as I can.' She fumbled to get the key in the lock, her baby's screams making every second seem like a minute. Eventually, she got inside and lifted a now furious Max out of his pram. She took him to the sofa and once again got herself into position to feed him. Being cocooned in the familiar space instantly calmed them both, and as soon as Max found what he was looking for, he latched on, silence covering the room like a thick, welcome blanket. Stella slowly relaxed her body and sank her back into the sofa. She closed her eyes, a wave of tiredness like she'd never known washing over her. Even her bones felt heavy.

Just then, her phone screen had lit up with a picture of her and Bridget – a favourite photo taken a few years ago on a particularly good holiday to Greece. The same holiday on which Bridget had cycled into an old stone wall on their way back from a particularly long rosé-fuelled lunch and meant they'd had to spend their last evening in the local hospital. Still, on the upside, Bridget's broken ankle had meant they were given the seats with extra legroom on the plane home at no extra cost. Seeing that photo was enough to bring a small smile to Stella's face. She reached for the phone and hit the green button followed by speaker.

'Hey, Bridget!' She tried her best to sound perkier than she felt.

'Are you all right, Stella? You sound terrible! Did I wake you up?'

'No, not at all, I was just, um...' Stella shifted Max a little and sat up. Clearly her attempt at sounding more with it hadn't worked. 'I'm just really tired, that's all.'

'Where are you?' Bridget shouted over the traffic roaring past her.

'At home.' Stella closed her eyes. Please come over, she wanted to say. But it was half past ten on a Monday morning. She knew she couldn't expect her friend to drop everything; she was probably on her way to some exciting job.

'I'm coming over. Can I bring anything? Do you need food?'

Stella was so happy to hear those words, she thought she might start crying again. 'But aren't you working?'

'I'm between appointments, I've got time to pop over. My next one's in a studio on your side of the river. That's why I called.'

'Well, if you're sure...'

'I'm sure, I'll see you in a bit. Can't wait to see you. Just don't expect me to do anything particularly helpful with the baby. I don't know how those things work.'

Stella managed a small laugh. 'See you in a bit.' She sighed with relief when Bridget hung up.

Half an hour later, the doorbell had rung. Stella opened the door, with Max asleep in her arms, to find Bridget on the doorstep with two bulging shopping bags. Bridget held them up, grinning. 'I bought most of the biscuit aisle.'

'Excellent, then you can come in. I'd put him down, but he'll probably start crying again, so if you don't mind, I'm just going to keep him here.' Stella nodded towards her sleeping boy.

'Suits me. I'll sort the biscuits and make you a cup of tea. Go and sit down. I'll bring them over in a minute.'

'I'm sorry, I look terrible,' Stella called as she made her way to the sofa.

'Don't be so ridiculous, you've just had a baby. But yes, as it happens, you do look like shit,' Bridget called back to her friend from the kitchen. She came back with a plate piled with an assortment of biscuits. Nestling in next to Stella on the sofa, she took her friend's hand. 'Come on then, how's it all going?'

Stella looked at her. 'It's really hard, actually. Seriously, this makes going to work look easy.'

Bridget squeezed her hand. 'I remember my mum saying the first bit is the toughest, but it gets easier. Until they start walking and talking, that is. Then you're in real trouble.' Bridget smiled, tucking a loose strand of Stella's hair behind her ear.

'I just wish my mum was here, you know? I feel like I haven't got anyone to ask what to do. There's Caroline, of course, but she's always made parenting look so easy. You lot haven't had babies yet – so selfish, by the way,' Stella scowled at Bridget, 'and Simon's been amazing, but now he's back at work...'

'Honestly, you'll meet other mothers, and before you know it, you'll be one of them, dressed in swanky leisurewear shouting loudly at your kids about being careful on the swing in the park.'

'I went this morning, to a mother and baby group. It was hideous and I'm never going to one again.' Stella motioned to the plate of biscuits with a nod of the head. Bridget reached over and picked up a piece of shortbread, handing it to Stella. She bit into it, crumbs falling onto Max's head.

Bridget wiped them gently off. 'Listen, you're just really, really tired. Think what your body has been through.'

'Well, I can tell you one thing for sure. I'm never, ever doing this again.' Stella closed her eyes.

'Kettle's boiled, tea?'

Stella nodded, slowly. 'Yes please.'

By the time Bridget came back from the kitchen, Stella was asleep, Max still cradled in her arms.

4

It came as a surprise to everyone, not least to Stella when, just over a year and a half later, she discovered she was pregnant with twins.

'Seriously?' Her boss had looked at her over his glasses from behind his desk.

Stella felt her cheeks redden. She'd been back at work for six months. 'Yes, I'm serious. Having twins isn't something I'd joke about, believe me.' She'd hoped to wait a little longer to make the news public at work, but her quickly growing bump made it almost impossible to hide.

'Well, I suppose congratulations are in order.' He managed a small smile, but Stella guessed he'd be trying to find a replacement for her the minute she left his office.

'Thank you. I'll let you know my leaving date as soon as I know it, but it won't be for a while, obviously.'

Stella had managed to get a place at a local nursery for Max and he was clearly loving it as much as she was enjoying being able to converse with adults about something other than toddler behaviour. But the daily struggle to leave the office on time to pick up Max from nursery before the late fees kicked in was real. Simon helped as much as he could, but his new job at a ferocious consultancy firm meant long hours and took him away from home at least one night a week.

As Stella's pregnancy had progressed, the juggle got more exhausting to manage. One evening, when Simon was away, book club had been due to meet at the pub as usual. When Stella had messaged the group chat to say she just didn't have the energy, Bridget called her straight back to tell her they would come to hers and would be bringing food with them.

Just after 7 p.m., the doorbell rang. Stella made her way slowly downstairs, having just got Max into bed. By now, she was the size of a small camper van – at least that's how she felt. She opened the door to see three of her favourite faces grinning back at her.

'Bloody hell, look at you! You look incredible!' Lucy cried out, wrapping her arms around Stella's neck.

'Please don't say I'm blooming. It's such a lie.' Stella rolled her eyes and hugged them each in turn as they came through the door. She was still the only one amongst them to have children and as they tumbled into the sitting room, discarding coats and kicking off shoes, she was momentarily envious of their freedom. To go out without booking babysitters – in fact, to have the energy to go out at all. But here they all were, now with glasses of wine in hand, passing round opened bags of crisps as they discussed what had been going on in all their lives since they last got together.

Stella sipped her non-alcoholic gin and tonic slowly, knowing the bubbles would no doubt give her indigestion, but she didn't want to be rude. Bridget had clearly put thought into bringing something for her to drink while they imbibed discounted Picpoul.

'Here, I got you these.' Lucy passed a small canvas tote bag to

Stella. 'Books from the office, I just grabbed a few on my way out, ones I thought you'd like.'

Stella peered into the bag. 'Thanks, Luce.' She didn't want to say that the chances of her picking up a book, let alone reading a whole sentence were slim to none. Ironic, really, given this was book club. She remembered their first meeting not long after they'd all moved to London, organised by Bridget. She'd got the four of them together around a table having been set the book a month before and Stella remembered the book they'd read like it was yesterday. It was *A Room with a View* by E. M. Forster and it remained one of her favourite books. The descriptions of the city and the characters in the book had stayed with her long after she'd turned the last page.

'So, how are you feeling?' Bridget sank back into the armchair opposite Stella. The once-sparse sitting room (although Stella preferred the term minimalist) was now populated with brightly coloured plastic toys. Along the mantlepiece were photos of Simon and Stella at various locations – on the beach at their wedding, at the bottom of the Eiffel Tower, at the top of the Empire State Building. Photos of Max sat in frames nestled in between books on the neat shelves.

'Truth? Knackered.' Stella laughed. 'But I'm so pleased you're here and not just because you brought food.' The smell of warm spices wafted from the kitchen into the sitting room. 'What is it, by the way?'

'Sarah picked up a load of tapas from Borough Market on her way here,' said Bridget. 'Smells amazing.'

Lucy got up from the sofa. 'I'll go and give her a hand.'

'There are loads of big plates on the shelves above the sinks,' Stella called after her as Lucy made her way down the hall to the kitchen. She turned back to Bridget. 'While I've got you...'

'Please don't ask me about him.' Bridget dropped her chin to the chest in mock despair.

'You know I'm going to ask you about him.' The 'him' Stella referred to was Neil, Bridget's boyfriend of two years and one that they all knew would never commit to Bridget despite her clearly wanting him to. He'd been married before; said he didn't want to do it again. 'Have you talked about, you know, what might happen?'

'Not exactly.' Bridget sipped her wine. 'I don't want to put any pressure on him.'

Stella could never quite understand how someone who always seemed so in control of her life, so self-assured and brilliant, could be so undemanding when it came to what she really wanted with the man she loved. It infuriated her, in fact.

'What about kids?' Stella shifted to get comfortable on the sofa, positioning another cushion in the small of her back.

'Yes. Well, not exactly, but I have mentioned it.'

'Bridget, don't you think that's deserving of a proper conversation rather than just being something you mention? I mean, if he's not wanting the same things as you... You deserve more, that's all.'

'You would say that because you love me, I know that. But I love him, Stella. And he might change his mind.'

'Bridget, this isn't about not having the same politics as your husband. This is about knowing what you want in life, and *I* know you want to have children of your own one day. And I don't think *he* does. What's more, I think you know he doesn't. And if you don't share the same fundamental hopes and dreams, then it's only going to get harder.'

'Maybe. But I'm just not ready to call time on us yet.'

'Just be careful,' Stella said softly. She reached out her hand to her friend.

'I will. Although to be honest, the same should have applied to you.' Bridget laughed her throaty laugh. 'I mean, seriously, Stella, twins?'

'Don't laugh. I wasn't even really sold on the idea of one when we had Max and now,' she gestured to her enormous bump, 'I'm going to have three under three. I feel a bit sick just thinking about it. Although that could just be the indigestion.'

'How's Simon? I feel like I've not seen him for ages.' Bridget tried to inject some enthusiasm into her voice.

They both knew Bridget wasn't a massive fan of Stella's husband, but they chose to ignore it. It was just easier that way.

'He's good, really busy with work. He loves his job, it's exactly what he wanted to do. Big team, bit of travel. He's away this weekend, in fact.'

'And what about you?'

'I'm not sure if I'm going to go back after these two...'

'I didn't mean work, I meant how are you getting on without him here. You must be exhausted.' Bridget looked at her friend, drained of her usual sparkle. Her dark hair hung loose on her shoulders, her skin pale.

'I'm fine, really.' Stella met Bridget's concerned gaze. 'Caroline's coming up at the weekend to help me get organised for the babies.' Stella stroked her stomach gently.

'That'll be nice?' ventured Bridget.

'That'll be annoying, you know it will.' Much as she loved her sister, Caroline could really get on her nerves too.

'She might be annoying, but she's good at all this stuff.' Bridget gestured at the toys.

'She is. You know I love her really. She's just a bit bossy, sometimes.'

Lucy popped her head around the door. 'Food's ready.'

Bridget got up from the sofa. 'Right, I'll pull you up. One, two, three...' She offered her hand to Stella and they joined the others in the kitchen, now awash with tea lights and a table covered in tapas.

That night, they'd talked as they always did, sharing stories and secrets. Sarah regaled them with indiscreet tales about famous people from her latest film set, Lucy shared her fears that one of her best-selling authors was about to defect to another publishing house and Bridget did her best to avoid answering any further questions about Neil. Stella was exhausted, but listening to her friends as they passed plates between them and topped up each other's glasses was just what she'd needed.

Later, as her head had hit the pillow, a message had popped up on her phone. It was from Simon, telling her he loved her and that he couldn't wait to see her when he was back in a few days' time. Too tired to type, she sent back a string of heart emojis and threw in an aubergine for good measure.

* * *

Amelie and Isla were born a few months later. One arrived screaming (Millie), the other quiet as a mouse (Isla). They slept side by side on their backs in the cot, but always facing each other, their tiny fingers often intertwined. Simon was ecstatic, Stella exhausted but elated. And just like that, they were a family of five. Six, if you counted the Labrador puppy Max had begged them for and Stella had agreed to have in a moment of weakness not long after the twins were born.

Once the first few months of nursing twins had passed, of which Stella could remember very little with any real clarity other than being shattered, she had managed to settle into some sort of routine, albeit revolving mostly around food. She found herself cobbling together endless meals for Max, while trying to get something puréed or mashed for the twins in the meantime. Stella started batch cooking to fill the freezer – years of forward planning and spreadsheets in her working life had left their mark – and before long, a few friends and neighbours with children the same age were asking if they could buy some of her meals to squeeze into their freezers. From fish pies to shepherd's pies, pasta bakes to chicken casseroles and vegetable stews, Stella cooked up all the things she knew Max loved eating but were a faff to make unless made in bulk, and the requests for more just kept on coming.

Soon she was sourcing proper packaging and labels with the help of an old friend from her supermarket marketing days, and with the help of another set up a website to take orders. Calling the fledgling business Star Pots, Stella asked a few of her fellow mothers to act as 'ambassadors' in return for free frozen toddler meals and before long word spread, her kitchen becoming a hive of activity with more people drafted in to help.

Just before she was due to return to work after her year's maternity leave was up, Stella had decided to hand in her notice and instead give the business a proper go. Simon was all for it, suggesting she give it six months and if the company didn't grow, she could always return to a salaried job.

With hours spent pounding the pavements, the twins in a buggy and a cooler bag of samples over her shoulder, Stella approached numerous independent shop owners and managers and soon learned to tell the difference, within minutes, between those who thought she was completely deluded and those who might just be persuaded to give her products a trial run.

After numerous false starts and more red tape than she could ever have imagined, even with her retailing background, Stella had slowly begun to secure listings in local cafes and deli-catessens frequented by parents on their way to and from nursery school. So she gave it a further six months and the orders just kept coming. Countless business fairs, school fairs and local pop-ups later, she was able to move the business out of her own kitchen and rent space in a professional test kitchen. She'd never been so exhausted, but as the business took shape, she loved what she did more than she ever imagined possible.

A few years later, with all three of the children now at school, she had found herself sitting in a meeting room of her previous employer at the supermarket pitching the business to the baby food buyer. By this time, Stella had built up a small core team around her, some of whom she'd worked with at her old company, covering product development, operations and marketing. Simon had left his job to come and run the financial side of the business, securing investors as Star Pots continued to grow. And once the brand hit the shelves of its first major supermarket, rival retailers had come knocking. The hours were gruelling, the workload immense. But through sheer hard work and determination, Star Pots had grown to become a brand as much admired as envied by its competitors.

Having put practically every penny they'd made back into the business since the day she'd sold her very first batch, and with the children getting older, Simon and Stella had agreed it was finally time to enjoy some of the rewards of their hard work, and decided to move to a bigger house. Their belongings were packed up from Simon's house, the one they'd lived in for the past decade, and moved into one they'd often walked past on their way to the common with the children, and the dog in tow, on their weekend outings. The house had always appealed to Stella, despite its overgrown garden clearly visible over the low stone wall and permanently drawn thick curtains in the windows at the front of the house. But she could see its potential and had eventually persuaded Simon that they should go for it.

They had moved in on a crisp autumn day and, over time, traces of the previous owners disappeared, from the heavy curtains, thick carpets and dark colours, replaced with restored, polished floorboards, off-white walls and a mix of old and new furniture. A new kitchen extension at the back of the house had created a large room with a glass ceiling over the long oak dining-room table, letting light flood into the room and spill over into the house. Stella had filled the small, decked area at the back with wild grasses and pots overflowing with ever-changing flowers and herbs and, with the help of a local landscape gardener, overhauled the front. By the following spring, newly planted cherry trees had filled the garden with their blossom and heavenly scent and whenever Stella walked in through the side gate and up to the front door, her stomach still flipped at the thought that the house was hers. They'd worked hard for it, but when she thought of Simon, their three children and the life they had together, she just couldn't believe her luck.

5

'So, how was lunch?' Stella pushed her stir fry round the plate. The children were in the sitting room watching television and Simon and Stella sat together at one end of the table, a glass of red wine each in front of them.

'Good, actually. Usual stuff – what are the projected sales, when's the new range going to be ready, when is it going to go into all stores rather than just two-thirds of them...' Simon picked up his glass and took a large slug of wine.

'Sorry you had to do it on your own.' She picked up her glass but didn't take a sip. She glanced up at him again, trying to push the question down that had been threatening to come out since she'd walked through the door. Simon has loosened the top button of his shirt, but the tie still sat around his neck, seemingly daring her to ask about it.

'How did the photo shoot go?' Simon held another mouthful on his fork.

'Oh, fine. Stand in front of kitchen counter. Cross arms and look businesslike but with a friendly smile.' She imitated the fixed smile she'd done for the camera that afternoon.

Simon laughed. 'Very convincing. When is the article coming out?'

'Hopefully in a few weeks' time, so that should help get a few more listings over the line. Nice tie, by the way.'

'Thanks.' Simon nodded at her plate. 'Are you going to eat that?'

Stella pushed it across the table towards him. 'You finish it.' She watched as he tucked into her leftovers. 'I haven't seen it before. Where's it from?' She tried her best to sound casual.

He picked up the tie with his free hand and looked at it. 'Um, I'm not sure. Can't remember.' He took another mouthful of food.

'What's the label?'

Simon looked up at her. 'What do you mean?'

'The label. Have a look on the back. That'll show where it's from.'

'What's so interesting about this tie?' Simon stopped, his fork mid-air.

Stella felt her cheeks reddening. 'I just wondered, that's all. Like I said, I haven't seen it before and it's just quite different. From your usual style, I mean.'

'What are you trying to say, Stella?' He waved his fork, the food on it falling to the plate.

'Nothing. It's just... I like it, that's all. And I wanted to know where it comes from. I thought maybe I might buy you more like that, it suits you.'

He shook his head and carried on eating. 'No idea.'

Despite desperately wanting to reach across the table and grab the tie to see, Stella decided to change the subject completely. 'We've been asked over to Caroline's for lunch on Sunday and I'd like us to go, we haven't seen her for ages.'

Simon looked up at her, his eyes pleading. 'Do we really have to?'

Stella was determined not to back down like she had the last time she'd tabled the idea. 'Yes, we really do. I know you find it boring, but she's my sister...'

'It's not her that's boring. She's just bossy. It's that insufferable husband of hers I really can't bear.'

'Come on, Philip's not that bad.' Stella laughed a little.

'He's the most boring man I've ever met. Always droning on about fiscal policy, and if it's not that, it's his bloody cricket club.'

'OK, so he's not the most exciting man in the world, but he's part saint to still be married to my sister, as far as I'm concerned.' Stella deployed humour to try to get Simon to agree. 'Come on, I've not seen her for months. I'll drive, so you can have a few drinks if that'll help you get through it. And we really won't stay for long, I promise.'

Simon sighed. 'Fine, if that's what you want to do, that's what we'll do.'

'Please don't make me feel guilty about it.' Stella reached across for his hand. 'The cousins love getting together, anyway.'

Simon stood up, taking his plate over to the dishwasher. 'I've said fine. But for the record, we're leaving straight after pudding, otherwise we'll be there all bloody afternoon.'

'Coffee.'

'What?'

'We'll leave after coffee. It's rude to leave before then.'

He sighed. 'Whatever. Anyway, I'm going to have a shower.'

'Now?'

'Yes, now. Is that all right?' There was an edge to his voice. She was clearly irritating him.

'Yes, of course. Sorry. I'm just tired.' She sighed. 'You go up, I'll finish here.'

Simon left the kitchen, calling for the children to turn the television off and go and get ready for bed as he passed them.

Stella loaded the plates into the dishwasher, telling herself that she didn't need to start questioning everything he did just because she didn't recognise an item of his clothing.

She herded Max and the twins up the stairs, reminding them to pick up their various piles of clean clothes as they passed rather than just step over them.

Hearing the water running in their bathroom, Stella crept into her and Simon's bedroom and crossed the floor to the pile of clothes on Simon's side of the bed. There, on top of his shirt, lay the tie. Stella picked it up and slowly turned it over. In capital letters, she saw the words HERMÈS and PARIS stitched onto the square white label. She looked at it for a moment before placing it carefully back just as she'd found it, making her way across the bedroom to the door. Just then, the water in the shower stopped. She turned and slipped quietly back down the stairs and into the kitchen.

Stella picked up her wine glass from the table where she'd left it and took a last sip before rinsing it and putting it by the sink. Perhaps it had been a present, or a treat to himself? But she knew, deep down, Simon wouldn't buy himself anything like that. Expensive ties just weren't his thing. He'd spend a fortune on season tickets for his beloved football team, but not ties. She tried to calm her mind, not let it race to places she didn't want it to go.

Grabbing her laptop, she perched on a stool at the kitchen island. 'Hey, Percy,' she said softly as the dog came and lay at her feet. He sighed heavily, as if he knew how she was feeling. Determined to take her mind off it, Stella flipped open the laptop and glanced down the long list of unread emails in her inbox, then started clearing it.

At first she didn't notice Simon come into the kitchen. He was dressed in shorts and T-shirt, his hair was wet, his skin flushed pink from the hot water. 'I'm going to take the dog out for a walk.'

He gestured to Percy, who didn't seem to be on the same page with the idea. 'Come on, boy.'

'But you've just had a shower.' Stella looked up, trying to read his face. She glanced towards the window at the darkness outside. 'And it's a bit late for that, isn't it?'

'I won't be long.'

'Simon, did I do something wrong?' Stella felt her stomach drop. She couldn't work out what she'd said, but his face told her he didn't want to be here. At least, not with her.

'I don't know what you mean. Really, I just want some fresh air, it's been a long day and I've been stuck with people I didn't want to be with for most of it. Anyway, he could do with the exercise, look at the size of him.' Simon waved the lead at the dog, making Percy finally shift from his resting position.

Stella could sense there was more to it, but she decided not to push him any further or he'd simply stop talking. Stella had grown up in a house where arguments were forgotten as quickly as they happened. Simon, on the other hand, hated confrontation. Silence was his preferred position, but over their years together, Stella had persuaded him that talking about things, anything, was far better than burying problems. At least, she thought she had. But there was something not right here and there didn't seem to be anything she could do about it right now.

'I'll see you in a bit,' Simon called as he left, closing the front door behind him.

Upstairs, Stella could hear footsteps on the landing.

'Mama? Please can you come and tuck me in?' a voice called down from the top of the stairs. It was usually Millie who found excuses to call one of them up to her, but this time it was Isla's voice.

'Coming,' Stella called back. She closed the lid of her laptop and headed up the stairs.

* * *

The sound of the key in the latch was enough to wake Stella from her sleep. She was still on the sofa, where she'd been since settling Isla hours before. She glanced at her watch. Simon had been out for almost three hours. She sat up, putting her hands to her face before pulling her hair back from it. Shaking her head gently, she blinked slowly, trying to bring herself back into the present.

She heard Simon walk straight through to the kitchen, despite the light being on in the sitting room beside her. Stella's heart sank. Whatever it was that was bothering him, he was still clearly cross about it.

Percy came in and nudged her with his wet nose, looking at her with his deep brown eyes. Stella stroked his head a few times and got up slowly, switching off the lamp beside the sofa. She walked through to the kitchen; Simon stood with his back to her, waiting for the kettle to boil.

'How was your walk?'

'Fine.' He stared down at his phone, then put it back in his pocket.

Stella took a seat at the same stool she'd been on earlier, the cold slab of dark marble between them suddenly seeming vast. 'Simon, please look at me. I feel like I've done something to upset or annoy you and I don't know what it is. If it's about the tie...'

Simon sighed heavily, then turned to Stella. 'It's not the tie. Stella, I'm sorry, but I can't stay here any more.'

Stella looked at him, waiting for him to say something else. Anything that might make those words make sense. 'What do you mean?'

'I mean I've got to leave.'

She searched his face for a look that would bring him back to her. But there was nothing, his face was impassive. 'Si, please tell me what's going on. I... I don't understand.'

'I'm sorry, but I just don't feel the way I used to. About you, I mean.'

She shook her head, a metallic taste filling her mouth. 'What are you saying? Why are you saying this? I don't, I mean I can't... What's happened? Please, Simon, talk to me. Tell me what's going on.' Her words tumbled out despite her efforts to put them in some sort of order. Her fingers trembled; her breath was short. She closed her eyes for a second, bright lights swam in front of them.

Nothing made sense. In a few seconds, Stella's whole world had shifted so far off-kilter, she could barely stand. Here she was, sitting opposite the man she thought was the love of her life in the house of their dreams with their three children sleeping upstairs. Until just a few moments before, life had been pretty much perfect. But now, seeing his face, the indifference as she struggled to say anything that made sense, it was anything but. Simon looked like he'd rather be anywhere but there, in the kitchen, with Stella.

He picked up his small black holdall from the floor, the one he usually used when he went to the gym. He slung it over his shoulder, telling her he'd call the next day. And then he was gone.

Stella sat in silence for a while, staring at the door. Whether it was moments or longer, she really couldn't tell. She went to stand but sank slowly to the floor, her legs unable to hold her weight. With her back resting against the island, she pulled her knees to her chest and then buried her face in her hands. Tears finally came, slowly at first, then falling uncontrollably, soaking through her fingers onto her clothes. Her cheeks burned; her heart raced. She wanted to scream, but no sound came.

Her thoughts turned to her children upstairs, asleep in their beds. What would she say to them in the morning? How could she tell them that their father had left because he didn't feel like he used to about their mother? How on earth was that going to play out in their beautiful, uncomplicated minds? The very thought of it was enough to force Stella to her feet and race to the sink. She heaved into it, but nothing came. Just despair from the pit of her stomach.

She turned back and looked across at the table again, set for breakfast, just as she'd left it before falling asleep on the sofa waiting for Simon to return from walking the dog. Now she wondered what he'd been planning on that walk. He must have already packed that bag before taking Percy out, after his shower perhaps.

Stella walked over to the table, wanting to sweep everything on it to the floor. Instead, not wanting to wake the children, she took a seat at the head, the chair Simon usually sat in. She reached for her phone and dialled his number. It went straight to voicemail. She tried again and again, then went to send him a text message. She looked at the blinking cursor, not knowing what to say. Her fingers trembled as she typed.

Please tell me what's happened? I don't understand.

The message was delivered but unread. Moments later, she typed another, asking him to please come home, then another and another. All of them were left unread. Finally, her mind exhausted, she slumped her head on to the table and cried herself to sleep.

6

Stella woke with a jolt, sunlight streaming through the glass ceiling. It took her a few seconds to make sense of where she was. Then, with crushing force, the events of the previous evening came flooding back. She sat up, still in the chair she'd been in all night. Everything looked just the same. The island in the middle of the kitchen, the huge wooden fruit bowl, the enamel jug filled with flowers Stella had bought from the shop on the corner the previous day. She looked at them now, wishing she could take them back. Take herself back to the day before, knowing what she knew now.

But what did she know? Simon had walked out. Told her he didn't love her any more. Or rather, didn't feel the same way about her. What did that even mean? Did he still love her? Or was it just that he didn't love her enough? What had she missed?

Questions crowded her mind. So many questions, but no answers.

Stella glanced at the clock on the wall. It was still early, time enough for her to go and shower and change before the children were up. She walked slowly to the kettle. Her back ached and her bones felt heavy, unsurprising given she'd slept at the kitchen table.

She heard footsteps above, one of the children on their way to the bathroom. She had to think, fast, about what to tell them. They'd wonder where he was; Simon was usually still there in the mornings. She reached for her phone and searched for her sister's number. Hitting the call button, she listened for the ringing, imagining Caroline picking up and wondering what on earth Stella was doing calling this early.

Caroline answered immediately. 'Hey, is everything all right?'

Stella swallowed hard. 'I need you to...' Her voice cracked, a wave of nausea washing over her.

'Stella, what's going on? You sound weird.' Caroline, as ever, got straight to the point.

'I don't really understand what's going on, but Simon's gone.'

'Gone where?' Caroline's voice was flat.

'I don't know.' Stella blinked, not wanting more tears to fall. She needed to try to find some order in the chaos. 'I honestly don't know. He said he... I'm not even sure what he said, but basically, he said he couldn't be here any more. And then he left.'

'Do the children know?'

'No, they were asleep. Caroline, I don't understand.'

'Have you called him?'

'About a thousand times.' Stella remembered sitting at the table the night before, hearing his answerphone message over and over again, watching to see if he'd read her messages. 'He's not answering. It's like he's just... disappeared.'

'OK, listen. don't say anything to the children for now, just say he's gone to work or something. Then we can try to figure out what the hell is going on.'

'I've got to get them to school.'

'Darling, it's Saturday. Leave them sleeping.'

'God, so it is.' She shook her head. 'Max has got football practice. I can't leave the twins here on their own. He'll be so disappointed if he misses it. Simon usually takes him.'

'OK, is there someone you can call to come over and stay with the girls while you go?'

'I'll call Bridget.'

'OK, good. Do you want me to come up later?'

Stella rubbed her forehead with one hand as if willing a sensible thought to come into her head. 'Actually, yes please.'

'I'll be there around midday. I can take the kids back with me for a night if you need me to. Just to give you some time to do whatever you need to do. Don't worry about packing for them, I can throw some things in a bag when I get there.'

'Thanks, Caroline.' There were times when Stella was grateful for Caroline's no-nonsense approach, and this was one of them. 'I'll call Bridget now. Speak to you later.'

'Stella, please try not to worry too much. I'm sure there's an explanation and he'll be back. Maybe it's just a wobble.' Caroline sighed. 'Hang on in there. I'll see you later.'

'Bye.' Stella hung up and tapped out a message to Bridget.

Please can you come over? Slight emergency. Max has got football and Simon not here. Don't want to leave girls on their own.

She looked at the message, then deleted it and typed a new one.

Simon's gone and I don't know what to do.

She pressed send. A few seconds later, her phone rang.

'Stella, what's happened?' Bridget's voice was croaky. Stella had obviously woken her.

'I'm sorry to call so early...'

'Don't be silly, what's going on?'

Stella told her.

'Didn't he give you any kind of explanation?' Bridget sounded incredulous.

Stella thought back to their exchanges the night before, searching for a clue, something to make it fall into place.

'I found a tie.'

'What tie?'

'One I hadn't seen before. I asked him where it came from, he said he couldn't remember.'

'That's hardly a reason to walk out.' Bridget laughed, the thought of it so ridiculous.

'I know. Which is why I think I must be missing something. It just doesn't make sense. I can't even...' Stella ran out of words.

'OK, I'll come over now. Give me half an hour, then you can go to football with Max. I'll hang out with the girls.'

'Thank you.' Stella felt a wave of relief. At least she could try to pretend that everything was fine for the children, even if it was just for one day. It felt like she was buying time to get to Simon, to find out what was going on, for him to explain. If she could only talk to him, she'd be able to make him see that whatever he was going through, they could do it together. From the moment they'd met, they'd been such a team. Together they could do anything: build a home, a family, a business.

Looking around the quiet kitchen, Stella wondered how she'd found herself in this horrible nightmare. She shut her eyes tightly for a moment.

'Mama?'

Stella opened her eyes to see Isla looking up at her, her hair a mass of tangled blond curls. One side of her face was flushed red, crease marks from her sheets still imprinted on them.

'Hello, you.' Stella reached down and gave her daughter a hug, wondering how he could have left them. If he didn't love her any more, so be it. But not the children. That wasn't fair. She wanted to scream it out loud. Instead, she held Isla closer for a moment before letting her go and trying to act like it was any other Saturday morning. 'What would you like for breakfast? I'm thinking pancakes, what do you reckon?'

Isla's eyes lit up. 'Yes please!'

'OK, I'll wake Max and we'll have some before I take him to football.'

'Where's Daddy?' Isla rubbed her eyes, yawning.

Stella's throat seemed to constrict in an instant. 'He's had to go to work this morning.' She busied herself looking for a jug in the cupboard, not wanting to make eye contact.

'But it's Saturday. Why is he working today?' Isla took herself over to the table and climbed onto the seat, the same one where Stella had cried herself to sleep just hours before.

Stella took a deep breath. She'd just have to tell a few white lies for now, until Simon came home and told her it was all going to be OK. That it was all a big mistake and not to worry, he'd realised he'd been an idiot. That here was where he wanted to be, with Stella, with his children. 'He's just very busy in the office at the moment. He'll be back later.' Stella winced slightly at the words, hating the fact that, actually, she didn't know when he'd be back. If he'd be back, even.

'Poor Daddy, that's not fair. Having to go to work on a Saturday.' Isla reached for the cereal on the table, taking out a handful of cornflakes and eating them from the palm of her little hand, like crisps.

Stella could feel the tears threatening to fall again. 'Darling, go and wake Millie up so she can have pancakes too. And Max, while you're up there.' She looked at the clock. It was nearly eight o'clock and, as if on cue, Percy started whining at the front door. 'Yes, all right. We'll go soon,' she called.

Just then, there was a knock at the door. Stella's heart leapt. But then, Simon wouldn't knock. He'd just come straight in. He lived here, after all.

She went to the door and opened it to find Bridget standing on the doorstep, her coat thrown over her pyjamas, sliders on her feet. She still had her bed socks on.

'I took a cab.' Bridget grabbed Stella into a hug.

Stella sank into her friend's embrace. 'Thank you.' For a moment, everything felt just the tiniest bit better.

* * *

The morning passed in a blur. Stella took Max to his usual Saturday football training session on the common, taking the dog with her. She watched from the side-lines, standing some way down from the other parents, sunglasses firmly in place. She'd left Bridget at home with the girls, all happily tucking into seconds of pancakes with plans to head to the sofa and watch TV in their pyjamas afterwards.

Stella hadn't been able to talk to Bridget about what had happened in any detail before she left, but with Caroline heading to pick the children up for the night, Stella knew there'd be time later. It was just a matter of getting through the next few hours.

She tried to concentrate on watching Max, but her hand gripped her phone tightly in her coat pocket, willing it to vibrate with an incoming message from Simon. The list of things Stella was worrying about was growing at pace. What if he wasn't coming back? What would she tell the children? It all felt so unreal. Just over twelve hours before, everything was normal. And now, everything she thought she knew had been thrown into question. She tried to breathe deeply, pushing down the panic rising in her chest.

A cheer came up from the small crowd watching the practice game. Stella looked up to see Max running down the side of the pitch, closely followed by his team, all slapping him on the back. He'd obviously just scored a goal and she'd missed it. He waved across at her and Stella waved back, giving him a thumbs up. The thought of Simon walking out on them made her feel sick. She wanted to take all the hurt and not let any of it touch her children. But if he didn't come back, she'd have to tell them sooner or later. She felt a wave of anger at the thought of it, her heart beating faster.

'What a cracking goal.'

Stella looked to her side to see a face she recognised as one of the fathers of another player.

'Sorry, I didn't mean to startle you.' He looked at her, suddenly embarrassed. 'You were obviously miles away.' He laughed gently.

'No, sorry, you didn't... I was just, um... yes, thank you.' She wiped quickly at her face, hoping there were no tears. She seemed unable to tell now if she was crying or not, she felt so numb.

'I'm Ollie's dad, that one over there.' The man pointed to the other side of the field. Stella had no idea which boy he was pointing to but nodded anyway. 'I think our boys are in the same class at school.' He put his hand out. 'I'm Charlie, by the way.' His smile was warm, sincere.

Stella looked at his hand for a second too long and by the time she put hers out, he'd taken his back, then proffered it again. An awkward handshake followed. 'I'm Stella. Sorry, I'm not usually...' She put her hand back in her pocket. 'Nice to meet you.' She managed a smile, then looked at the floor. She didn't know what to say. How could she act normal? 'I'm sorry, I've got to...' She took her phone out of her pocket and waved it.

'Oh, of course. Sorry. I just thought I'd say hello.' He smiled. 'Another time.' He waved and turned, walking quickly back along the pitch towards the other end.

Stella immediately felt bad. There was no phone call to answer. No messages, either. Just an unbearable silence. She looked at her last text message to Simon.

Can we at least talk? Please?

The light grey letters on the screen below her words told her he still hadn't read it.

7

Caroline appeared at the house just after midday, horrified to find the twins – not to mention Bridget – still in their pyjamas.

'Can I get you a coffee, Caroline? Stella's on her way back, she's just messaged me. Five minutes, she says.' Bridget led Caroline through to the kitchen, suddenly wishing she'd at least wiped the surfaces clean of pancake batter as she clocked Caroline sweep her eyes over the mess.

'Actually, that would be lovely, thank you.' Caroline took a seat at the kitchen table, moving a cereal packet to one side as she did. 'So, what's happened?'

Bridget hit the button on the coffee machine and it whirred into action, the sound filling the room. 'Well, she didn't say much, to be honest. All she said was that he left last night and she hasn't heard from him since. Hopefully it's just an argument, I'm sure he'll be back later.' Bridget decided against telling Caroline about the tie. It seemed so ridiculous.

'But that's not like them, is it? I mean, this hasn't happened before, has it?' Caroline reached out to take the steaming coffee cup from Bridget. 'Thank you.'

Bridget sat down with a sigh. 'Not that I know of. I've never thought of them as great arguers. I mean, I know they argued a bit more when the kids were tiny, but I think we can put that down to tiredness.'

'Well, that's par for the course.' Caroline laughed a little, then caught herself. Bridget didn't have children of her own and Caroline didn't know if this was through choice or not. A few seconds of awkward silence followed. Both were relieved to hear the sound of the key in the front door.

'That must be her.' Bridget got up and went to meet Stella.

Max ran into the kitchen, his cheeks flushed pink. 'Hi, Auntie Caroline.' He crossed the room and gave his aunt a hug.

'Wow, look at you! You've grown so much since I saw you.' She squeezed him back. 'How does pizza and sleepover at ours tonight sound? Jake's back from university for the weekend, hopefully.' Caroline's sons, Jake and Arthur, adored Max and he, of course, loved hanging out with them. And Caroline relished having the twins to herself, deprived as she was of female company in her own household.

'Sounds good, thank you.' Max nodded enthusiastically. His eyes narrowed momentarily. 'Is Mum not coming?'

Caroline fixed her smile in place. 'She's got a lot of work to do later, so I said I'd take you all off her hands for a bit. She'll come and get you tomorrow. Hopefully she can join us for Sunday lunch.'

'Oh, OK.' Max nodded. 'I'll go and get changed.'

'Put some pyjamas in a bag, toothbrush too,' Caroline called after him.

Stella walked into the kitchen just as Max left. 'Hey.' She managed a smile.

'Hey, how are you doing?' Caroline stood up and kissed her sister on both cheeks.

'Fine. Well, not really.' Stella shrugged. 'Thanks for holding the fort, Bridge.'

'You're welcome.' Bridget smiled. 'I did tell the girls to get dressed, but I'm not sure I've quite got the knack when it comes to being forceful.'

'No, you're definitely the fun one compared with me.' Stella laughed gently. 'I've just told them to go up. I'll go and see how they're getting on.'

Caroline took her cup over to the sink. 'No, let me go. I'll give them a hand. I take it you haven't heard anything?'

Stella shook her head. 'Nothing. Not a word. Honestly, I have no idea where he is. He's not answering his phone, it just goes straight to voicemail. He's not even read my messages.'

'I don't understand why he'd just go like that. That's so... dramatic,' said Caroline. Her barely concealed dislike for Stella's husband had always been a sore point, one that they both tried to avoid as much as possible.

'Please, Caro. Don't do that, it's too soon.' Stella sat down next to Bridget at the table, sinking into the chair.

'Sorry, I didn't mean...'

Stella waved her hand. 'I know. I've just got to think. Except I can't even...' She sighed, her eyes lowering to the floor. 'I just don't get it.' She looked up at Bridget. 'Am I missing something? Do you know something I don't?'

'No!' Bridget was quick to respond. 'Stella, if there is something wrong, he needs to tell you. You can't be expected to second-guess.'

'And I'm sure there's a perfectly simple explanation to all this.' Caroline tried to sound sincere. 'I reckon by the time you pick the kids up tomorrow, Simon will be here and everything will be back to normal.' Seeing her sister so blindsided was horrible to watch. 'Right, I'll go and chivvy the children and we'll get going.

Just promise to keep me posted, let me know when he's back.' She paused. 'Or gets in touch, at least.'

Stella looked up at her big sister. She couldn't ever imagine Philip leaving. He wouldn't dare. But, as overbearing as she could sometimes be, there was no denying Caroline was good in a crisis. 'Thank you.' Stella smiled, but it didn't reach her eyes. She felt totally numb.

Bridget got up and went to give Caroline a hug. 'Thank you, I'll look after her at this end, I promise.'

* * *

With overnight bags packed and loaded into Caroline's car, Stella and Bridget waved to the children as they drove off down the road. They'd seemed quite happy to be going away for the night, although Stella could tell Max suspected something was up.

Bridget put an arm around her as the car disappeared out of view. 'You OK? Sorry, silly question. What I meant was, would you like a glass of wine?'

Stella looked at her friend and smiled. This time, it did reach her eyes. 'I think I need a brandy.'

Bridget laughed. 'I'm on it. Go and collapse on the sofa, I'll bring it to you.'

Stella headed to the sitting room and curled up at one end of the big sofa as instructed, Percy at her feet. She checked her phone again. No messages, no voicemail, no emails. She ran through a list of people she could call to see if they knew anything. But then, what would she say? If she said he was missing, they'd say she should call the police. And she knew that he wasn't missing. He'd chosen to go because he didn't want to be with her. That's what he'd said and for now she had nothing else to go on.

* * *

That afternoon, Sarah messaged the book club group chat asking if anyone fancied a trip to the cinema the following week.

Stella's phone pinged when the message arrived. She grabbed it, hoping with her whole being that it would be a message from Simon. When she'd read it, she held the phone out to Bridget.

'Can you tell them what's happened? I want them to know.'

'You sure? They'll insist on coming over, you know that?'

'I know, I want them to if they can. I want to be with you all.' Stella wiped at her face with the scrunched-up ball of tissues she held in her hand.

* * *

An hour later, they sat, the four of them, quite literally holding Stella together while they tried to figure out where her husband might possibly be – and why he'd left in the first place.

'And there really weren't any warning signs?' Lucy asked again.

'Honestly, no. I know I probably sound mad or maybe like I'm kidding myself, but I thought that everything was fine. There was the usual stuff – we've been really busy at work and we should have probably made more time for each other without the children being around, but then it's always like that, I guess.' Stella shrugged her shoulders, looking at them for reassurance.

Sarah leaned forward to pour herself more wine from the half-empty bottle of white on the table. 'Maybe he's having some kind of midlife crisis.'

Lucy nodded, holding her glass out to Sarah for a refill. 'Maybe he just needs to buy a motorbike or whatever and be done with it.'

Stella shook her head. 'But this behaviour, it's just not him. He's so... measured. Normally, I mean.' She paused. 'There is something I haven't told you.'

'The tie?' asked Bridget.

'What tie?' asked Sarah and Lucy in unison.

Stella uncurled her legs from under her and sat forward, putting her empty glass on the table. 'Might be nothing, but there's just something that doesn't feel right.'

'I don't think you should read too much into it,' said Bridget, hoping she sounded more convincing than she felt.

'Well, he had on a new tie yesterday and it was so noticeable because the style wasn't like something he'd normally buy himself. For one thing, it was expensive, way more than he'd normally spend on himself.' Stella thought of how Simon managed their business finances, questioning every request to spend money. His fastidiousness sometimes drove her mad, but she knew she should be grateful that she didn't have to worry about that side of the business.

'Did you ask him about it?' Sarah ventured.

'Yes, but he just brushed the whole thing off, made out it was no big deal. But afterwards I couldn't stop thinking about it, so I went to have a look when he was in the shower. It's a Hermès tie, for god's sake.'

'That's so not like him!' said Lucy, laughing a little, then immediately feeling bad for doing so. 'Sorry, Stella, I'm not saying he doesn't... just that he's nothing if not conventional with his wardrobe.'

'I know, that's the thing. It's really not him. That's why I noticed, I guess. And what's weird is the way he clearly tried to gloss over the matter. If someone gave him the tie quite inno-cently, why not tell me?'

'But asking him about a bloody tie is hardly grounds for bolting for the door, is it?' Bridget's eyes narrowed.

There was a moment's silence. Stella knew what they were all thinking so she decided to say it out loud. 'You all think he's having an affair.'

'Oh, come on, we don't know that, Stella, there might be a really simple explanation for all this,' said Bridget, stroking Stella's hair softly.

Stella looked straight ahead. 'An affair is the only explanation that makes sense though.' Her voice was firm.

In a swift movement, she got up from the sofa and left the room. She raced up the stairs two at a time, went into their bedroom and opened the wardrobe where she assumed she'd find the tie, but it wasn't there. He'd clearly taken it with him.

Stella walked over to the big chest of drawers under the window overlooking the common. People were out making the most of the unexpected sunshine. She picked up a photo frame from the top of the chest and looked at it, their wedding photo. She'd always loved that photo, taken on the beach, the sun so bright it had put their faces in shadow, but the smiles on both of their faces were unmistakably happy.

'Where are you?' Stella spoke the words into the universe in the hope that, wherever he was, Simon might hear them and remember how much he loved her. Or at least had loved her once. Tears fell from her eyes, slowly at first, but soon her cheeks were wet from crying.

She opened the top drawer and started searching through his socks, then opened the next drawer down, pulling his clothes out onto the floor, waiting for a clue to land at her feet. She went to the cupboard and lifted his clothes out onto the bed, reaching into the pockets of his suit jackets and trousers. Next, she riffled through the drawers in the small table on his side of the bed, dropping everything onto the carpet. All these years, they'd never had secrets, but as she went through his things, it was like going through the belongings of a stranger.

Picking up the photo frame again, Stella lay back on the pillows and closed her eyes. One word filled her mind, crowding out everything else. She whispered it over and over again: why, why, why, why, why? The photo frame fell to the floor with a dull thud.

By the time Bridget, Sarah and Lucy came up the stairs to check on her, they found Stella curled in a ball on the bed surrounded by clothes, her body shaking with silent sobs. Lucy sat beside her and gently rubbed Stella's back while the other two quietly put the room back together.

8

At first, the days passed slowly, each minute crawling by. But before Stella knew it, Simon had been gone for a week, then two, then four. Despite not wanting to get out of bed most mornings, Stella forced herself to keep going, not least for the sake of the children. She was functioning rather than living, but it was the best she could do. She spent hours going through their paperwork, trying to find something, anything, that might tell her where or why he'd gone. She found some old mobile phone records, trawling through them with a highlighter, ringing any numbers she didn't recognise. With each fruitless search, Stella's hope slowly diminished.

After a week of telling them their father had simply gone away for work, Stella knew she'd have to tell the children the truth. At least, what she knew to be the truth. She had sat them down at the kitchen table after school one day and delivered the news that their father had gone. She told them she didn't know where or why and she didn't know when he was coming back, but, hopefully, he'd be back soon and then he could explain it himself. It took all her self-control to not unleash a torrent of words at the very thought of what Simon had done, tell them that he'd ripped her whole world apart without so much as saying goodbye, but she held it in.

Max had nodded, his eyes fixed on the table. Stella could see he was trying hard not to cry, his fingers digging into his palm. Millie had looked confused, Isla sad. Then, after a few moments, they'd asked what was for tea.

Bridget, Sarah and Lucy had taken it in turns to drop in on Stella every day for the first few weeks, making endless cups of tea and tidying up the kitchen. They brought food, not that Stella could eat much of it. Caroline had been typically practical, driving up each week to spend a day at the house with Stella, changing sheets and sorting out the washing.

'There must be someone else you can call who might know where he is?' asked Caroline one afternoon as she folded laundry at the kitchen table.

'I've tried everyone I can think of. I've tried his friends that I know, our old colleagues. No one's heard from him.' Stella sat at the table, her laptop in front of her. The screensaver, a picture of the children and Simon on a Greek beach from a particularly lovely holiday taken just a few years before, seemed like it was from another lifetime. She looked at her husband's face, smiling out at her, so familiar and yet suddenly completely unknown.

'What about his family? There must be a relative somewhere?'

'He didn't have any. Not that I know of, anyway. Just us.'

'Facebook?'

'He loathed the idea of Facebook. Doesn't even have an account.'

'What about your bank account, has he taken any money?'

'No, he's not touched our joint account. I know he had his own account; we always kept our own accounts as well as a joint one for our mortgage, bills and everything else like that.'

'And are you managing with work?' Caroline reached for a biscuit from the tin that sat between them on the table.

Stella smiled a little. 'Yes, everyone's been brilliant.' Most of her colleagues had been with her since Star Pots' early days and even though Stella was the public face of the company, they really were a team. She'd told them Simon would be away for a while and that they'd have to manage without him for the time being. She hadn't elaborated and they didn't question her further, knowing that Stella would tell them in her own time what was going on if she wanted to. A temporary finance manager was being recruited, so, other than keeping an eye on the business, Stella was able to keep in touch from home. 'But, to be honest,' she sighed, looking up at Caroline, 'I'm going to need to get back to it sooner rather than later, given that we've still got bills to pay and it looks like I'm the only one paying them for the time being.' Her stomach dropped at the thought, but she knew they were in a far more fortunate position than most with some savings in the bank, a roof over their heads and family and friends who seemingly wouldn't leave her alone, for now at least.

'You know, I didn't want to say anything, but I've never...'

Stella shook her head at her sister. 'Caro, please don't. I know you've never liked Simon.'

'It's not that I didn't... don't like him, it's just that I couldn't ever really get a grip on who he was as a person. He's without history. I mean, who doesn't do Facebook? What about that other one? Link Up or whatever it's called.'

Stella fixed Caroline with her eyes, tears threatening to fall again. 'Please, don't,' she whispered. 'I feel bad enough as it is.

Honestly, I have no idea why he's gone. No idea. And no, he didn't do LinkedIn either. Hated stuff like that.' Stella looked up at the ceiling, as if expecting an answer to come from somewhere. 'I know you all thought I married him too soon, that I was too young. That we had children too quickly.'

'Oh, come on, Stella, we've never said that.'

'No, but I know you and Dad think so.'

'Have you told Dad yet?'

'Not yet. Have you?' Stella looked at her sister.

'Of course not, that's up to you. He'd want to know though. You know that don't you?'

Stella sighed. 'I don't want to worry him.' She didn't want to admit that the reason she'd held off was because she'd fully expected Simon to be back by now, having realised how much he missed and loved them.

But that hadn't happened. Instead, she'd been left with no clues as to when he'd be back. If he'd be back. Not only that, Simon seemed to have taken her courage and strength with him, leaving her fumbling from one day to the next, wondering how long her life would feel like it was on hold. She felt utterly wretched.

Caroline stood up and made her way across the kitchen. 'I'm going to make you some tea and then you're going to sit on the sofa and read a magazine or watch some mindless television or something. I'll get the children from school. And I've brought you some supper, so I can leave that in the fridge for you to heat up.'

'Thank you.' Stella sighed again, grateful for her sister's kindness.

'Is Bridget coming over later?'

'Yes, she's dropping in on her way back from work apparently. But, honestly, you really don't have to organise round-the-clock care for me, I'm fine.'

Caroline looked at Stella, her face drained of colour. Her hair was drawn back off her face, her cheeks sallow. 'Darling, you are not fine. And if this was happening to any of us, you'd be doing the same thing. Now, do as you're told and take this to the sofa.' Caroline handed her a steaming mug of tea.

Stella knew there was no point in arguing and, anyway, she simply didn't have the strength. 'Thank you.' She returned Caroline's smile, took the mug and made her way into the sitting room.

'Right, I'm going to take Percy for a quick walk, then I'll go and get the kids. You rest, I'll see you in a bit.'

Stella heard the front door close behind Caroline. She lay back on the sofa and closed her eyes, wanting sleep to come so her mind would stop whirring. Her head ached.

She reached for her phone just to check again to see if there was anything she might have missed. Perhaps there was something in their text exchanges before he left that might explain why he'd gone, something she just hadn't spotted before, although she'd looked endlessly already. Practically knew their last exchanges by heart, having gone over them so many times. Things had been a little tense with work and children, but nothing that had given Stella cause for concern. She scrolled through her phone, seeing his words swim before her eyes. Maybe she'd been kidding herself all along? Maybe he had never really loved her at all? Even so, you didn't just walk out on your family. That was unfair. Unforgivable, even.

Tears fell down her cheeks, but for the first time since he'd left, they were tears of anger. She felt a rage she hadn't known before, making her heart thump against her chest. She was, Stella realised, absolutely bloody furious with him.

* * *

'I think this is a good thing,' said Bridget. She paused, pointing her fork at Stella for effect.

'What do you mean?' Stella took a small mouthful of Caroline's – delicious, it had to be said – lasagne. It was the first time for weeks Stella had felt like she really needed to eat. Anger had made her hungry.

'Feeling like this, you know? It's the first time you've actually said you're cross with him for leaving.'

Stella took a slow sip of the red wine in her glass, warm bramble fruit flavours filling her mouth. 'It's almost like I don't want to believe anything other than it's just temporary. Because if I do, I have to acknowledge there's a big problem.' She put her glass down. 'And if I do that, it means we can't just pick up where we left off when he does finally come back. Does that make any sense?'

'Kind of.' Bridget took another mouthful. 'God, your sister's good.' She gestured to the food.

Stella nodded and smiled.

'I'm going to say something and I don't want you to get cross with me, OK?' Bridget looked at Stella. 'You can't just sit here waiting for that to happen.'

'What do you mean?'

'You've put your life on hold for the last month or so and still there's been no word.'

Stella grimaced. 'Thanks for reminding me.'

'No, I don't mean... What I mean is, do you think it's time we started thinking about what life might look like without him. Because say he does want to come back, would you want him to? After doing this, I mean?'

There was a pause. Stella took another sip, then shrugged her shoulders. 'I honestly have no idea.'

'You're living your life in a holding pattern, waiting for Simon to call you. And that call might not come, darling. I'm sorry to have to say it out loud.'

'I know.' Stella put her glass back on the table. 'Bridget, believe me, I know. It's all I think about, every single bloody second of the day. I just want to know why.'

'Well, we love you and we think it's time we started making plans of our own, not right now, of course, but soon. Put in a weekend where we go away, just us girls.'

'Book club?'

'Exactly.' Bridget smiled.

'Why do I get the feeling you lot have already got a plan?' Stella managed a small laugh.

'We might have talked about something. We just thought you could do with a complete change of scene for a few days, go somewhere where you don't have to think about anything but having a nice time.'

'And where, exactly, were you thinking?'

'Florence.' Bridget grinned at her friend. '*A Room with a View*, remember?'

Stella smiled. 'Our first book.'

'Technically, our only book.' Bridget laughed. 'But we did always say how one day we'd all go. And that was meant to be before anyone got married. That was before you had kids, and before I seemingly forgot to have kids.'

Stella squeezed Bridget's hand. Bridget had been trying to conceive for a while, having finally talked Neil round to the idea of starting a family together, enduring rounds of IVF over the last couple of years. Nothing had worked, and as time had gone on, Bridget had talked about it less and less, until one day she had declared herself quite happy without children as long as she could borrow her friends' to hug as often as she wanted. Of course, they all knew Bridget was covering a deep well of sadness, but over time she had taught herself not to peer down into it too often.

'It's a lovely thought, but I'm not sure a mini-break to Florence is going to help me right now. And anyway, I can't leave the children. Not at the moment, it's too soon.'

'We're not thinking right now, but perhaps in a couple of months' time. Let's just find a weekend and put it in the diary, then we've got something to look forward to. It might all be different by the time we go, anyway.'

'You mean he might have reappeared? I'm not so sure.'

'He might. But I'm not going to let you just plough on regardless. You'll need a break at some point and Florence is the perfect place to have it.'

Stella sighed. 'I did love that book. And the film. Haven't seen it for years.'

'So, is that a yes?' Bridget looked at her hopefully.

Stella knew from her friend's face they'd clearly discussed it in detail. She found herself nodding, partly because she was too tired to argue. 'Yes, it's a yes.'

'It's a yes!' Bridget exclaimed, jumping up on to her feet. 'Wait until I tell the girls.' She reached for her phone and tapped out a message on the group chat. 'I'm not saying a holiday is going to fix everything, of course it's not. But it might just give you some space and time to think about things when you're not so close to them, you know? Failing that, we'll just fill you up with ice cream and negronis for a few days.'

Stella's phone pinged. Her hand shot out to pick it up, but, of course, it was just the notification from Bridget.

She said yes!!

A string of heart and pizza emojis from Lucy followed. Then came a reply from Sarah:

CAN'T BLOODY WAIT X

Stella knew Bridget was right, she couldn't just sit and wait for her missing husband to figure out whatever it was he was doing, wherever he was doing it. She had a family to look after, a business to run, a house to manage. Much as she hated the idea, she had to carry on without him for now.

'Mama?' Stella looked up to see Isla standing by the kitchen door in her nightie.

'Hi, sweetie, are you OK?'

Isla made her way across the kitchen in her bare feet, clutching her favourite teddy, and instantly climbed onto Stella's lap.

Stella instinctively put a hand to her daughter's forehead. 'Goodness, you're boiling. Come on, let's get some medicine down you.'

She led Isla over to the sink and reached up into a cupboard, taking out the bottle of Calpol and grabbing a spoon from the drawer.

'Here, in one.'

Isla dutifully downed the spoonful.

'How about you have a small glass of water, too?'

Isla nodded.

'Come on then, I'll take you back upstairs and tuck you in.' She took her daughter's hand again. 'Back in a sec,' she called to Bridget as they made their way down the hall.

'I'll clear this up,' Bridget called back and stood up to clear the plates.

She looked around the kitchen, with its fridge covered in children's drawings and photo frames on the side filled with happy smiling faces. She felt so sad for her friend, wishing she could tell Stella when this would all be over. But all Bridget could do for now was wait and hope.

9

The sound of her phone ringing woke Stella from her slumber. She'd lain awake for much of the night, trying to find sleep. It had danced just in front of her, only to move away when she thought she might be getting close. And just when she had fallen into a deep sleep through sheer exhaustion, it was time to get up again and get everyone ready for school.

Stella reached for her phone. It was her father. Being an early riser, he always assumed everyone else would be up and busy by now. 'Hey, Dad.'

'Sorry, early I know.'

She glanced at the clock. It was almost eight o'clock. 'Shit, is that the time? I must have overslept... Thank goodness you did ring. Dad, listen, I'm running late. Can I get the kids to school and call you back?'

'Yes of course, I was just going to suggest I meet you for lunch today, that's all.'

She could tell by his voice that he knew what was going on.

'Did Caroline tell you?' Stella asked.

There was a pause. 'She did. But please don't be cross with

her. I'd asked if you were all right as I hadn't heard from you for a bit, and you didn't answer my last message.'

'Oh no, I'm sorry, Dad. I meant to reply but I didn't really know what to say and the last few weeks have gone by in a bit of a blur and, well, I'm just sorry not to have called before now.'

'Stella, please don't apologise. I just want to know that you're OK.'

'I'm OK,' Stella lied.

'So, can you spare me an hour today? Lunch on me at the usual.'

The usual was the same restaurant they'd been going to as a family for years. Birthdays and anniversaries were always spent there, at a table halfway down one side with a view of the room and the river beyond, the open kitchen to the right.

Stella hit the speakerphone and talked as she threw on some clothes. 'I've got a meeting this morning, but I can be there by 1 p.m. How's that?' Stella decided not to mention to her father that the meeting was with a solicitor for the time being. Much as she didn't want to admit it, she knew she couldn't put it off any longer.

'Sounds perfect.'

'Is Susie coming?' Stella hoped her stepmother might be, for moral support more than anything.

'Just me, I'm afraid. She's already got plans.'

'OK, no problem. Send her my love. I'll see you there at one o'clock.'

'See you then. Bye.'

He'd gone before she had a chance to say goodbye, an old habit of his.

Racing into the children's rooms, she woke them up in turn, urging them to get dressed quickly. Ever since it had just been the four of them in the house, Max had taken it upon himself to be more helpful, getting ready a bit earlier so he could help get the twins sorted. It was as if he knew his mother was hanging on by a thread, wanting to help her so it wouldn't break.

Dropping the children at school in the first few weeks after Simon left had been awful. Stella avoided eye contact with any of her usual school-gate friends for fear of them asking how she was. Liz, one of the mums with a daughter in the same class as the twins, had asked Stella if everything was all right when she'd picked them up from Liz's house after school one day. Stella had done her best to reassure Liz that everything was fine, knowing she must have looked pretty awful for her to ask, given they were simply acquaintances rather than good friends. She'd managed to meet with Max's teacher after drop-off one morning briefly, asking her to let the staff know that the children's father was away indefinitely and that she'd be grateful if the teachers could let her know if Max brought it up at all, or behaved differently, and the same with the twins. The teacher had been kind and sympathetic in a professional way, for which Stella was grateful, assuring her that all seemed well and that school would keep an eye on them.

But before long, Stella saw what she thought looked like pity in some of the eyes of those nodding their hellos to her. Word must have got out, she concluded. She knew it was only a matter of time before someone heard something from someone, whether it was via one of the children's friends or someone at work or even, she thought, somebody who knew Simon. She'd never know for sure. And the not knowing, about anything, was exhausting.

Fixing her sunglasses in place, Stella pulled her jacket tighter around her and made her way back to the car. Glancing at her watch, she saw she just had time to go home and walk Percy, when she could call and talk to the office at the same time, before changing and heading into town to see her solicitor at their offices. This would be her first proper outing since Simon left that required actual clothes rather than tracksuit bottoms and an old jumper. Her house had become her haven, filled with her family – apart from her actual husband, of course – and friends and leaving it to face the world outside felt daunting. But she couldn't ignore her solicitor's messages any longer, the office had been trying to reach her for weeks.

Stella walked through the park at a pace, Percy trotting behind her, trying to focus on her surroundings rather than the tangle of thoughts in her head, but failing miserably. Back at the house, she stood in front of her wardrobe. She pulled out an old favourite black blazer, pairing it with a pale pink silk shirt and a pair of black skinny trousers. The jacket hung from her frame, her hair lacking its usual shine. Stella resorted to the darkest bronzer she could find in her make-up drawer, covering her face in colour and applying blusher and a slick of lip gloss. She looked at her face in the mirror. Not great, but it would have to do, she thought. Turning her back on her reflection, Stella made her way downstairs. She went to the kitchen to fetch her handbag, deciding the breakfast table would have to stay a mess until later. Closing the heavy front door behind her, Stella made the short walk to the Tube station.

It felt like another world since she'd last done this and as she joined the stream of people moving down the tunnels to the platform, her chest tightened. She tried to slow down her breath, focusing on putting one foot in front of the other.

Standing on the platform, waiting for the train, Stella was reminded of all the countless times she'd stood on that very same platform with Simon as they'd headed to work together. She'd always loved the way they could stand together on the train, communicating through looks rather than words in an overcrowded carriage. But now she stood alone. She imagined him suddenly appearing, running down the steps and leaping on the train just before the doors shut.

Just then, the Tube train appeared from the blackness of the tunnel, lights looming. Once the doors had opened, she stepped into the carriage and managed to find a seat, grateful to be able to sit for a moment and steady her breathing. Looking around, she took in the faces, all staring at screens, some with faint smiles on their faces, others nodding their heads to the sound of beats flooding their ears. Why was she looking for him? She knew he wasn't going to be here on the first train that she happened to get on. But there was something about being back in the world outside her own four walls that felt strange, like she just might be in the same space as him at some point. A wave of nausea came over her, making her skin feel clammy.

Stella looked up to see the name of her stop flash by the window, once, twice, three times. The train slowed and she stood to get off. As she waited by the door, she looked at the passengers waiting on the other side to get on. *Stop looking for him, he's not here,* she told herself. Was this how it was going to be for the rest of her life?

She shook her head a little, as if trying to rid it of the image of his face. But it wouldn't go. He might have physically left her, but mentally he was everywhere. The irony was almost too much to bear.

* * *

Two hours later, as Stella sat at the table in the restaurant waiting for her father to arrive, she looked out across the crowded room. As ever, there was a mix of business and pleasure taking place at various tables. At the larger ones, people in suits talked while barely noticing their food. At smaller tables, couples sat exchanging forkfuls from each other's plates. Waiters moved quickly between tables, trays of food and drink held high. Calls to action from the chefs could be heard from the kitchen at the far end and the warm smell of garlic, rosemary and butter wafted out across the room.

Stella picked up the menu, a simple piece of paper with the day's date at the top. Glancing down the page at the dishes on offer, she felt her stomach rumble. She'd not eaten that morning, going straight to coffee instead.

Looking out across the restaurant towards the river outside, she watched the world go on in front of her, the happy hum of people talking and laughing around her. It seemed impossible that she'd ever feel that carefree again. Just then, she looked up to see her father walking across the restaurant towards her, a familiar smile on his face. 'Hi, Dad.'

'Don't get up, Stella.' He motioned for her to stay sitting, coming round to kiss her cheek. As he sat down, a waitress appeared with two flutes of Prosecco, along with a small plate of bruschetta, dripping in oil. 'Lovely, thank you.' He smiled at the waitress, then turned to his daughter. 'So, how's things?'

Stella tried her best to look and sound breezy. 'Oh, you know… things have been better.' She smiled, tears springing instantly to her eyes. 'Sorry.' She managed a half laugh, half cry. 'I thought I'd last a bit longer before…' She wiped at the tears threatening to fall.

'I'm so sorry.' Her father reached across and gently put his hands over hers. 'We're really sorry. Susie sends her love, of course. How long has it been?'

'Dad, I'm so sorry I didn't tell you. I didn't want to worry you. To be honest, I thought he'd be back by now.'

'How long, Stella?' His voice was calm, gentle.

'Almost six weeks.' She picked up her glass and took a sip, the bubbles hitting her tongue like a thousand tiny sherbet raindrops.

'And you've really not heard a thing from him?'

'Nothing, Dad.' Stella sighed. 'He said he wasn't happy. It's not like he just disappeared with no reason. Except that he didn't really explain it and that's the bit that's so hard. I just don't know.'

'How are the children?'

'They've been amazing, really. Better than me, that's for sure.' Stella wiped quickly at her eye, brushing away another tear. 'The thing is, Dad, I'm just exhausted. How the hell did you do it?'

'What do you mean?'

'When Mum died... I'm not talking about emotionally, though any tips on that are gratefully received.' She managed a small smile and sat back in her seat. 'I mean, how the hell did you manage to look after us both on your own?'

He looked at his daughter, thinking how much she reminded him of her mother, with that same brown hair and bright, hazel eyes, and it broke his heart to see her hurting this way. 'I know it's tough and I wish I could tell you when it will get better, but the only option is to just keep going. One day at a time. That's what I did and eventually, after a while, it does get easier. But for now, just do what you need to do.'

The head waiter appeared to take their order. 'Hello, Mr Morris, Stella. How are you both?'

'Well, thank you, Joseph, how are you?'

'Very well, thank you. We have your favourite on the menu today. Fresh in this morning.'

'Dover sole?' Her father's face lit up. 'Yes please.'

The waiter nodded and turned to Stella.

'And I'll have the calamari – we can share, Dad – and then the risotto verde.' She smiled up at Joseph.

'And another couple of glasses of this, please.' Stella's father tapped his glass.

'Dad, I shouldn't.'

'It's only Prosecco. And they're small glasses.' He smiled. 'My treat.'

'Thanks.' She picked up a piece of bruschetta, popping it into her mouth. It felt good to be out, doing something normal rather than sitting, waiting for a text, an email, a call, or spending hours trawling the social media accounts of his friends in the hope of tracking Simon down.

'So how was your meeting?' He too reached for the plate.

Stella shrugged her shoulders. 'It was with my solicitor. I just thought I should see her, let her know what was going on and it was fine, really.' This wasn't quite true. During the meeting, her solicitor had broken the news to Stella that the house and business were in both their names, so at some point she and Simon would have to discuss what to do about that. It had seemed so unreal to be talking about the man she had thought she knew so well as if he were a stranger. Her solicitor had gone on to talk about protecting her assets, but she hadn't really been able to take it all in, scribbling a few notes in the hope that the advice might make more sense to her when she came back to it later. She was usually all about the detail, but it all felt so surreal, unbelievable in fact.

'Well, that's something I suppose.'

'I kind of wish he'd done something dramatic before leaving, at least then I'd know why.'

'You don't mean that, Stella.'

'The funny thing is, I really do.'

'Stella, I realise I may be a little biased, but you are my brilliant, funny, fearless daughter.' He held his hand up when she tried to protest. 'Please, it's important you hear this. Obviously, only Simon knows why he decided to leave. Hopefully, one day he can explain his actions, but until then don't punish yourself trying to work it out. It'll drive you crazy. You need to conserve your energy for you and the children. And we're all here to help, OK?'

Stella nodded slowly, her head down. 'I know, Dad. I'm just so bloody furious about it.' She lifted her eyes to meet her father's gaze. 'How could he do this to us?'

Her father shook his head a little. 'Life has a habit of really blindsiding us every now and again. What I do know is that all we can do is keep going and hope that things will get better.' He picked up his glass. 'They usually do.'

Stella held her glass up to his. 'I wish Mum was here.'

'I know.'

They raised a silent toast between them.

As she walked back home, along the river with the spring sun on her face, Stella passed couples on the footpath, old and young. Life went on around her and she wondered, as she did about a million times a day, where Simon was. What was he doing? Who was he with? And, of course, the hardest question of all – why wasn't he with her?

She remembered her father's words and looked up at the pale afternoon sky. She took out her phone and, before she overthought it, quickly tapped out a message to book club. If she really was going to try to take her mind off Simon, perhaps Florence was a good idea after all.

10

As soon as Stella had said she was ready to go, the other three had swung into action. Lucy was on flights duty, Sarah and Bridget took on the task of finding a hotel and Stella was told to do nothing but organise childcare for a couple of weeks' time, from Friday afternoon until Sunday evening.

With offers from both Caroline and her father and Susie to help look after the children and the dog while she was gone – honestly, they were all thrilled to hear she was going away – Stella felt happy leaving the organising of everything else to her friends. Frankly, she didn't really care where she was going. Anywhere would do, as long as it took her mind off her current situation even for just a little bit.

Stella returned to the office for a couple of days a week but found it almost impossible to engage with what was going on. Instead, she sat in meetings, nodding and smiling in what she hoped were the right places. She'd always been so driven and focused at work but now struggled to complete even the simplest of tasks without considerable effort.

The children, however, had continued to amaze her with their resilience. Max had even told her to stop asking if he was all right, telling her not to worry about him. Sometimes, when she tucked them into bed at night, the twins would wonder aloud when Daddy would be back. As much as Stella wanted to tell them he'd be home soon, she caught herself and took a breath, not wanting to give them false hope. Then, as calmly as she could, she'd reply that she wasn't sure yet, but as soon as she knew, she'd tell them. But for now, they just had to manage without him.

On the morning of their flights, Stella had dropped the children off as usual before returning home to walk Percy and make some calls while doing so. Then, sitting down at the kitchen table, she attempted to clear her inbox. She sipped at her coffee and tried to focus on the words in front of her, but, predictably, infuriatingly, Stella's mind wandered back to Simon. Determined to get him out of her head, she shut her laptop and went upstairs to pack a suitcase. She still had a few hours until Bridget picked her up. Max was off to stay with his best friend for the weekend and Caroline had insisted she collect the girls from school, clearly thrilled at the thought of a few days in town with the twins. 'Philip can look after the boys. I'll take the girls to a musical or something,' she'd said before telling Stella in her inimitable, matter-of-fact way that she simply must go and have a wonderful time and not to worry about them for a second.

Stella went upstairs and stood for a moment in the middle of their bedroom, wondering where their small suitcases were. As far as she could remember, they'd always been kept under the bed, but there was no sign. She opened her cupboard to check, knowing there wasn't room for them given the amount of shoe-boxes in there. For some reason, she was incapable of throwing away shoes, even if they hadn't been worn for years.

She closed the doors and walked over to Simon's wardrobe. Apart from that first afternoon when she'd pulled at whatever she could find, she'd barely been able to look at anything of his without feeling either sick, angry or both.

Stella took a breath and opened the doors, her stomach flipping over on itself at the sight of his clothes hanging as if nothing had happened. Stella spotted one of her favourite pairs of his shoes on the rack below the clothes, conker-brown brogues he'd worn when they'd first met. It was so strange to see all his clothes still there, like props left behind after a play had ended its run.

Stella looked up at the shelf above, spying what she was looking for, a small black case that she'd sometimes pinch back when they used to have the odd weekend away. Technically it was Simon's, but she liked the size of it, perfect for carrying on to a plane.

Using the stool from her dressing table, Stella climbed up and reached for the case, pulling it down and throwing it onto the bed. She opened it and smoothed down the fabric inside, trying to concentrate on what she needed to pack. According to the group, the weather in Florence was going to be ideal, warm but not yet hot. She grabbed some underwear, socks, a couple of loose cotton shirts, a pair of cropped trousers and a couple of her favourite summer dresses. She added a pair of sandals to the suitcase, threw in her washbag, taking out the liquids, and squashed it on top.

Just before closing it, Stella turned and grabbed her favourite long cashmere wrap from the shelf. She laid it across the rest of the clothes and pushed down on the lid of the case again to do up the zip. As she did so, she felt the outline of something small and square in the front pocket of the case. Opening the zip of the pocket, she reached inside and pulled out an old brown leather wallet. Thinking it must have been left there since Simon's last trip, she opened it up to see if there was anything still inside. Just as she'd expected, the wallet was now empty, though the shape hinted that it had at some point clearly been put to good use.

Stella opened it out fully, peering into the pocket at the back where banknotes must have once been. Again, empty. She went to close the wallet, wondering just how old it was, when she spied a tiny speck of white paper tucked down to one side. Reaching in, she slowly pulled out the scrap, taking care not to rip it as she did. Holding it in her fingers, Stella wondered just how long it might have been sitting there, hidden away. Putting the wallet down, she carefully unfolded the paper. Two sides had straight edges, the third was ripped. Realising it was the corner of a newspaper page – she could tell from the texture, though there was no date, annoyingly – she peered at the name and number written in small letters in faded black ink. It read: Emily Parker. Underneath was a number, an old landline number, Stella guessed, although it didn't look like one from anywhere she knew.

Stella sat on the edge of the bed, still holding the scrap of paper carefully in her fingers. She racked her brain, trying to recall whether she'd heard that name before, while pretty sure it was completely new to her. Stella looked at the writing again, as if searching for a clue about the person who wrote it. The hand-writing was neat and deliberate, not at all like Simon's scrawl. What secrets did Emily Parker hold?

She reached across and grabbed the phone from beside the bed. Holding the handset in her hand, she punched at the numbers on the piece of paper in front of her. Her heart raced in her chest and for an agonising few seconds Stella braced herself, though she didn't know what for. Then a noise came down the line, so loud in Stella's ear she almost dropped the phone, a long flat tone telling her the number didn't exist.

Dropping the handset into her lap, Stella gently shook her head, laughing to herself a little as she did. Had she really expected to find the answers she so was so desperate for from a stranger in one phone call?

She looked around the room, then flew downstairs to the kitchen and took a seat at the table, opening her laptop as she did so. Typing the name into the search bar, she waited to see what the internet would throw up. Soon, the screen was full of Emily Parkers, most of them far younger than Stella. She started clicking on some of the profiles, desperate to find a link to Simon. Over and over again, she clicked on a stranger's face, only to be led down a rabbit hole of more people she neither knew nor recognised.

It wasn't until the doorbell went that she glanced at the time and realised it was after midday. She'd been sitting at her laptop for over two hours.

Stella went to the door, hearing Bridget's voice before she got there.

'You're early!' Stella couldn't hide the surprise from her voice. She glanced at her face in the mirror, slightly appalled by the dishevelled person looking back at her.

'I know, bit overexcited. Thought I'd come early and give you a hand.' Bridget walked past Stella into the kitchen and sat down at the kitchen table, looking Stella up and down. 'I assume you're going to get dressed properly before we go on our mini-break to one of the most beautiful places in the world?' She turned and squinted at the screen in front of her. 'Who's Emily Parker?'

Stella swiftly shut the laptop and scooped it up, along with the small brown wallet beside it. 'Oh, it's a work thing.' She knew telling Bridget now would mean a cross-examination and, given she didn't yet have any answers, she decided it was better to wait before telling her friend. 'I'm just going to go and finish packing, won't be long. Help yourself to coffee, you know where every-thing is.'

Stella went upstairs and put the wallet in her bedside drawer, deciding that whatever secrets Emily's name might hold, they'd just have to wait until after Florence.

* * *

Twenty minutes later, Stella's packed bag sat at the bottom of the stairs. Percy was sulking in his basket in the corner of the kitchen, having spied the bag, refusing to make eye contact with Stella as she gave the kitchen one last look over.

The doorbell rang on the dot of 2 p.m. Lucy's voice came through the letterbox. 'Hey, you ready?'

Stella bent down and ruffled the dog's neck as she passed him. 'Oh, Percy. You're making me feel guilty. I'll be back in a few days, I promise.' He looked up at her with his enormous soulful eyes, then quickly looked away before laying his head down once more with a long sigh.

She opened the door to find Lucy and Sarah waiting for her, huge smiles on their faces.

'Ready.' Stella smiled back and, for the first time in what felt like forever, was actually looking forward to what the next few days might bring. She'd not given the trip much thought until now and realised she didn't even know where they were staying. Of course, she'd offered to help, but the others had insisted on making the arrangements. As they piled into the car and made their way to the airport, the sound of chatter filling the air, Stella felt her body relax a little.

'Will we be there in time for dinner?' asked Sarah.

'I should think so, the flight's only a couple of hours,' said Bridget. 'Lucy, you're in charge of finding us somewhere to eat, given you know the city best.'

'But that trip was years ago!' She'd visited Florence as a

teenager with her family on holiday. 'I really can't remember very much about it. We did get dragged around the museums, but I remember being more interested in the ice cream, to be honest.'

'I'm thinking double scoops, twice a day. At least.' Sarah laughed.

'I've got a couple of recommendations from one of my authors on where to go to find good restaurants.' Lucy scrambled around in her bag for her phone. 'I've written them in my notes somewhere.'

'I love that we're heading to a city filled with some of the most incredible art in the world and all we're thinking about is what we're going to eat and drink.' Stella was laughing now too.

'Obviously.' Lucy winked at her cousin. 'We couldn't possibly admire *David* on an empty stomach.'

11

They arrived before sunset, the taxi speeding towards the city centre and crossing the Arno before weaving its way through increasingly narrow streets towards their hotel. The sun bounced off the water, glinting as the river beckoned them on towards the heart of Florence. Stella took in the glorious skyline with the unmistakable orange dome of the cathedral, the bell towers and surrounding hills. It looked almost dreamlike.

Bridget and Sarah had settled on a small, family-run place on the south side of the river. They'd managed to bag the last two rooms and the location was perfect. As the group of friends spilled from the taxi into the entrance of the hotel, they took in their surroundings with excitement. They were in an old converted private house, complete with impossibly shiny, wooden parquet flooring and enormous chandeliers hanging from the high ceilings. A mix of antique furniture alongside more modern pieces made the space inviting rather than grand and when they walked through to the lounge, two enormous windows over-looked an exquisite garden at the back, a great swathe of green bordered by cedar, oak, horse chestnut and cypress trees. At one end, a large bell tower rose above the trees like a lone candle left on a cake.

The owner, a stylish woman in her sixties, greeted them warmly. 'Hi, I'm Ginevra. Welcome to Florence.' She had a wide smile, her grey hair swept up into a neat bun at the back. 'Let me show you straight to your rooms so you can drop your bags, then we can sort out the paperwork afterwards.' She led them up the stairs and along a narrow corridor to their rooms. Although small with sloped ceilings, both had a free-standing bath, much to the friends' delight. Lucy and Stella took one room, Bridget and Sarah the other, and they agreed to meet on the terrace over-looking the garden to discuss their intended plan of action for the evening.

The sun still shone in the early-evening sky, clouds scudding gently by.

Sarah made her way up to the terrace to find Lucy already sitting at a table, sunglasses on, her fingers quickly swiping at her phone screen.

'I've got drinks coming. Goodness, isn't this glorious?' Sarah looked out across the garden below.

'Stunning,' said Lucy, without looking up. 'I've found some-where for us to go for pre-dinner snacks, too. It's a tiny square not far from here.' She peered at the screen, 'Piazza della Passera. Then I thought we could head up to the Ponte Vecchio to see the sunset over the river, then a quick spin around the outside of the Duomo before heading back this side for dinner.'

'Sounds perfect,' said Sarah, though she didn't like to say she would be happy just sitting exactly where she was for the entire evening with this view. Sarah glanced behind her, then back to Lucy. She lowered her voice. 'How do you think Stella's doing? Do you think she's all right?'

Lucy looked up, perching her sunglasses on her head. 'I think so. Obviously, there's the whole brave-face thing going on. I honestly can't imagine how she must feel, but I'm just hoping this break really does help take her mind off everything, even if just for a little bit.'

Sarah pulled a chair out from the table, taking a seat next to Lucy. 'I know. I do remember how awful this bit of the process is, not that mine was anything like as bad.'

'Oh god, of course you can. I'm so sorry, Sarah.' Lucy looked mortified. For a moment, she'd totally forgotten that Sarah had been through a divorce years before.

'Please don't apologise, it's really fine. And anyway, that was a long time ago, now.' Sarah sat back in her seat and put her face up to the still warm sun. 'Also, he was a massive arsehole, which kind of helps, to be honest.' She laughed.

'I know, but still, it must have been hard deciding to leave in the first place.'

'You're right, it was. There were so many times when I told myself life would be easier if I stayed. Things weren't that bad. But that was the problem, really. They weren't bad, but they weren't that good, either. They were just... OK. And I didn't want to feel just OK for the rest of my life. I knew I didn't love Stuart enough and I still think, if he was completely honest with himself, he would say he didn't really love me enough either. We'd just drifted along for so long. Which is bonkers really, because we ended up both being unhappy but not honest enough to admit it.'

'So, what changed?' Lucy had always wondered, but Sarah was usually so private about her relationships, they'd never really discussed the circumstances of her divorce in detail.

'Hurtling towards my mid-forties and realising I was, touch wood,' Sarah looked around for wood before briefly touching the side of her head, 'around halfway through my life and I didn't want to sleepwalk through the rest of it. We so easily could have done, but I knew it was better for both of us to part as friends, not stay together until we really hated each other, you know? And it's not like we had children to worry about.'

Lucy nodded, but they both knew Lucy didn't know. In fact, Lucy had absolutely no idea how that could happen, given she was married to a man she clearly adored and who, in turn, seemed to love her with all his heart. Lucy had met Al in the first week of her job when he'd held the door of the lift open for her and they'd talked all the way to the sixth floor. Turned out he'd pretended to be going to the sixth floor just so he could find out where she sat (she later realised he worked in the finance department on the second floor). He'd regularly invented reasons to be on the same floor as Lucy in the hope of bumping into her (without success) until a few weeks after that they'd once again been in the same lift going down. Sadly, that time they hadn't been alone and despite having mentally rehearsed asking her out for drinks, Al hadn't had the chance to speak to her before she'd left the lift.

Eventually, their paths had crossed at an impromptu drinks party thrown on the fourth floor by a team celebrating a particular signing and, this time, Al went straight over to Lucy as soon as he saw her. They'd gone out for drinks after work that evening and became firm friends for almost two years before Lucy looked at him one day and realised her feelings were a lot stronger than friendship. When she finally plucked up the courage to tell him, helped by two enormous glasses of warm Pinot Grigio at a book launch she'd dragged him along to, he'd asked what had taken her so long, although frankly she could have said the same to him. Nearly twenty years of marriage and two children later, despite being quite different on paper, they were entirely complementary as a couple. A formidable team with a relationship built on respect and the fact that Al made Lucy laugh like a drain.

'Anyway, this trip's definitely not the place for me to talk about my ex-husband,' whispered Sarah, nodding her head towards Stella and Bridget, now making their way across the terrace to join them at the table, followed by a young waiter bearing a tray with glasses and an unopened bottle.

'Well, this is a bit bloody all right, don't you think?' Bridget took in the view before grinning at her friends and taking a seat on the other side of the table.

'Look at you, Stella,' Lucy whistled.

Stella smoothed down her pale blue cotton dress. Her hair was still wet and her skin pink from the shower she'd just taken. She folded herself into the free chair and crossed her legs, the silver espadrilles on her feet catching the light. 'Stop it.' She smiled at her cousin across the table.

'Skin and bone, though.' Bridget reached across and gently pinched Stella's arm. 'I'll make it my personal mission to fatten you up over the next few days.' She picked up her glass of Prosecco as the waiter finished pouring the other glasses.

Sarah frowned at Bridget. 'Hey, don't make her feel worse, she looks great.'

'No, I know she's right. The heartbreak diet might be the only one I've ever done with instant results, but I really don't recommend it. Bloody nightmare.' Stella laughed at her own understatement. 'Anyway, here's to us being here. Thank you for making this happen.' Stella looked each of her friends in the eye and clinked their glasses in turn. 'Here's to getting lost for a few days.'

'To getting lost,' they chimed, before taking their first sip under the Tuscan sun.

* * *

'Are you sure it's this way?' Sarah called to Lucy, who was now walking ahead with her phone in her hand looking up at the buildings around her, then back to her phone again.

'Yes, Ginevra said it was this way. Said we couldn't miss it.' What they were looking for was a small trattoria in the square Lucy had mentioned, suggested by the hotel's owner as the perfect place to find something to eat before heading out to see the sunset over the Arno. 'She said it's run by an old friend of hers, best bruschetta on this side of the river apparently,' said Lucy, still walking at pace.

They'd left the hotel and walked along quiet streets lined with sand-coloured buildings, their shutters painted green. Neighbourhood shops sat closed behind metal grilles, their huge dark wooden doors were firmly closed. The streets were low-key and quiet until, as they rounded a corner, they found themselves at the edge of a cobbled piazza. At one end stood a large church with a plain light stone façade and a simple round window at the top. In the middle of the piazza, an impressive octagonal fountain provided a place to sit in the shade of the trees, and cafes and restaurants lined the edges, tables spilling out onto the cobbles.

'I think we need to come back here later for a drink,' said Sarah, gazing up at the tall buildings around her, admiring the arches at the top. 'I like the look of that one there.' She pointed up to what looked like a rooftop bar.

'Lucy, hang on,' Stella called out to her cousin, now marching across the piazza ahead of them.

'It's just up here. If we get there now, we'll have time to get something to eat before walking up to the bridge to see the sunset,' Lucy called back.

'Nothing's going to get between her and a plate of food,' Bridget laughed, grabbing Stella's hand and pulling her on.

They walked down a few more quiet streets before coming to a tiny square. Benches lined the outside, bicycles strewn against the back of them. People sat in groups, talking and laughing, and in the middle, a huddle of small children drew on the stone floor in chalk.

'Please say it's this one, I'm starving.' Sarah looked ahead at a restaurant on one corner, the tables outside already busy.

'Oh, it looks gorgeous,' said Stella, slightly out of breath.

They were quickly shown to a table by the waitress and Lucy noted how most of the people at the other tables were both young and Italian. She took this as a personal triumph. 'Always a good sign when you're surrounded by locals, I think.' She nodded conspiratorially to her friends.

A waitress brought menus and Stella suggested they order a selection of dishes and share.

Lucy nodded. 'As long as there's tomatoes and bruschetta involved, I'm happy. What about to drink – more Prosecco?'

'Surely it's got to be a negroni given it was invented in Florence.' Stella looked at the drinks list as she spoke.

'Good choice, our bartender here makes a very good negroni.' The waitress smiled at them knowingly.

'Sounds good, thank you. We're all in.' Sarah looked at them, to be met with nods of approval all round.

The air was still warm and the sky above showed signs of a setting sun. Their first negroni loosened their limbs, the second their tongues. Before long, plates of crostini topped with cavolo nero, bruschetta piled with bright red tomatoes and slices of salami covered the table as they talked easily and laughed a lot.

They quizzed Sarah on the modern minefield of internet dating now that she was very much back on the field of play post-divorce and listened open-mouthed at Sarah's descriptions of what some men expected to know before even committing to a first date. She horrified them with tales of personal grooming expectations in places they'd never even considered and had them in hysterics at the tale of one potential date who sent her an unexplained picture with a sock covering his genitalia.

Bridget brought up the time she'd got talking to the most beautiful-looking man she'd ever seen in a bar in Greece when she and Stella had gone on holiday, years before, when they were both still single. 'He leaned across and kissed me right there, in front of everyone. Except for Stella, who'd missed it because she was in the loo. When she returned, I decided not to tell her what had happened for fear of appearing to be a total lush.'

'Which obviously you were.' Sarah grinned.

'Anyway,' said Bridget, 'a few moments later, I went to the loo and returned to find Stella at the bar kissing the same man, so I went up and tapped Stella on the shoulder, who turned round mid-kiss and looked absolutely mortified.'

Stella put her hands over her face, laughing. 'Shit, I'd forgotten all about that.'

'However,' continued Bridget, dramatically, 'the guy simply shrugged and said he didn't realise we were friends, then said given he'd kissed us both, how did we feel about carrying on? And that's when Stella picked up his beer from the bar and poured it into his crotch.'

'You didn't!' cried Sarah and Lucy in unison.

'Too right I did.' Stella nodded, laughing.

More drinks arrived and it was only as they finished their third negroni that Lucy looked up and realised with a cry that they'd missed seeing the sunset.

'We'll see it tomorrow, I promise.' Stella squeezed her cousin's hand across the table. She sat back in her chair and looked up at the sky, now a beautiful dark blue. Her cheeks ached from laughing, a feeling she'd almost forgotten. Simon popped into her head, almost as if passing through to make sure she hadn't forgotten about him. She closed her eyes.

'Are you all right?'

Stella opened them to see Lucy looking at her, brows knitted together.

'I will be. Thank you.' She smiled and took another sip of her drink. 'Now we're here, shall we stay and order some pasta to share? Those aperitifs have left me still hungry.'

They duly ordered more food, sharing plates of penne with tomato and vodka sauce covered liberally with Parmesan, followed by short, sharp espressos and a shot of limoncello on the house for each of them.

They reluctantly left the restaurant and started walking slowly back towards the hotel, passing through another small square on the way. On the corner, above an enormous arched doorway, Lucy spotted a plaque. 'Look!' she cried, pointing up at it. 'This is where Elizabeth Barrett Browning lived!'

'How on earth did you spot that?' Sarah laughed.

'I just looked up and there it was. I love her poetry. I used to read it endlessly when I was younger.' Lucy sighed.

'So you did, I remember,' said Stella.

'When did she live here?' Bridget squinted up at the plaque, trying to make out what it said.

Lucy read the words. 'Weird, they've spelt her name wrong. It's double "t". Anyway, she lived in Florence with her husband for years, absolutely loved it here. What was her famous quote, something about Florence being like a chimney?'

'Florence is my chimney corner, where I can sulk and be happy.' Stella's voice was quiet, but the words were crystal clear.

'How did you remember that?' Lucy turned, her eyes wide with admiration.

'I'd love to say I remember you reading it to me, but there's a framed print of it in our hotel. I spotted it on the wall when Ginevra showed us round.' Stella shrugged her shoulders, a whisper of a smile on her lips.

Sarah put her arm around Stella's shoulders and Bridget hugged her from the other side. They stood for a moment looking up at the poet's old windows onto the city before walking on, arms looped together.

12

Stella woke to the sound of birds, so loud she thought they might be in the room. Creeping out of bed, she walked to the window, not wanting to disturb Lucy, who was still fast asleep on the other side of the bed. Her cousin wore a black eye mask with the words 'FUCK OFF' embroidered on it in white stitching. It had made Stella laugh the night before and was the last thing she could remember before falling asleep.

But it wasn't long until the familiar dreams, or rather nightmares, had taken up residence in Stella's head. Walls had closed in on her as she threw clothes into a suitcase, trying desperately to get everything packed before she ran out of time and space. As ever, she'd woken up from the nightmare just as everything went dark, her breathing shallow, her chest soaked in sweat. Her heart was beating so fast, it felt like it might just burst out of her chest.

Stella opened the window overlooking the garden so she could put her face to the still cool air outside. The sun was yet to throw its light over the city. She glanced back at the clock beside the bed; it was half past five in the morning. Knowing sleep wasn't going to come back to her now, she pulled off the T-shirt she'd slept in and threw a clean dress over her head. She quickly splashed water on her face and cleaned her teeth as quietly as she could before grabbing her cardigan and her bag, slipping her feet into her trainers.

She went downstairs, the young man behind the reception desk greeting her with slight surprise before nodding and opening the front door for her. She assured him everything was all right, telling him she just wanted to go for an early-morning walk.

'In that case, can I suggest you head up to the Duomo? It gets so crowded during the day, but at this time, you'll be able to walk around the whole of the building, the outside I mean, and there will be no one there.' He smiled at her.

'Thank you, great tip.' Stella smiled back and stepped out of the hotel, turning right and heading to the end of the street, before turning left towards the river. The streets were empty, bar the odd scooter zipping past.

Within a few moments, Stella reached a bridge and saw the Arno, its gentle waters reflecting the pale blue of the cloudless sky and the colours of the buildings on either side. The morning light had started its creep across the city from the east, lighting up the ochre walls one after the other as it went.

Stella stopped halfway across the bridge and looked along the river at the Ponte Vecchio with its matchbox houses stuck along the sides. Above the arches, the large windows of the Vasari Corridor at the top of the bridge hinted at the hidden treasures Florence held within the walls of the buildings around her.

Walking over the bridge, Stella headed north across a deserted square and on past the imposing rough stone walls of the Strozzi Palace and the shuttered shopfronts of Gucci, Armani and other famous Italian designer names. Turning a corner, the buildings seemed to get older, the streets narrower, the shops giving way to cafes and restaurants, all still closed at this early hour. A street cleaner stood by his truck smoking a cigarette, an old man walked past with a small dog on a lead, nodding a silent hello as she passed him.

Stella walked on for a few moments and then, up ahead, glimpsed the pink, white and green stone of the Duomo. The orange domed roof and bell tower to its right loomed into view, the sheer size and scale taking her breath away. It was a sight she'd seen so many times in films, but it looked almost too beautiful to be real, even though it was right in front of her eyes.

She walked around the octagonal basilica first, its green horizontal stripes making it look like confectionery. Then she walked the perimeter of the cathedral, with just a few passing Florentines and a young American couple getting their Duomo-at-sunrise Instagram money shot for company.

The peace of it all, alongside the sheer magnificence of the building, made Stella feel small but present as she took in her surroundings. The benches that sat along the sides of the cathedral were still empty and so she sat alone, marvelling at all the shapes and patterns of the building. For months, her world had shrunk to one of pain, of getting through each day without crying in front of the children, of answering work queries and pretending to care. But here, for a moment, she felt still and calm.

Slowly, more people started appearing around her as if they'd been given their stage call. Stella took out her phone and tapped out a message to Caroline, asking if everything was all right and asking her to kiss the girls for her. She looked at the screen showing her list of favourite contacts, the names all so familiar. Bridget. Caroline. Dad. Lucy. Sarah. Simon. Seeing the last name still made her stomach lurch. She hovered over the phone, wanting to delete it, erase all trace of him. Having spent months desperately trying not to let herself text him again, knowing there'd be no reply, in that moment she wanted to remove him altogether. Her finger trembled over the screen, willing it to hit DELETE.

But she knew she couldn't just erase him, for the children's sakes. They still loved him. And if she was honest with herself, she still loved him. That's why it hurt so much, this physical pain that seemed to pull on her heart. An ache that just wouldn't go away.

Stella shook her head gently and raised her eyes from the screen in her hand up to the building and the sky beyond. She stood and looked around, deciding it was time to find some coffee and maybe something to eat. It was still early, not yet seven.

She stretched her legs out and reached her arms up before standing and heading back towards the river down a long pedestrian street. She wasn't surprised to see the shops still shut but walked on in the hope that one of the cafes might be open. She soon found herself on the edge of Piazza del Signoria with the enormous hulk of the Palazzo Vecchio and its clock tower to one side. There were statues everywhere: a fountain with a statue in the middle to one side, *David* on the other (she knew it was a copy; Lucy had told them the night before and insisted they must go and see the real thing while they were in Florence) and underneath the arches yet more statues. Two stone lions sat either side of the entrance leading up to the open hall and seeing there were still no cafes open, Stella walked over and perched on the steps, looking back across the square. She glanced at her watch. Now she'd started thinking about something to eat, she realised she was quite hungry. There were still relatively few people about, but the tourists were starting to arrive in the square. Surely, they'd be thinking about breakfast too.

'It's weird, right?'

Stella turned to see a young woman sitting a few steps further up. She had long dark hair and bright red lipstick on. She spoke with an English accent.

'You'd think of all the places, Florence would be somewhere you could get coffee easily, but the funny thing about this place is that nothing really happens before eight o'clock in the morning. It's quite civilised, when you think about it, I mean.' The woman smiled at Stella.

'I was wondering why there was nothing open. You sound like you're used to it. Do you live here?' Stella turned to face her.

'For about four months. I've been working as an au pair. Well, worked.' She pulled a face.

'Oh no, what happened?'

'Turns out the husband had other ideas about what services an au pair offers.'

'How awful.' Stella instinctively reached out a hand but was too far away to touch the woman. 'I'm so sorry to hear that.'

'It's fine, really. I got out before anything happened but found myself without a job or somewhere to live, so I'm staying with a friend and I've got an interview this morning for another job. As a tour guide, actually.' The woman picked up a dog-eared guide-book beside her. 'I've been swotting up all week. Ask me anything.' She laughed.

'OK...' Stella looked around. 'Who's the guy in the fountain?' She pointed at the one to the side of the Palazzo Vecchio.

'Neptune, commissioned by Cosimo de' Medici, of course, most of the statues were, to be honest. This one was to celebrate his gift of clean water to the city because Neptune is the god of freshwater. Apparently,' the woman nodded towards the statue, 'his features were modelled on Cosimo's.'

'Very good,' laughed Stella. 'Anything else?'

'How are you with gory stories?'

Stella grimaced. 'How gory?'

'See that clock tower?'

Stella glanced up.

'Another family called the Pazzis tried to overthrow the Medicis, but the plot went wrong and they only managed to kill one of the Medici brothers who ruled at the time. So, when the perpetrators were finally caught, they were hung from ropes out of the windows of the building.' The woman looked up at the Palazzo.

'OK, that is quite gory.' Stella too looked up towards the tower, then down to the windows below.

'That's not the gory bit. When they hung them out of the window, one of them started biting another one, literally sinking his teeth into the leg of another, eyes practically popping out of his head, in a desperate bid to stop himself from hanging to his death.'

Stella pulled a face. 'That is truly horrible.'

'Sorry, I didn't mean to put you off your breakfast. Talking of which, looks like you're in luck.' The woman pointed over to the cafe on the far corner, its shutters now up. 'I've got to go, but promise me one thing, you'll order a cornetto con crema with your coffee. Honestly, there's no better breakfast.' The woman went to stand up.

'I will, thank you,' said Stella. 'Good luck with your interview. And for what it's worth, I think you're going to be brilliant.'

'Thanks.' She smiled back.

Stella watched as the young woman headed across the square, her stride purposeful, until she was out of sight, then Stella stood and made her way across to the cafe. Taking a seat at a table outside, she watched as more people poured into the square. Soon, the sound of teaspoons hitting saucers surrounded her like a morning orchestra. She ordered her breakfast exactly as instructed and the waiter appeared with it swiftly, placing the cup along with two cornetto pastries on a small plate on the table in front of her. Stella devoured them, catching the flaky pastry in her hand held below her chin. She licked her fingers, then picked the remaining flakes from the saucer with her fingertips and ate them too. The coffee afterwards was strong and bitter, a perfect contrast with the sweetness of the cornetto.

Stella took in the blue of the sky above, the people milling about the square, the sheer splendour of the setting. Just then, her phone buzzed in her pocket. It was Lucy, checking to see if she was all right. Stella sent back a photo of her empty coffee cup and said she'd be back in fifteen minutes.

* * *

Lucy dropped her phone onto the duvet, which was so deliciously light it was like sleeping under a marshmallow. She sank back into the pillows and sighed. She thought of her cousin, of her laughing the night before.

They'd always been especially close, her own mother like a surrogate to Stella when she lost hers. They'd play endless card games as children, talking for hours as teenagers about what they might be when they grew up. She smiled to herself, remembering how they'd planned to live next door to each other when they were older so that their families could be friends and they could carry on seeing each other all the time. But life hadn't turned out like that, of course.

Stella and Simon really had seemed like the perfect couple. The fact that they worked together, building up a successful company, was a feat in itself. Lucy worked in the same industry as her husband, and they sometimes talked about work at home, but she couldn't imagine actually working with him. There was no way she'd be able to leave the argument about who'd left the top off the milk or forgotten to put the bins out at home and be able to act like nothing happened at the office. But, then again, Stella and Simon were very different people. Stella had always been meticulous about whatever she did, while Simon was driven by ambition. Thinking about it now, his focus on goals was one of the things Lucy had liked about him at first. But, over time, she had watched him become more involved in Stella's business, and before long he had talked about it more than she did. Like it was his business.

Lucy stopped herself. If Simon hadn't done a disappearing act on Stella, she probably wouldn't be thinking like this.

Her phone pinged. Fumbling for it among the covers, Lucy picked it up and squinted at the screen. It was a message on the group chat from Bridget.

I THINK I'M DEAD!!!

Lucy typed out a response, telling Bridget she wasn't dead; it was just a hangover and that she'd see both her and Sarah for breakfast on the terrace in half an hour. Bridget replied saying that she thought she might have food poisoning, emphasising the point with all the appropriate emojis. Lucy smiled, pulled the eye mask back over her eyes and turned on her side to doze until Stella returned.

13

Stella crossed back over the narrow Ponte Vecchio bridge towards their hotel, the old wooden shopfronts of numerous jewellery stores lining the bridge either side. Above each one, a yet unfurled canopy with the trader's name: Biscioni, Gherardi, Cardini, Fantoni. Halfway across the bridge, Stella stopped, looking down the river towards the bridge she'd crossed earlier that morning, now busier with people heading into the centre. She took a moment to take in the river, the sounds of a city coming to life around her. Taking a deep breath, she had to concede that a change of scene really had been a good idea. Her head felt a little clearer, despite the previous night's negronis, her body didn't ache as much as it usually did recently. The endless questions and fears that seemed to run through her brain on a loop had been temporarily muted, too. Florence, with its sheer beauty, really was doing its best to help cheer Stella up.

Stella crossed the road at the end of the bridge and headed down a narrow street running parallel to the river, before turning left towards the hotel, or so she hoped. She found herself crossing the beautiful Piazza Santo Spirito from the night before, now clear of tables and people.

Her phone vibrated in her pocket. Reaching for it, she sat on a stone bench just in front of the church and pushed up her sunglasses to read the screen. It was a message from Caroline.

Hope you're having a lovely time. Taking the girls to see Matilda the Musical today! My treat. Max is fine too… spoke to the mum last night. Have an ice cream for me x

Stella smiled to herself. Much as her older sister annoyed her sometimes, she didn't know what she would have done without her since Simon had left. As sisters, they'd really had their moments over the years, but now they were older, they appreciated one another more than ever before.

Stella sent a message back, thanking Caroline for everything, asking her to kiss the girls for her and promising to eat lots of ice cream on her behalf.

Returning to the home screen, the familiar picture of the five of them stared back at her. She knew she should change it – looking at it was always painful – but she just couldn't bring herself to. Just then, a missed call notification popped up. It was from the office. Stella knew they wouldn't bother her unless it was urgent but wondered why anyone would be in the office on a Saturday. She dialled the number back. It was answered after the first ring.

'Hi, it's Stella, I missed a call.'

'Hi, Stella, it's Lily.'

Lily had been covering Simon's role at Star Pots for the last few months. Something about her tone made Stella's stomach flip.

'What's happened?'

'I'm so sorry to call you, I know you're away for the weekend, but I thought you'd want to know as soon as possible.'

'What is it?'

'I've found a hole in the accounts. Quite a big one, actually.'

'What do you mean, a hole? How big?' Stella's heart raced. She felt sick.

'Well, it took a bit of time to uncover. It's been done cleverly. Over time, so, at first, I just didn't spot it. But it looks like someone – and I'm pretty sure it's the work of one person – has been skimming profits for some time.'

'How much are we talking?' Stella could barely get the words out.

There was a pause. 'Thousands. Tens of thousands, actually.' Lily sighed. 'And that's just what I've uncovered so far. I'm so sorry, Stella.'

'Who else knows about this?'

'Just me at the moment, I wanted to be sure before I came to you.'

'It's Simon, isn't it?' Stella stared up at the small round window in the wall of the church in front of her. She spoke slowly and deliberately now, trying to control the anger she could feel rising in her chest.

Lily spoke quietly. 'I've put a stop on any funds leaving our accounts until you're back, but, to be honest, nothing's been taken for a while. I think it was a pattern that stopped when...' There was a pause.

'When Simon left,' Stella finished Lily's sentence. She closed her eyes for a few seconds, then opened them again. No, it wasn't a dream. She was still here in Florence, being told that her husband had been stealing from her, from their business, for months, probably longer. How could he do this to her? She wanted to scream, smash the phone, run. But, instead, she took a deep breath and thanked Lily, reassuring her she'd done the right thing by calling, and saying they'd go through it all next week as soon as she was back in the office on Monday. Until then, it was to be kept between them.

Putting the phone back in her pocket, Stella put her sunglasses back on, her hands trembling slightly. Slowly, she got up and walked back to the hotel. She decided to keep the news to herself, not wanting to ruin the only full day they had together in Florence. In that moment, she started to feel something she hadn't really felt until then. Of course, she'd felt angry at him leaving, raged about him walking out on them all without a second glance. She'd also felt wretched, betrayed and broken. Now, as she walked slowly across the Piazza's grey stones, noticing the patterns under her feet, she felt a sense of release. Until now, she'd made endless excuses, mostly to herself, about why he'd done what he'd done. Maybe she hadn't been loving enough, attentive enough, attractive enough? But now she knew. She had always been enough. The problem was he was not what she'd thought.

* * *

By the time Stella got back to the hotel, the others were all up on the terrace sitting at a table at one end, eating breakfast. Sarah and Bridget were insisting that the other one take the last pastry from the basket in the middle of the table.

'There you are!' said Lucy, waving at Stella as she made her way to the table. 'How was your walk?'

'Illuminating.' Stella smiled.

'Did you have breakfast already? We can ask for some more of these.' Sarah pointed at the now empty basket. 'Or do you want a coffee, at least?'

'I'm fine, thanks. I had one by the Palazzo Vecchio. Weirdly, it's not as easy to find coffee here as I thought. Literally nothing opened until about eight o'clock.'

'What time did you head out?' asked Lucy. 'I didn't even hear you go.'

'You were dead to the world, Luce.' Stella sat down and reached for an empty glass, before pouring herself some orange juice.

'Are you OK?' Bridget peered at Stella, looking concerned.

Stella fixed a smile on her face. 'I'm fine, really. Probably just tired, to be honest. So,' she decided to change the subject as quickly as possible to avoid the tears pricking at her eyes from falling, 'what's the plan?' She picked up her glass and took a gulp, the flavour of freshly squeezed oranges a welcome change to the stale taste she'd had in her mouth since the phone call.

Bridget passed a paper napkin across the table to Stella. 'Here's the plan, expertly drawn by Sarah this morning.'

Sarah laughed. 'Lucy told me what to draw.'

Stella looked at the napkin, showing a scribbled map of places to visit, illustrated with quickly done drawings depicting various sites. It looked like a treasure map.

'We start by walking across the bridge to here,' Bridget pointed at a dome, 'then on to see *David*.' Her finger came to rest on a drawing of a penis. She looked at Stella seriously, tapping her finger repeatedly on the illustrated landmark.

Stella looked at her friend. 'You're ridiculous.'

'But funny,' said Bridget, winking at Stella.

'He's got massive hands, I seem to remember.' Lucy held hers up to emphasise her point.

Stella nodded. 'OK, great, we go and see *David* and his massive hands. Then what?'

'I don't mind where we go as long as there's ice cream,' said

Sarah. 'And no negronis.' She winced at the thought, remembering how they'd seemed so harmless the night before. What deceptive little drinks they'd turned out to be.

'Then we must go to Vivoli, which is the oldest gelato shop in Florence apparently,' said Lucy. 'I think it's near Santa Croce.'

'Isn't that the church in that film, the one with Tom Hanks?' asked Sarah. 'I worked on that film.'

'In Florence?' asked Bridget.

'No, Pinewood Studios. I just remember having to paint stuff to make it look old. Chairs, tables, you name it.'

'Did you meet him?' Bridget's eyes were wide.

'Again, sadly not. Well, not properly, anyway. I knelt at his feet once, painting a chair leg that needed some work in between scenes. I don't think he noticed I was there. That's all part of the job, to be kind of invisible.'

'How disappointing.' Bridget's face fell.

'So, *David*, then ice cream, what else?' Stella peered at the paper map on the table. She pointed at a drawing of a knife and fork.

'That's the big Central Market, we thought we could go and get lunch there or pick up a few things to take to the Boboli Gardens, save ourselves for a proper feast when we go out later,' said Lucy. 'What do you think?'

'I think it all sounds absolutely perfect.' Stella meant it. Anything to take her mind off what she now knew. 'Right, I'm just going to have a quick shower, I'll be ten minutes.' She got up to leave the table. 'Meet you all downstairs.'

They said of course and carried on chatting until she was out of earshot.

'OK, something's happened. Did you see her eyes? She looked as if she'd seen a ghost,' whispered Bridget to the others once Stella had disappeared from view.

Lucy nodded slowly. 'I think you're right. But you know what Stella's like. Brave face and all that. She'll tell us when she's ready.'

Sarah sighed. 'I hate seeing her like this. It makes me want to find Simon and ask him what the bloody hell he's doing.'

Bridget reached across the table and put her hand over Sarah's. 'I know you know more than us what this feels like. It must be hard seeing her go through it too.'

'Divorce is horrible.' Sarah literally shivered at the memory. 'But being with the wrong person is worse. Not that I can tell her that yet.'

'She'll get there.' Lucy sighed. 'Stella is one of the strongest people I know.'

They sat in silence for a moment, each lost in their own thoughts.

Upstairs in her room, Stella stood with her face under the hot jets of water from the shower, tears falling so fast she feared they might never stop.

14

The four women set off from the hotel, Lucy in charge of navigation. Stella had arrived in the hotel reception with her sunglasses firmly in place and smiled and nodded as each of her friends quietly asked if she was OK. They knew the answer, but they also knew their job was to carry her through the day as best they could.

Within moments, they reached the bridge Stella had crossed that morning, stopping to look back along the river at the Ponte Vecchio, by now busier with tourists. Cotton-wool clouds hung casually above the city in the bright blue sky, a gentle breeze moving them along slowly.

They walked up through the narrow streets into the heart of the city, through small squares and along roads lined with shops, many still yet to open. Sarah took in her surroundings. 'The whole place has a decidedly unrushed feel about it, like no one's in a desperate hurry. Don't you think?'

Lucy coughed. 'Well, kind of. I didn't want to freak you all out by making lots of plans, but I have booked us tickets to the Accademia this morning, so we don't have to queue.' Lucy held up a piece of paper.

'When did you do that?' Bridget turned round. 'I mean, thank you, obviously. But that's so organised!'

'I'm sorry, I can't help it.' Lucy laughed. 'We're booked in about fifteen minutes, so perfect timing. I just knew if we didn't, then we wouldn't get in, and if there's one thing I really want to see while I'm here it's *David*. Just to see if he's as big as I remember.'

Bridget and Sarah raised their eyebrows at Lucy. 'No, not like that.'

Stella laughed. 'Thanks, Lucy, that's really thoughtful of you. And you're right. We should absolutely see the real *David* while we're here.' Silently, she wondered who the real Simon was but pushed the thought to the back of her mind, not wanting it to spoil the day ahead of her.

They walked on, turning a corner to see the Duomo in front of them, so tall it momentarily blocked the sun from view. They stopped and stared, taking in the details, from the vast bronze doors of the Baptistry to the arches, frescoes and sculptures on the front of the cathedral. By now, crowds of tourists moved slowly around the outside of the buildings, eyes turned upwards to take in their surroundings rather than down towards their phone screens. Groups gathered around various tour guides, the gentle hum of humanity on a city mini-break all around. The queue to enter the cathedral snaked around the outside of the building.

'We can come back and do this later, it should be quieter this afternoon,' said Lucy. 'Let's keep going.' She nodded towards a street leading north away from the cathedral. 'The Accademia's up this way.'

'I've never seen anything so...' Sarah whispered, still standing gazing at the Duomo. 'Unbelievable.' She tried to take it all in, the scale seemingly impossible to comprehend.

'I bet the view from up there is amazing.' Bridget pointed at the clock tower to the side of the building. 'Come on, or we'll lose the others.' She grabbed Sarah's arm and they turned towards the road Lucy had gestured to and walked quickly to catch their friends up.

Restaurant tables on the narrow pavements were being set for a day's trading, awnings now covering them. The women continued past shops selling perfume, leather goods, books and art supplies. Scooters and bicycles jostled for position on the sides of the roads, left by their owners as they went about their business in the city.

Thanks to Lucy, they bypassed the queue of people waiting to enter the Accademia, an unassuming building from the outside with no-nonsense square windows and a simple wooden doorway. Inside, it was a completely different story. A long hall led them towards the heart of the museum, a statue depicting women looking tangled and tortured dominating the space. Lucy nodded towards it. '*Rape of the Sabine Women*.' She gazed at it for a few seconds, then carried on walking towards a second hall. 'This way.'

'I feel like I'm on a school trip,' whispered Bridget to the others.

They dutifully followed Lucy into the next hall and there, beyond it, bathed in natural light pouring from the ceiling above stood Michelangelo's *David*. Sarah, Bridget and Lucy walked on towards the bright white marble stone, but Stella was drawn to the sculptures on either side, seemingly half-carved, unfinished. She walked up to the first one on the other side of the room, peering at its form as she got closer to it. The figure looked as if he was desperate to escape from the rock holding him in place, the force of movement almost palpable. The rock still bore the marks of a chisel.

Lucy appeared at Stella's side. '*The Awakening Slave*,' she said, nodding.

'What are the others?' asked Stella, her eyes still scanning the statue.

'The series is known as the Slave Sculptures. Michelangelo did them, but they were unfinished. There's this one, the *Bearded Slave* up there, *Atlas* over there and *The Young Slave*.' Lucy pointed at each in turn. 'I love how they're incomplete, don't you? Like, we haven't got the whole story. There's more to come once they're set free, if you know what I mean.' Lucy carried on looking ahead.

'Are you trying to tell me something?' Stella kept her eyes on the statue.

Lucy turned to Stella and winked. 'Come on, let's go and have a look at *David* and his enormous right hand.' She took Stella's hand and pulled her over towards the others.

An hour later, saturated with sights of statues and paintings, they stepped back into the sunlight, the warm air a sharp contrast to the coolness of the museum. Stella had enjoyed it more than she'd expected; not only that, but she was also delighted to note that, yet again, she was starving. 'Anyone else hungry yet?'

'Me. Are we far from that market you made me draw on the map?' Sarah asked Lucy.

'I don't think so, hang on.' Lucy tapped at her phone for a moment, then looked up and pointed along a road. 'Five minutes or so that way. Follow me.'

'Ooh, McDonald's,' Bridget sighed as they passed the most

tastefully displayed golden arches she'd ever seen, set into the natural golden arches of Florence's back streets.

Stella threw Bridget a look. 'You have got to be kidding me. We come to one of the greatest cities in the world, stuffed with glorious food and you want a Big Mac?' Stella laughed.

Bridget shrugged. 'I'm hung-over. Don't judge me.'

'I promise you, where we're going you will never want to eat one of those again,' said Lucy, airily.

'Hang on, you've already got a plan, haven't you?' Stella eyed her organised cousin.

'Might have.' Lucy grinned at them. 'I published a book with a really brilliant cook recently and she told me about a place in this market that sells a meat sandwich that, she says, literally changed her life.'

'Wow, that's a big claim.' Stella pushed her sunglasses on to her head. 'What's so special about it?'

'Apparently, the secret is in the salting of the brisket before it's cooked. Then they cook it slow and low for a long time before serving it in a bun with salsa verde and something else... chilli oil, I think. And if we ask nicely, they'll dip the bun in the broth before we eat it.'

Stella's stomach rumbled just thinking about it. 'OK, I'm sold.'

'But ice cream later, yes?' said Sarah, hopefully.

'You sound like the girls.' Stella thought of the twins, even though she knew they'd currently be having the time of their life with their beloved aunt.

They walked on, following Lucy down more narrow streets before turning a corner, and there in front of them, hiding part of the Duomo in the distance, stood the Central Market, an imposing two-storey building surrounded with arches and, sitting on the top, a huge cast-iron and glass box.

'It looks like an Italian Smithfields with a French twist,' said Sarah.

'Now, I'm not entirely sure where the sandwich place is, but I'm sure we'll find it if we wander around for a bit.' Lucy led them up the steps into the building to be met with the sight and smells of seemingly endless food stalls. They walked past counters covered in cheese, meats, vegetables, bread, olives, pasta, fish, wine and more cheese. There were whole stalls devoted to mushrooms piled so high, they could barely see anyone behind.

Above them, another floor of tables sat under yet more cast-iron arches. The market was busy but not crowded and after admiring various displays of vegetables so beautiful they looked more like painted porcelain than actual vegetables, they found what they'd come for. There, on a corner, stood a stall with the name Lucy was looking for, Da Nerbone, painted in large gold letters on the green wooden board above.

Lucy pointed. 'Bingo.'

They dutifully joined the queue, eyeing the handwritten menus stuck to the wall behind the counter as a team of people worked fast behind it, shouting instructions to one another behind clouds of rising steam from various pots and pans. When it came to their turn to order, while the others squinted at the menus, Lucy went ahead and ordered four *panino bollito* with all the sauces.

After a few moments, the women stood, each with a hot bun wrapped in paper in their hands, having watched as each one was filled, slathered in sauce and finally dipped in the broth. Gripping their goodies, they walked back outside and headed to a spot on the stone steps outside the building. Sitting side by side, they peeled back the paper and bit into their lunch. For a split second, none of them made a sound as the flavours of the salted meat, the juice-soaked bun and the zing of the sauces hit their taste buds.

'Oh my god,' Sarah was the first to exclaim through a mouthful.

'You were right.' Bridget turned to Lucy. 'That definitely beats a Big Mac.'

'So good,' sighed Stella, licking her fingers.

Lucy smiled at her cousin. 'Glad you like it.'

They sat for a few minutes, savouring every mouthful and licking their fingers once they'd finished.

Sarah screwed up the paper in her hand and tossed it into a nearby bin. 'That was absolutely delicious, just what I needed. Right, where next?'

'How about we head back across the river via the Palazzo Vecchio where I was this morning, we could have a look at the Cinquecento and then on to the Boboli Gardens. They can't be that far from here.' Stella stood up and brushed the crumbs from her front.

Bridget tapped at her phone. 'Not far at all. Bit more culture, then a little lie in the sun.'

'Sounds good to me.' Lucy offered her hand to Sarah and pulled her up.

They set off back towards the general direction of the river, passing through piazzas and crossing car-free streets towards the imposing tower of the Palazzo Vecchio. They took in the glory of the Hall of the Five Hundred, the enormous paintings covering the walls and ceilings almost too much for the naked eye to manage. Bridget's attention was briefly stolen by the tiles on the floor, and she wondered aloud whether she might find anything similar in the Fired Earth shop back home. Stella and Sarah laughed, Lucy simply rolled her eyes.

Once they'd seen enough, they headed along the Piazzale degli Uffizi, booking tickets for a tour early the next morning at a small kiosk, before joining the stream of visitors crossing the

Ponte Vecchio. Up ahead lay the vast Pitti Palace, behind which sat their destination, the Boboli Gardens.

By now, the sun was high in the sky. Together, the four friends walked into the gardens through an amphitheatre-shaped entrance, past a tall stone obelisk and up towards the top of a gently sloping hill, statues gazing back at them wherever they looked. On they went, up the hill towards a lake with a huge bronze figure sitting atop an elaborate carved stone base in the middle of the bright green water.

'Who's that?' asked Sarah as they got closer.

Lucy considered it for a moment. 'It must be Neptune, like the one we saw outside the Palazzo Vecchio.'

Stella pointed at the steps ahead. 'Carry on to the top?'

'The view should be gorgeous from up there,' said Bridget, picking up her pace.

They walked up a huge flight of wide stone steps towards another statue at the top, this one of a handsome woman holding aloft what looked to them like a handful of wheat, before turning to take in the view. Below them, beyond the fountain and the Pitti Palace, lay the city of Florence and surrounding hills.

'There's something quite extraordinary about this place.' Stella sighed.

'Like Valium. What's through there?' Bridget smirked, then pointed at a building hidden behind a tall hedge.

'Can't say I was thinking of Valium, but yes, sort of.' Stella laughed.

They followed Bridget up towards the building ahead and took a path that led them into a small, manicured garden filled with pink roses. The scent reached them before they'd even made it to the garden, carried on a barely-there breeze. Another small fountain sat in the middle of the garden and beyond the far wall cypress trees and Tuscan villas dotted the rolling green hillsides.

A castle, complete with imposing turret, dominated the horizon and on the other side, behind them, a yellow palazzo building with green shutters on the front and statues on the roof sat like an impossibly perfect backdrop.

They stood for a moment gazing at the landscape, breathing in the scent of the roses as they did so. Slowly, they wandered back down the path, then turned left along a long tree-lined avenue, past statues overlooking lawns and hidden in hedgerows. Soon, they came across another even bigger lake, this time, not just a fountain in the middle of it, but a whole landscaped garden.

'This place is like a dream.' Stella made her way to a stone bench to the side of the lake and took a seat.

Bridget sat down next to her. 'Fancy a glass of Prosecco?' She reached into her bag and pulled out a bottle and four paper cups.

'Where on earth did you get that?' Sarah said, laughing at her friend's genius.

'In the market when you lot were admiring yet another pile of mushrooms.'

They toasted Florence with their paper cups before taking a sip of the still-chilled Prosecco.

'Delicious!' Sarah's eyes lit up.

'Gorgeous,' added Lucy. 'Thanks, Bridge.'

The garden was quieter at this end, most of the tourists not making it far beyond Neptune. They sat in a line on the stone bench, their faces to the sun.

Stella looked up at the sky, now cloudless, and took another sip of her Prosecco, letting it sit on her tongue for a few seconds before swallowing. She looked at the floor and took a breath, knowing she needed to share what she'd found out with them. 'I need to tell you something.'

They all turned to look at her.

'Simon's been stealing from the business.' Stella looked up.

'For a while, probably. I'm sorry to bring it up now, I wasn't going to. I just found out this morning and being here with you all, I feel like he's making me carry a secret and I don't want to have to do that. It's not fair, on you or me.' Stella took another sip from her cup.

'Stella, I'm so sorry. That is the last thing you need,' said Lucy, softly.

'Completely. What a bastard.' Bridget closed her eyes, shaking her head.

'I was just actually getting my head around the fact that he's gone, that he doesn't want to be with me or the children any more and there's nothing I can do about that. But to find out he's...' Stella shook her head.

'How did you find out?' asked Lucy.

'Lily rang this morning from the office, she's been looking after the financial side of the business since he left. She said she hadn't wanted to tell me when I was here, but at the same time she's obviously had to freeze the accounts, so I needed to know. Otherwise, I might have got a notification from the bank and not known what was going on. Anyway, he's been taking money out over time, cleverly, so it didn't get spotted. God knows how long it's been going on for, Lily's looking into that now. But she thinks it's quite a lot of money.' Stella looked up, blinking away tears. 'What I don't understand is why. After all, we had enough. It's not like we had any money worries.' Stella wiped at her eyes briefly. 'Why would he steal from us? From a business we built together?'

Bridget took a slow sip from her cup, wondering whether the words that were about to come out were the right ones. She decided to say them anyway. 'Maybe that's why he did it. Because it was your business originally, I mean. Not his.'

Stella looked at Bridget. 'But why would he do that?' Stella simply didn't get it.

'I've no idea. But Simon is turning out to be someone we really didn't know. He's been able to turn his back on you, and on his children. That is *not* normal. You cannot blame yourself for this. It takes a certain kind of person to do what's he's done.' Bridget practically spat the words out.

'Yes, a massive arsehole,' snapped Lucy. She looked at Stella. 'Sorry.'

Stella sighed. 'But that's not who I married. And that's what I just can't understand. Did I just not see him for what he was? Seriously, have I been a complete bloody idiot all these years?' Stella passed her cup to Bridget. 'More please.'

Bridget filled it to the brim, bubbles frothing over the top. 'No, Stella. You are not an idiot. None of us saw this coming. I admit I wasn't his biggest fan, but that's more because he didn't seem interested in us as your friends. He always wanted you to himself.'

Lucy shot Bridget a look and shook her head slightly.

Bridget got the invisible memo and changed tack. 'Look, Stella. We can only imagine how hard this is for you and we want to do everything we can to help you. But stop blaming yourself. None of this is your fault.'

Stella nodded slowly. But the reality was now as clear as the blue sky above her head. He'd stolen money and left. The question was: why?

15

Slowly, the friends headed back into the city centre in search of ice cream, crossing the next bridge along from the Ponte Vecchio to get there. They'd stopped halfway across for a few moments to look back towards the bridge and watch the changing reflections in the river below them.

'I love the way the river cuts through the city, like it's a way out at any time,' said Sarah, to herself as much as anyone.

'What do you mean?' asked Stella.

'Well, think of Siena, with its walls keeping you in. But Florence is so small, neat even. Hills on either side but the river gives you the option to leave whenever you like. I kind of like that about it.'

On they went, by now in search of both ice cream and a loo (the Prosecco had taken its toll). The road they took into the city led them to the huge Gothic church of Santa Croce with a large piazza in front of it, surrounded on all sides with three-, four-, five-, six-storey buildings, all with a distinctly medieval feel. It was quieter than the area around the Duomo, and they wandered into the church, a great echoing cavern, and walked around the vast space inside, stepping into the various chapels lining the walls. They passed Dante's monument and Michelangelo's tomb, a rather ugly structure they all agreed, given the man was one of the greatest artists to have ever lived. However, Giotto's frescoes made up for it, delighting them with their calming colours and compositions.

As they walked back across the piazza, their thoughts turned from statues to ice cream, Lucy checked her map on her phone and led them off the piazza and along a narrow street, until there, opposite a small church, they found what they'd been looking for: the ice cream shop of Lucy's childhood dreams.

They entered the tiny space, most of which was taken up by a curved wooden counter topped with stainless-steel tubs holding ice creams of every colour behind glass. Stella went straight in with her order – one scoop of chocolate and one of pistachio – and took her tub outside while she waited for the others. Sitting on a stone bench, just in front of a small church, she stuck the small wooden spoon into the soft ice cream, taking only the fresh, fragrant pistachio first, and let the flavours fill her mouth. Then came a small mouthful of chocolate, sweet and unctuous.

Sarah joined her (vanilla and hazelnut), then Bridget (chocolate and Stracciatella) and finally Lucy with what looked like a cup of coffee.

She took a seat at the end and showed them the cup. '*Affogato*,' she said, nodding at it. 'Ice cream with a shot of coffee on it. Two birds, one stone.' Lucy took a noisy slurp, followed by a sigh as the combination of sweet ice cream and strong, bitter coffee worked its magic on her taste buds.

They sat eating their ice creams, dipping their spoons in each other's tubs to get a taste of everything. Then, once every last drip had been scraped from the sides, they dropped their tubs into the bin, while Lucy returned her cup to the counter.

'What's that?' Stella pointed at the small stone window in the wall just about a foot above the floor in between the two doors of the shop as Lucy came back out.

'It's a wine window,' said Sarah, looking pleased with herself. 'I read about them once. Apparently, when the plague swept through Florence in sixteen hundred and whatever, these popped up all over the city so wine merchants could still serve wine to customers by handing the glass through the wall.'

'What a brilliant idea, I think we should have them reinstated. Minus the plague, obviously,' said Stella. 'Actually, what are we going to do this evening? I mean, thinking of drinks.' She drained her cup. 'And food, obviously.'

'How about back to the hotel to put our feet up for a bit and we can head to that lovely square we walked through last night, find one of the restaurants there,' said Sarah.

'Does that mean you're not going to make me climb that bloody bell tower?' Bridget looked at Sarah, her eyes hopeful.

'Not today, but honestly, I think we really must do it tomorrow before we leave. We can't come all this way and not see the city from above. We can either do the Duomo or the bell tower, your choice, but we've got to do one of them.' Sarah's eyes fixed on Bridget until she got a nod of agreement back.

'OK, fine. We'll climb stairs first thing in the morning.' Bridget shrugged.

They wandered slowly back across the river, their surroundings now feeling pleasingly familiar. Plans were made as they parted outside their rooms to meet back at six, ready to head out to watch the sunset from Piazzale Michelangelo, about a half an hour walk from the hotel.

Once back in their rooms, Lucy headed straight to the bathroom for a shower and Stella flopped onto her bad and picked up her book. She managed barely a chapter before falling asleep, her early start that morning catching up with her. She woke to the sound of Lucy's voice, gently asking if she would like her to run her a bath. Stella nodded sleepily, thanking Lucy.

As she lay in the huge roll-top tub, her feet up on the taps at the other end, Stella tried to remember the last time she'd had an uninterrupted bath. Looking out of the small window across the garden, she counted her blessings that she had her friends around her. She thought of her children, wondered how deep the wounds were, how long they'd take to heal. There was so much to think about, but at the same time, Stella remembered her father's words. One day at a time.

She heard her phone ping in the bedroom.

'Do you want me to see who that is?' asked Lucy.

'It's OK, I'll be there in a minute.' Stella stepped out of the bath and dried herself before wrapping the thick white hotel-fluffy towel around her. She came back into the bedroom to find Lucy tapping away on her phone. 'Everything OK?'

'Yes, just watching one of my authors on Instagram. She's a wellness author, but the irony is she's barely been off social media for the last five years. Honestly, you'd think people would have worked out it's all smoke and mirrors by now.'

'Social media got my business off the ground.' Stella picked up her phone.

'Oh, I know it can be a force for good, but seriously, there's so much rubbish on there too.'

'Then don't look at the rubbish.' Stella tapped in her pin number.

'I have to, they're my clients.' Lucy sighed and dropped her phone onto the duvet. 'Right, I'm going to put some make-up on and do my hair.' She took a handful of her thick, dark curls and pulled at them. 'How long have we got?'

'About ten minutes.'

'I'd better get a move on, then.' Lucy swung her legs round and disappeared into the bathroom.

Stella swiped at the last message, which she saw was from Caroline, a picture of the twins sitting in a restaurant with enormous pizzas and fizzy drinks in front of them, huge smiles on their faces. The caption said:

Having a lovely time! Hope you are too.

She typed a reply, saying that she too was having a lovely time, she missed them all and couldn't wait to see them.

Stella looked at the screen on her phone. She tapped on the Instagram icon and opened the app. She did have a private account but hardly ever used it. One of her team managed the business account, but she knew her way round well enough to search for someone. Slowly, Stella typed a name into the search bar.

A list of Emily Parkers came up, just as they had before when she'd googled the woman's name on her laptop. Stella scanned the tiny icons, wondering if she might be looking at the woman's face without even knowing it.

Lucy came back into the room. 'Who are you stalking?' She peered over Stella's shoulder.

'I'm not really sure.' As much as Stella wanted to carry on searching, she knew deep down it was fruitless. There just wasn't enough to go on. Emily Parker might have changed her name by now. And anyway, she might just have been someone from Simon's past who didn't hold any answers for Stella at all. She shut the app and put her phone in her bag.

'Well then, how about we go and watch the sunset instead?'

Stella got up and grabbed her cardigan from the back of the

chair by the window. She looked out over the gardens, so peaceful and still. 'I think that's a much better idea.'

* * *

Having met in the hotel lobby and exchanged pleasantries with Ginevra, the four friends set off up the hill towards the Piazzale Michelangelo, past gushing fountains, up stone steps and finally reaching the huge square at the top, all a little out of breath.

'God, he gets everywhere,' said Bridget, looking up at the huge statue of David, as he gazed at city below.

They found a spot by the balustrade and stood side by side, taking in the view in contented silence. The enormous Duomo dominated the skyline, the square tower of the Palazzo Vecchio to one side, the Santa Croce to the other. The tall, flat buildings lining the Arno were in shadow, but the sunlight had thrown a magnificent orange glow over the roofs and the gently moving river seemed to change colour before their eyes, reflecting the sky as the water snaked slowly under the bridges. The sky changed from pale pink to deep orange as the sun dipped below the skyline, bathing the buildings in light before darkness crept in, fading out the cypress-covered hills beyond.

'Well, this is quite the show.' Sarah sighed. 'I tell you what, though, I'm ready for something to eat.'

'Me too,' said Bridget. 'To Santo Spirito?'

'To Santo Spirito,' said Stella, smiling.

The crowds that had gathered to watch the sunset dissipated as quickly as they'd grown and the friends set off back down the hill towards their chosen destination for dinner, a restaurant Ginevra had suggested.

'But, first, we're having a drink at a rooftop bar,' Lucy said, picking up the pace at the thought of a chilled glass of white wine and a big bowl of olives.

They walked along the streets of Oltrarno towards the square, the tables filling it already busy with people by the time they arrived. They followed Lucy to a building on the corner, which turned out to be a rather smart-looking hotel, and made their way to the top floor, where the lift door opened onto a long, narrow terrace under huge stone arches overlooking the Tuscan country-side, the city behind them.

They settled on a table at the end, taking their seats on two rattan sofas topped with plush, cream cotton cushions. Stella ordered a bottle of white and moments later a bottle was brought to the table in an ice bucket, along with four enormous glasses. The waitress poured their wine and they clinked their glasses with another toast to Florence.

'This is delicious, what is it?' asked Sarah.

'Vernaccia di San Gimignano,' said Stella. 'It's a Tuscan white, I saw it on telly recently. Not this actual one, obviously. The one they had was from Sainsbury's. But I recognised the name on the wine menu, and it was only about a third of the way down the list, so not too expensive.'

Lucy took a sip. 'It's absolutely delicious. Tastes of lemon peel.'

'And almonds,' said Sarah. 'Gorgeous.'

Bridget looked around. 'This balcony has got something of the Romeo and Juliet about it, don't you think?'

'That was Verona,' said Lucy.

'I know that.' Bridget tried to look convincing. 'I just mean you can imagine it happening here. Like, that scene couldn't happen anywhere but on a balcony in Italy.'

'Well, it worked pretty well on a fire escape in New York City for Tony and Maria,' said Stella, reaching for an olive.

'I loathed that film,' said Bridget.

'How can you say that?' said Sarah, exasperated.

'Easily. You invest in the characters, totally fall in love with Tony and Maria and then *he dies!* And there's not even a glimpse of a happy ending, nothing! After more than two hours! It still makes me cross thinking about it.' Bridget took a sip of her wine.

'Well, life's not a fucking fairy tale...' said Stella. They all looked at her, not quite knowing what to say in the short silence that followed. 'Although, I have to say, I hated that film too.' She shrugged her shoulders, laughing as she did.

Bridget laughed and raised her glass to Stella. 'Then I'm glad it's not just me.'

When they'd finished off the last of their wine, the friends left money on the table and headed downstairs and across the square. Tiny lights danced above them in the trees, the noise of talking and laughing filling the warm air. Stella took it all in and thought of her own storyline, knowing, deep down, that it was up to her to determine what happened next. But, for now, she resolved to think of nothing but Florence, her friends and the evening ahead.

16

The friends were greeted at the restaurant like long-lost relatives by the owner and quickly shown to a table halfway along one side of the crowded room. The walls were painted a deep red, dotted with old paintings and pictures. Low lights hung above the wooden tables and a mirrored bar at one end seemed to house a bottle of every spirit ever invented, jostling for space across three small shelves. The whole place felt like a beautiful Tuscan secret – and they were lucky enough to be in on it.

They were swiftly brought menus and between them they ordered a mix of bruschetta and crostini to start with, followed by a couple of Fiorentina steaks with garlic and rosemary-flecked roast potatoes to share. The waiter brought a carafe of red wine to the table, a cherry-scented Chianti Classico recommended by the owner when he'd taken their order, and before long the table was covered with the most delicious-looking food. They ate and talked, wiping up the juices from their plates with the saltless bread on the table. After the main course, the waiter placed a plate with a selection of local cheeses in the middle of the table, then small bowls of tiramisu, impossibly light and moreish. They finished with a small glass of vin santo and cantucci biscuits, followed by short, sharp coffees and a small glass of grappa on the house, which they simply couldn't refuse.

'I honestly think I'm going to burst,' said Bridget, loosening the top button of her trousers.

'That was so delicious, but I know this,' Sarah picked up her glass of grappa, 'is going to make me feel horrible tomorrow.' Regardless, she knocked the rest of it back, then shook her head and shivered as the liquid went down her throat and made its way around her body, coursing through her veins.

'I can't remember the last time I had grappa.' Stella laughed as she put the empty glass on the table, shaking her head just as Sarah had done.

'God, I can,' said Bridget, grimacing. 'Disastrous holiday with Neil last year. We had dinner in a little restaurant, drank grappa and had a row on the way home.'

'What about?' Lucy lifted her glass to her mouth, screwing up her nose at the smell of the drink.

'The usual. I raised the question of more IVF, he got cross, then we argued.' Bridget shrugged her shoulders. 'It's easier to just not bring it up now.'

'You know you shouldn't be made to feel like that.' Sarah gently placed her hand over her friend's hand across the table. 'He really doesn't know how lucky he is to have you.'

'Absolutely,' said Lucy, nodding.

'You know, I'm not just saying this, but there are many, many upsides to being single.' Sarah's eyes glinted.

'Like?' Bridget sat back in her chair.

'Well, for starters, you can do what you want, when you want. You can eat what you want, when you want. You don't have to sit through anything rubbish on telly. Or put up with anyone stealing the duvet.' She picked up a biscuit. 'Stuart used to take up the whole bed. No snoring, or leaving hairs in the sink in the bathroom. But,' she raised her finger, 'it's not just the freedom of doing whatever you want. It's more than that. It's not having to please anyone else. I had two years, maybe three, of feeling like utter shit most of the time. But then I realised there are so many good bits about being on my own, as in not half of a couple. To be honest, I stayed for so long because I feared what life might be like without him. I know it's not the same as you, Stella, and believe me I'd do anything for you not to be hurting like you are now, but I promise you, life will get easier. In time, that is. Being on your own is terrifying, but it also means, eventually...' she looked up and took a breath, 'complete bloody freedom.' Sarah smiled and took a bite of the biscuit in her hand. 'And I tell you, once you've had a taste of that freedom, you won't want to give it up easily. Certainly not for anyone who puts a sock on their willy, that's for sure.'

The four of them laughed until tears rolled down their faces.

Lingering over the last of their wine, the friends carried on chatting. It was only when the waiter began mopping the floor around them, they realised they were the last ones there. Having gathered their belongings and thanked the owner and his staff for a wonderful dinner, they stood for a moment in the square, lights still twinkling in the trees. The tables outside were still surrounded by groups talking and laughing.

'How about we walk to the bridge and back before we go back to the hotel, take in the view at night?'

'Good idea,' said Sarah. 'I need to walk some of this off.' She patted her stomach.

Bridget did up her trousers. 'I'm definitely up for a walk, I'll never get to sleep feeling this full.'

They headed towards the river and walked to the Ponte Vecchio along the now familiar route. The air was still warm, the night sky a beautiful deep inky blue sprinkled generously with stars. Halfway across the bridge, now almost empty of people, they stopped and stood underneath the huge stone arches, looking east along the river towards the Ponte alle Grazie, rolling Tuscan hills in the distance. Below them, the water moved slowly, small ripples making the light on the surface dance to an invisible tune.

They stood side by side, each lost in their own thoughts for a few moments. Much as Stella tried to not think about him, she couldn't help but wonder, as she so often did, where Simon was, what he might be doing, who he might be with. Emily Parker's name hung in her mind. Despite the wonderful evening they'd had, the thought of Simon left her feeling hollow once more.

She felt Lucy's arm around her shoulders. 'Thank you,' Stella whispered. 'I'm all right, I promise. I just can't help but think about him. Where he is, you know?'

'Of course you do, it would be weird if you didn't.' Bridget put her arm around Stella too, squeezing her shoulder.

'It's just... I'm tired of trying to figure out what happened. He left me with nothing to go on.' Stella sighed. 'I didn't want to talk about it tonight. I'm sick of talking about him, sick of thinking about him, to be honest. But it's so unfinished. I've tried everything, but until he gets in touch – if he gets in touch...'

'He will, I'm sure.' Sarah spoke softly.

Bridget nodded. 'He'll be back. But leaving without trace like that is...' She stopped short of saying the word unforgivable out loud.

Stella took a deep breath. 'I know it sounds ridiculous, but I found a name written on a piece of paper in an old wallet of his. It might be nothing, but it did make me wonder... I know so little of Simon's past. He has no family but us, none of our friends have heard from him. It's the only name I have that might be able to tell me something.'

'What's the name?' Lucy asked, her mind already putting two and two together and realising that's who Stella was searching for on her phone earlier.

'Emily Parker.'

'And that doesn't ring any bells?' asked Sarah.

Stella shook her head, watching the gentle movement of the river below them. 'None.'

The name hung in the air for a moment.

Stella moved back from the wall and stood upright. 'Right, enough. I need to dance.'

'Seriously?' Sarah's eyes lit up.

'Absolutely. It's our last night and I'm not going to bed until I've danced.' Stella grinned at them all. 'There was a bar that looked like people were dancing, we passed it as we left the square.'

'Then what are we waiting for?' Bridget clapped, delighted at the idea.

They walked back across the bridge towards the square, promising themselves they'd still be first in the queue to climb the 414 steps of Giotto's Bell Tower in the morning. As the bar came into view, people spilling out onto the square, the four of them picked up their pace and headed into the throng. Soon, all thoughts of Simon left Stella's mind as, for the next couple of hours, she swayed to the rhythm and moved to the beat with her arms in the air. Nothing else mattered but the music.

17

By the time Lucy stretched and opened her eyes on Sunday morning, Stella was already out of bed. Lucy looked across the room to see Stella sitting in the small armchair by the open window of their hotel room, the cerulean sky beyond. Bells rang in the distance, floating across the landscape through the open window.

'Hey, how are you feeling?' Lucy's voice was croaky. She lifted her eye mask and rubbed at her eyes. 'Ow.' She reached for her head. 'Did you sleep well?'

'I slept, like properly slept. Better than I have for ages.' Stretching her arms above her head, Stella uncurled her feet from underneath her. 'It's been lovely, sitting here. When I spoke to Caroline yesterday, the girls seemed so happy. And Max is having a great time, apparently. And, actually, that's all I really care about, them being OK in all of this.'

'They will be, Stella. With you, they will be.'

'I hope so.' Stella sighed and looked back out of the window. Birds pecked at the grass on the lawns below. 'You need to get up.'

She glanced at her phone to see the time. 'For some reason, we thought it was a good idea to meet early this morning.'

'Excuse me, for some reason, you thought it was a good idea to dance until two in the morning. I haven't done that for bloody years.' Lucy winced as she sat up.

'I know, sorry.' Stella laughed. 'I'll have a quick shower.'

'Perfect, go for it. I might just close my eyes for another ten minutes.' And with that, Lucy deployed her eye mask once more.

Stella quickly showered and dressed, throwing a green linen dress over her head and pulling her hair into a loose ponytail. She woke Lucy, telling her not to fall back to sleep, then grabbed her bag, placed her sunglasses on top of her head, slipped on her plimsolls and headed downstairs.

Bridget was already at the table on the terrace with a pot of coffee, an untouched glass of orange juice and basket of pastries in front of her. She spoke as Stella approached the table without looking up. 'Parker, did you say?'

For a moment, Stella didn't know what Bridget was talking about. Then she remembered and nodded her head slowly. 'Yes. Why?'

'And where did you say he was from? Originally, I mean.'

'Oban, in Scotland. Well, not far from there. Not that he ever went back after we met.'

'Do you think she might be around the same age as him?'

'I've no idea.'

'Well, I've found an Emily Parker on Instagram who looks about our age and has got a few old pictures of Oban on her feed. She runs a restaurant on Mull now.' Bridget turned the screen round to show Stella. 'Look.'

Stella took the phone from Bridget, taking in the open, smiling face looking back at her, colour in her cheeks, her blonde hair wind whipped by the wind. Behind lay a deserted beach, the sand stretching back to a blue-green sea white-tipped with waves. The woman's green eyes shone, as if they had a light behind them. From the shape of her mouth, it looked like she was saying something to whoever was taking the photograph. Stella touched the screen and the face disappeared. She handed the phone back to Bridget and sat down opposite her. She reached for the untouched orange juice. 'Do you mind?'

'Go ahead. I've gone straight to coffee.'

'So, what do I do now?' Stella nodded at Bridget's phone.

'Figure out if you really want to go down that path. I know what you're saying, if she does know him, she might know something you don't. But at the same time, it also might bring more questions than answers. Or answers that you might not want to hear. Or no answers whatsoever. Stella, she might have nothing to do with him at all.'

Stella broke off a piece of the pastry on the top of the pile in the basket. 'I know. But I can't just sit and wait for him to decide when he might, if at all, give me an explanation. I need to do something. He left me, our family, our whole bloody life and stole from us. I need to know why. I can't go on living a kind of half-life, waiting for someone to tell me what happens next.'

'So there's your answer.' Bridget spoke through a mouthful of pastry.

'What do you mean?'

'Don't wait for him to dictate what happens next. You know he's done wrong, in so many ways. If – or rather, when – he turns up and tries to mess it up again, you tell him you know he's taken money and that if he's sensible he'll do as you ask, whatever that might be.'

Stella poured herself a coffee. 'I still feel like I'm missing something.'

'Then you should find Emily Parker, but only if you promise

you'll go into any search knowing that you might not find the answers you're looking for.'

'Promise.'

'OK, then.' Bridget drained her coffee cup. 'Right, where are the others?' She glanced back towards the door into the hotel. 'We've got to get a move on if we're going to fit everything in before we have to leave.'

As if on cue, Lucy appeared at the door. 'Ready for some Botticelli?'

'Steps first, remember.' Stella raised her eyebrows.

Sarah appeared behind Lucy, moving slowly, sunglasses on. 'Anyone else regretting the dancing?'

'Not yet, but I've got a feeling climbing the steps is going to remind us that we're not twenty-two any more,' said Bridget, as she got up to stand.

They made their way back into the heart of the city, crossing the square and over the Ponte Vecchio bridge, still quiet at the relatively early hour. Stella and Bridget walked ahead, Lucy and Sarah a little behind.

'Bridge, please don't say anything to the others about what we talked about this morning,' said Stella, quietly.

'They'd definitely try to talk you out of it, you know that, don't you?'

'Exactly. That's why I don't want them to know just yet.'

'Whatever you think.' Bridget nudged her friend, smiling.

They soon reached the bell tower and, just as they'd hoped, had beaten the queue.

About half an hour later, they stood, breathless, at the top of the bell tower looking out over the Duomo and down to the terra-cotta roofs of Florence. In the distance, the cypress-covered Tuscan hills sat beneath a cloudless sky, looking like a film set that might suddenly be moved. Below, small figures could be seen walking around the outside of the Duomo. They picked out the places they'd been in the previous days, from the flat white front of the Santa Croce to the medieval tower of the Palazzo Vecchio and, on the other side of the river, the Pitti Palace and Boboli Gardens beyond.

'I think I might have to come back and live here one day, like Elizabeth Barrett Browning,' sighed Bridget.

'To sulk and be happy?' laughed Sarah, offering Bridget her water.

'It's just so refreshing being in a place with so much beauty all around. Makes me think I can change things if I want, you know?'

'I think I do.' Sarah smiled. 'Are you OK?'

'Absolutely.' Bridget nodded.

Once back on the ground, the four friends had a coffee while giving their legs a chance to recover from the descent, then made their way through the streets to the Uffizi Museum. Their pre-booked tickets allowed them to bypass the queue, which was already long despite the relatively early hour, and walk straight in. As they admired Botticelli's *Venus* and Michelangelo's *Holy Family*, took in the wonder of Titian's *Venus* and Leonardo da Vinci's *Annunciation*, they lost themselves to the paintings for a while as they walked the corridors of the building, moving from medieval to Renaissance in a matter of footsteps.

Once they'd seen enough, they headed back over the old bridge before stopping for pizza in Santo Spirito. They ate in the warm May sunshine overlooking the square, sharing pizzas covered with ripe, roasted tomatoes and perfectly melted cheese on deliciously thin, crispy bases. In that moment, Stella thought life seemed so simple. Perfect, even, surrounded by her friends. She didn't want the day to end.

By the time they boarded the plane late that afternoon, Stella's mind was still full of the beautiful sights, smells and tastes of

Florence. And as they flew over the city, sunlight lighting up the Arno like a golden path running through the middle of it, she felt she was going home with a just a little more resolve to move forward than she'd had when she arrived. But, first, she knew she had to go back and look for some answers to her questions. Only then could she leave Simon in the past.

She felt someone squeeze her hand. It was Lucy, leaning across and pointing out of the window. 'Look at the Arno. So beautiful.'

'Thank you, Lucy.'

'What for?'

'This. For making me come to Florence. I've loved every minute.'

'Brighter days ahead, I promise.'

Stella smiled and squeezed her cousin's hand back. 'Can you give me a firm date on that?'

They laughed and watched through the window as the city below them slowly disappeared from view.

18

'OK, that'll do for now.' Caroline shut the oven door and turned to survey the kitchen. It had looked like a flour bomb had gone off just a few hours before, but now, every surface gleamed. The chicken pie she'd made with Max's help was in the oven and all three children were in their pyjamas watching television in the sitting room. Stella had messaged earlier to say she'd be home soon, so Caroline sat at the kitchen table with a hot cup of tea and soaked in the silence for a few moments. She thought about heading home and her heart sank. Having a weekend away from the unspoken tensions in her own marriage had been a blessed relief. Not that anyone would know there were any problems. Caroline was very good at putting on a brave face. In fact, she'd been doing it for so long, it was second nature now.

It wasn't that Philip was a bad man. Quite the opposite, in fact. He was a very good man. Worked hard, loved his children, had a solid moral compass, all the things Caroline should be grateful for. It was just that, if she was really honest with herself, life with him had become so predictable. And more than that, she felt like he didn't really see her any more. Or rather, the person he saw was sensible Caroline, safe Caroline, slightly bossy Caroline. He didn't see the woman who needed to be told she was loved and wanted. The only time she'd tried to talk to Philip about how she was feeling, he'd looked so uncomfortable, she'd changed the subject, telling him it didn't matter.

As if sensing her sadness, the dog came and sat beside her, resting his head on her lap and looking up at her with his soulful brown eyes. He sighed heavily. 'I know, me too,' Caroline said, patting his soft head gently. 'But what am I supposed to do? I can't explain it to him, I wouldn't even know where to start.'

There was a knock at the door. Percy scampered across the kitchen floor, barking at the noise.

'Mummy!' The twins raced to the door, clamouring to reach the latch.

'Here, let me open it.' Caroline reached from behind them and opened the door to Stella.

Dropping her bags to the floor, Stella scooped up both of her daughters in her arms. 'Hello, my darlings!' she cried, tears springing to her eyes. 'I've missed you so much!' Stella stood up again and embraced her sister as the girls clung to each of her legs. 'Thank you so much, I can't even begin to tell you...'

'Don't even think about it, it was the least I could do.' Caroline hugged her sister tightly. 'To be honest, I've had such a lovely time.' She stood back and ruffled the girls' hair. 'I wouldn't normally say this, because other people's children are never as nice as your own, but in your case, I really do love them just as much. Sometimes even just a little bit more.' Caroline laughed, winking at the girls.

'Mummy, we went to see *Matilda*!' shouted Millie, her green eyes shining with delight.

'I want to tell her!' protested Isla.

'You can both tell me, just let me get inside and have a quick chat with Auntie Caroline before she goes.' Stella turned back to her sister. 'Is Max back?'

'Yes, he's in there. I think he had a good time, too. No gaming rules at his friends' house, apparently.'

Stella laughed. 'The dream, as far as Max is concerned.'

'Hi, Mum.' Max appeared at the door. He went to Stella and hugged her gently.

'Hello, my boy,' whispered Stella, squeezing him back. 'How are you doing? I missed you so much. Did you have a lovely time? You look tired, I won't even ask what time you went to bed.'

'Mum, I'm not a baby.'

'Exactly,' said Caroline, nudging Stella. 'Go and sit in there with them and I'll bring you a cup of tea.'

'Are you sure you've got time? I thought you said you needed to get home, I'm sorry we're a bit late, but the traffic was terrible coming back.'

'No, really, I've got time. Philip's quite capable of fending for himself for a bit longer and the traffic might have calmed down in half an hour. So, go on, go and sit down and I'll be with you in a minute.'

Stella sat on the sofa in the sitting room with the twins, listening as they gave her a very detailed account of their trip to the theatre, while Max sat on the floor with the dog. She glanced around the familiar room, the noise of her children's chatter filling it, and felt an enormous sense of protectiveness wash over her. More than anything, she wanted to keep the children safe and happy. Whatever mess her marriage had created, she resolved to remember the joy too. And it was here, with her, in this room.

Caroline came in with Stella's tea and handed it to her, telling the girls to be careful as she did. She sat in the armchair opposite and got comfortable. 'So, tell me all about it.'

Stella looked at her sister and sighed. 'It was just magical. Honestly, one of the most beautiful cities I've ever been to. But I tell you what,' she squeezed the children either side of her, 'I'm so happy to be home.'

The women drank their tea and Caroline asked all about the trip; where they'd been, what they'd seen, sighing at Stella's descriptions. She'd been to Florence briefly years ago and had always wanted to go back. 'Oh, look at that view!' she cried, peering at Stella's phone. 'Is that from the top of the Duomo?'

Stella looked across at the screen. 'No, we climbed the bell tower instead. Then you get the view back towards the Duomo.' Stella swiped at the screen. 'See? There.'

'Oh, look at that. So beautiful.' Caroline took in the roofs, the skyline, the hills in the distance. Even in miniature, it still managed to take her breath away.

'To be honest, I was a bit lazy about taking photos because we had Bridget there. She was snapping away with her camera, so no doubt we'll have lots of lovely ones. I'll share them when I get them.'

'Before I go let me show you what's in the oven for you all tonight.' Caroline motioned to Stella, signalling towards the door.

'Oh, OK. Sure.' Stella followed Caroline to the kitchen. She lowered her voice. 'Is everything all right?'

'Yes, nothing to worry about. I just thought I'd mention that the girls were a bit tearful about Simon. Nothing serious, but they asked me when I thought he might be coming home. I said I didn't know. I wasn't sure exactly what you'd said to them. I know you've been as honest as you can, but I didn't want to say the wrong thing. So, anyway, I just said that as long as you all looked after each other in the meantime, they shouldn't worry.'

'What about Max, has he mentioned it at all?' Stella's heart leapt at the thought of her children being upset. She wished

Simon could hear this conversation, see the hurt he'd caused with his actions.

'No. In fact, I asked him if he was all right, if there was anything he wanted to talk about, and he said he was fine. Oh Stella, I'm so sorry, I didn't mean to upset you.'

Stella held the palms of her hands to her eyes, stemming the tears. She shook her head. 'Please don't apologise. It's not your fault. It's just...' She remembered how much better she'd felt on the plane just a few hours before, but now she was back in the house, it was as if nothing had changed at all. 'I tell myself it's all going to be all right, but actually, I feel like I might go under at any moment.'

'What did your solicitor say? I mean, why can't we just get the police to find Simon, force him to admit what's going on?' Caroline's voice rose in an angry whisper.

'Sadly, it doesn't work like that. Their advice is to wait for him to get back in touch, or turn up, or whatever he's going to do. And much as I wish I could, I can't go to the police. It's not like he's done anything wrong.' Stella's stomach flipped at the words, knowing them not to be true. But she wasn't ready to tell Caroline about the money for fear that her sister would insist on going to the police right then and there. Stella couldn't face the thought of that quite yet, wanting to at least give Simon the chance to explain. He was the father of her children after all.

'Well, what are you going to do? You can't just sit around waiting for him to turn up, that's not fair on you.' Caroline sat down at the kitchen table, which, of course, she'd already laid for them.

'Funny you should say that because that's exactly where my thinking got to in Florence. I've been telling myself he'll come back for so long. But now I know that's not the case. And so, I'm going to go and see someone.'

'Who?'

'An old friend of his. At least I think she is. Or was, anyway. I found a name – Emily Parker – and number in one of Simon's old wallets. I, well Bridget, found someone with the same name, looks around the right age and lives near Oban. Obviously I could be barking up completely the wrong tree but it's pretty much all I've got to go on for now.'

'I knew it. He's having an affair.' Caroline's face fell, even though she'd been expecting to hear this from Stella for months.

'Maybe.' Plenty of late-night googling of reasons why men leave their marriages had told Stella this was the most likely reason. 'But I have no proof of that. And anyway, this is about trying to find out a bit more about him in the first place. He has no family, I've tried all his old friends and none of them have heard from him. Nothing. He's literally disappeared, and I need to know why. So I thought I could just ask her a few questions, see what she says.'

Carline looked dubious. 'How do you know where to find her?'

'Bridget found where she works on Instagram.'

'So, what are you going to do?'

'Go and find her, tell her what's happened to me, then ask if she knows anything that might help me understand it all.'

'You do realise you sound...'

'A bit mad?' Stella smiled.

'I was going for desperate, actually, but yes, let's go with mad.' Caroline smiled gently back. 'Where does she work?'

'Mull.'

Caroline's eyes widened. 'That's hardly a day trip. Wouldn't it be easier to just send her an email?'

'I want her to know I'm not a freak.'

'I think if anything is going to freak someone out it's showing up unannounced on Mull.'

'Maybe, but if I just email, it's too easy to write me off. I just want to see if there's anything she can tell me that might help me understand, something from his past, maybe.'

'I'm not sure I understand what you're hoping to find. And I still think you're going to freak her out.'

'But if she sees I'm simply hoping to ask some questions... I honestly think this is the best way to do it.'

'When do you think you'll go?'

'I want to try to get up there sooner rather than later, but I just need to spend some time in the office, then I can plan a trip. I think I'll need three days, tops. It's a day to get there, really.'

'Want me to come and look after the kids again?'

'No, you've done more than enough to help. Dad and Susie had offered to come this weekend, but you'd already booked your spot. So, I thought I'd take them up on their offer when I go.'

'OK, but if you do need me too, please say. You know I love being here.'

'I know, thank you.'

'In the meantime, one day at a time, as Dad would say.' Caroline sighed. 'Right, I'd better get going. I'll just let Philip know, so he knows I'm on my way.' She typed a message into her phone. 'Traffic should be fine, now.'

As Stella waved goodbye to her sister, she felt a real pang of sadness. She was used to her sister being so busy, so bossy, but something was a little off, even if Stella couldn't put her finger on it. She returned to the kitchen and took the warm pie from the oven, placing it on the island. She reached to get some plates from the cupboard, calling the children as she did so. They sat around the table together to eat, the twins talking over each other as usual. Stella told Max the gory story she'd been told by the woman on the steps in Florence, albeit a slightly tamer version, and promised them that one day, they'd all return to Florence together so she could take them to the same ice cream shop.

Once the children had been managed into bed, uniforms and lunch boxes located, Stella took her suitcase upstairs, plonked it on the bed and opened it, ready to unpack. There, on top of her clothes, was a note with her name on the front in Lucy's writing.

Remember to face the sunshine x

She looked out across the common, a bright moon casting a silver-blue glow across it. After reading it again, she folded the note back over and smiled to herself, tucking it into the mirror on her dressing table.

19

Just a day into life back at home and Florence seemed a world away to Stella. Being a single parent was exhausting. The washing, the cooking, the cleaning, the shopping, the organising, it was seemingly never-ending – and that was before any actual parenting was accounted for. Even though Stella had done the majority of the domestic heavy lifting before Simon left, at least there'd been someone to share the mental load with. But spending time in an unfamiliar place, even for just those few precious days, had allowed Stella room to think about what she needed to do next and she returned to the office with a renewed sense of purpose, determined to take the business from strength to strength. Her family depended on it.

On her first morning back in the office after Florence, Stella gathered her team together. For the last few months, she'd been joining most meetings remotely, but she'd decided it was time to tell them the truth about what was going on. And she knew she had to do it face to face.

Their response left her wondering why she hadn't told them

about Simon leaving sooner. No one asked where or why he'd had gone; they simply accepted it, offering words of support, and asking what they could do to help. She felt like a huge weight had been lifted from her shoulders, though she decided not to tell them about the missing money for now, not until she knew exactly what it meant for the business. It was a significant amount, but Stella didn't want to worry her team any more than she absolutely had to. For now, she just had to keep going. The irony was that now everyone knew, she didn't feel like she had to pretend, which, she now saw, was ridiculously exhausting. The meeting moved on to discussing other points on the agenda and Stella felt more present with her team than she had for months. There was much to do, with the impending launch of the book and a new app in development.

After the session was over, Lily stayed behind so they could go through the numbers in more detail. Stella closed the door and sat down next to her.

'So, how bad is it?'

Lily sighed. 'Well, here's a summary of what's been taken and when.' She turned her laptop screen towards Stella. 'As you can see from the dates, it's been happening for a while. The amounts are substantial, but not enough for them to be picked up unless you were looking for them.'

'Which, of course, no one was because that was his job.' Stella squinted at the screen.

'Exactly. The thing is, Stella, he's been very good at hiding it. So, if you look here,' Lily pointed at the screen, 'you can see how he's marked this transaction down using a normal expense code, but there's no record of us having purchased anything of the same value. And there are lots like this – little and often was his way. But if you add them up, it comes to this.' She pointed at a figure at the bottom of the screen.

Stella looked at it, her stomach flipping at the sight of the number. She shook her head. 'How could I have missed this?'

'That's the point. He's been very clever.' Lily looked at Stella. 'I mean, assuming it's him.'

'It's him,' said Stella, softly. 'It has to be. So, no one else knows about this?'

'No. I've changed all the passcodes in the meantime, just to make sure no one else has access to the accounts. Is there anything else we need to do now?'

Stella pressed the tips of her fingers together, looking at the screen. 'We'll have to tell the board members, but not just yet.' Much as she wanted to call the police there and then, for Simon to be found and punished accordingly, at the same time she didn't want to put the children through any more than they'd already had to endure. Their father leaving was hard enough. Knowing he'd stolen from them made Stella feel like he was stamping on her already shattered heart for good measure. 'I just need some time to think and I'll let you know. In the meantime, please can we keep this between us.'

Lily nodded. 'Of course. I'm sorry, Stella.'

'It's not for you to apologise. Thank goodness you spotted it in the first place.'

Later that afternoon, as she sat in her office going through her emails, Stella found herself typing Emily Parker's name into the search bar on Instagram again. Looking at the face smiling back at her from a windswept beach, Stella studied it closely. 'What do you know?' she whispered.

Just then, one of her sales team knocked on the door, reminding her they had a meeting about potential new accounts in the diary. 'I'll be there in two minutes, thanks, Jemma.'

As they sat round the large white oval desk in the middle of the office going through the list of forthcoming meetings, a new name popped up.

'Haven't we been trying to get in the door with them for a while?' asked Stella.

'Yes,' said Jemma, 'but they saw the piece you did in the paper a few weeks ago and got in touch. Turns out they're expanding and would like a meeting with you, whenever you can make it.'

'Whereabouts are they?' Stella had a feeling she knew.

'Glasgow,' said Lily. 'They supply loads of independent shops across Scotland.'

Stella looked at Jemma and nodded. 'Let's get it in my diary as soon as we can. No time like the present and all that.'

* * *

A week later, Stella sat at her kitchen table, Bridget, Lucy and Sarah all staring at her. Since Simon left, they'd insisted on doing book club at Stella's house. They said it was so that she didn't need to worry about organising a babysitter, but Stella suspected it was more so they could keep an eye on her and make sure the house wasn't a complete tip.

She'd just told them about her plan to go to Mull and find Emily Parker and by the looks on their faces, they clearly all thought she'd lost it.

'I can't believe you're actually going!' Bridget practically choked on her mouthful of crisps.

'So, what else do you know about this Emily?' asked Lucy, still slack-jawed.

'Look, I'm sure you're all thinking this trip isn't going to solve anything, but I'm not expecting it to, I promise. At the very least, I'm thinking it might just help me move on a little bit, hopefully.

And I really, really want to be able to do that.' Stella raised her glass. 'Anyway, cheers.' She took a sip of her wine.

'Stella, don't change the subject. What have you found out about her?' said Sarah, pulling the crisp bowl towards her and scooping up some houmous on a crisp.

'You really want to know?' said Stella, putting her glass back down on the table.

'Yes!' they all chorused as one.

'Well, she's a chef at a hotel there. She's been there for a few years according to the website, but her bio mentions that she's worked in quite a few places on the West Coast. The hotel looks gorgeous, actually, it's an old castle on the north coast of the island.'

'So, will you just go to the hotel?' Sarah asked.

'I thought I'd stay for the night after my meeting in Glasgow.'

'What if she's not there?' Lucy motioned for the bowl of crisps from Bridget.

'Well, then I guess I just have a nice night in a hotel in a place I've never been before. So, it doesn't really matter. If she's there, great. If she's not, then...' Stella tailed off.

'Then what?' said Sarah. 'Stella, are you sure about this?'

'Honestly, it's fine. If she's not, then I'll take it that it wasn't meant to be. But if she is, I'll just ask her a few questions. No big deal.' Stella stood up and opened the oven door, checking the roasting chicken. 'Anyway, I want to hear how your week's been. Bridge, you first, what's going on?'

'Oh, nothing really. Usual. Work, sleep, repeat.' Bridget shrugged. 'Florence feels like a dream. I wish we could have stayed. I felt so inspired there. Talking of which, do you want to see the photos?'

'God, yes! I literally took three photos and one of those was a mistake. It's me looking into the camera from below. Hideous.' Lucy pulled a face.

Bridget grabbed her laptop and opened it. 'Right, let me just...' She turned it round so they could all see. Crowding round the screen, they watched the slideshow Bridget had put together, their smiling faces popping up in between shots of the city. Blue skies and green shutters, umber-coloured walls and arched wooden doorways, ice creams and negronis, stone staircases and paintings, each image taking them further back into the streets and sights of Florence.

'Please can we do that again one day? It was just the best,' said Stella.

'Only as long as it's not to help one of us get over another break-up.' Lucy laughed.

'Maybe we can do a belated trip to celebrate my break-up?' said Sarah. 'Even if it was quite a long time ago.'

Bridget snapped her laptop shut. 'Right, come on. I'm starving and that chicken smells so good. Shall I get some plates?'

'Yes please, take them straight from the dishwasher.' Stella pointed at the door under the kitchen island as she made her way over to the oven.

'Ooh, I've just remembered I picked up something for pudding.' Sarah reached into her bag on the floor by her feet and pulled out a big bag of cantucci biscuits and a small bottle of vin santo. She held them up like trophies.

'Where did you find those?' said Bridget.

'Lidl,' replied Sarah, her face beaming.

'Here you go,' said Stella, placing the roasting tin on the table. She handed Lucy a carving knife and fork. 'Can you do that bit. I'm just going to throw some salad leaves into a bowl.' Just then, the twins appeared at the door in their pyjamas. 'Hey, you two, what are you doing up? You should be in bed.' Stella went to usher them out of the kitchen and back up the stairs, but they dodged her and accosted the guests.

After managing to draw out hugging people round the table for a good five minutes, both girls were shepherded out and back upstairs by Stella. She tucked them in and kissed each of them on the forehead, the sound of her friends round the table downstairs.

She looked in on Max, still awake and playing something on his iPad. 'Hey, no screens in bed.' Stella walked over to him and put her hand out. He handed it over without a fuss.

'Mum, when you go to Scotland, you will come back won't you?' Max's voice wobbled a little.

Stella's heart jumped in her chest. 'Yes, of course! And it's not until next month, we haven't even got a date yet. I'm just going for a couple of days. I promise you that's my last work trip for a while and you'll have a lovely time with Grandpa and Susie, you know they'll spoil you rotten.'

Max brushed his blonde hair from his face. 'Is Dad ever coming back?'

Stella looked at him, his cheeks flushed, his eyes wide. She knew she couldn't lie to him. 'The truth is, I don't know. I wish I did, but I don't. So, until we do, let's just keep going.'

'One day at a time.' Max gave his mother a small smile.

'Yes, my love. One day at a time.'

20

———

'OK, ready?' Emily Parker stood in her swimming costume, wetsuit boots on her feet and a towel wrapped round her body. She looked at her friend standing next to her, similarly dressed but with a more apprehensive look on her face.

'Em, is this going to hurt?'

'No! Well, not once you get used to it.'

'Wait, you said...' cried her companion.

'Lou, I promise you, you'll feel amazing once you get used to the water. And we'll only stay in for a minute. Here, take my hand.' With that, Emily grabbed her friend's hand and together they walked across sand the colour of buttermilk and into the blue-green sea.

'It's bloody freezing!' Lou shrieked as the water hit her legs.

'Just keep walking and when I say swim, we swim.' Emily's voice was calm, determined.

'Jesus!'

'Now, swim!' Emily launched herself forward into the water, taking a few strokes before turning back to face Lou. 'Come on, you can do it!' Emily had been in the sea almost every day since the spring, but for a first-timer like Lou, it took some getting used to. 'Honestly, keep moving and your body will soon get used to it.'

With a gasp, Lou followed Emily and sank her body onto the water. 'OH MY GOD!' If someone were to stick a thousand pins into her body all at the same time, Lou imagined it wasn't far off what she was feeling right at that moment.

'Come on, you're in! Keep going! Keep moving!' Emily was laughing as she encouraged her friend. 'You're doing brilliantly!'

'I cannot believe... I... agreed to... this. What... was... I... thinking?' Lou managed to say in between breaths.

'Look at you! You'll be swimming to Rum in no time!' Emily nodded her head at the island beyond. 'Let's swim this way for a bit.' She turned and swam parallel to the beach, leaving Lou on her inside. 'How are you feeling now?'

'Actually, I think I'm getting used to it. Still stupidly cold, though.'

'I swear you will be buzzing after this.'

'I'm just hoping I can feel my face after this,' said Lou, managing a small laugh.

Ten minutes later, the two women sat on the beach, wrapped in towels. They had the rock-strewn beach almost to themselves – a couple of other swimmers in full wetsuits were still out in the water – and sat with a flask of hot, milky coffee between them. The sky above was the clearest blue, streaked with thin, wispy clouds. They watched the gannets plunge into the sea, quickly followed by guillemots darting in to see what they could find. A stiff breeze blew across the bay, making the fine hairs on their bare arms stand up on their salty skin. They both had their eyes closed, faces turned to the sun as it tried its best to warm them up a little more.

'OK, I have to admit you were right. I really do feel amazing.' Lou took a sip of her coffee. 'Ooh, actually, I've just remembered.' She reached round and pulled a small container from her bag. 'Here, hold this.' She passed her coffee cup to Emily to hold and opened it, showing Emily what was inside. 'Fresh madeleines made this morning. I might have siphoned off a few.'

'Those look amazing, thank you.' Emily took one, feeling it was still warm. She held it up to her nose, inhaling the scent of warm cake. She took a bite and sighed. 'Mmm, so good.'

'Light as air, even though I say so myself,' said Lou, laughing.

'So,' said Emily, through another mouthful of cake, 'do you think you might hang around for a bit at Glengowan?' Emily smiled as she said this. She'd worked at the hotel long enough to know that few managed to stick it out for longer than a year, two tops. Tucked away on the north coast of the island, the hotel was remote, even by Mull's standards. And in the ten years she'd been working there, first as a sous-chef and now as head chef, she'd come to know within just a matter of days whether the newbies would last. She'd been hoping that Lou would stay, not least because she was a brilliant sous-chef but also really fun to be around.

As much as Emily loved her job, it could get lonely at times. Her hours were long, not to mention antisocial; trying to forge a normal social life on the island was tricky. She had a great team, but most were much younger than her, or older with families of their own. When she'd first arrived on the island, she had made an effort to meet people outside of the hotel, but given the physically demanding nature of the work, all she really wanted to do on her one night a week off was sit in silence in her cottage in the grounds of the estate with a book in front of the fire or binge-watch something on her laptop, preferably in bed. She'd joined a bridge club – it had been the only option for something that counted as a social life – but that had petered out after a while. As for meeting someone romantically, she'd given up on that idea years ago.

Emily's few hours off during the day in between service were precious and she used the time to explore the island, usually by foot. Unless the rain was horizontal, she'd throw on her sturdy boots and walk. Sometimes she'd hear about a spot she didn't know from a local and drive back down the single-track road to explore a new corner of the landscape. She had walked up mountains and along coastal paths down to deserted beaches, watched colonies of seals sunbathe on rocks and sea eagles circle the skies above her. The island was rugged and feral but breathtakingly beautiful at the same time. It ruled the people on it rather than the other way round and, in time, Emily had come to love it more than anywhere she'd ever lived. When she first came, she'd been running away from a life that hadn't worked out as she'd hoped. But now, she felt as if perhaps this had always been the plan. She couldn't imagine living anywhere else.

Lou popped the last of her madeleine into her mouth. 'I'm definitely here for a while, I think. I do love it, but I'm not sure how you've lasted so long. Don't you ever want to go somewhere a little less cut off?'

Emily looked out to the sea again and took in a deep breath. To her, the view was still as magical as when she had first laid eyes on it. 'That's the thing. I'm not sure I can ever leave now.' She reached into her bag and pulled out her watch, glancing at the time. 'We'd better get back, it's nearly eleven.'

'OK, chef.'

'You only have to call me that in the kitchen.'

'I know. Habit.' Lou shrugged.

As they drove up the long drive towards the castle on the hill, the sun now high in the sky, the sounds of Joan Baez's 'Diamonds and Rust' drifted from the car radio. Emily's hands gripped the wheel just a little bit tighter. How was it that a few bars from a song could take her back in a matter of seconds to a time she'd almost forgotten about? Almost.

Service that night had been straightforward, they were busy but not bursting, which was just how Emily liked it in the restaurant. It was the start of summer, not yet the school holidays, and the guests were a mixture of young couples having a few days away, older couples on week-long tours of the West Coast and a fair share of tourists from abroad. The last few years had been tough, but people seemed to be getting their confidence back when it came to travel and once they'd made it to the hotel, they were ready to have a good time.

Emily loved cooking at this time of year, with local langoustines and mussels all in abundant supply. One of her favourite dishes to cook – and eat – was a simply done piece of fish – whatever had been brought in that day – with brown butter and a bit of dulse, freshly cut off the rocks at low tide.

With service over and the kitchen cleared down, Emily did one last check of the rota for the following day before saying goodnight to her team and heading off back to her cottage. It was a short walk from the castle, down the drive and off to the left, and with the moon almost full, hanging in a cloudless sky, she didn't need to use the torch of her phone as she sometimes did.

As she approached the front door of the cottage, she heard the familiar barking inside and, as she got closer, sniffing. She opened it to be met with the wet nose and wagging tail of her dog, Bertie. He was an old liver-and-white springer spaniel, bought not long after moving to the island from someone she'd got talking to in the pub she'd worked at in Tobermory. They, in turn, had introduced her to someone who worked at the castle, such was the way of the island.

When Emily had decided to move to be nearer to her new job, the formidable hotel owner, Margaret, had insisted Emily take the cottage in the grounds for a peppercorn rent. She too was a spaniel owner and Emily suspected it was Margaret's soft spot for Bertie that had helped secure her living arrangements.

Margaret had been left the castle by her philandering husband – everyone knew about his affairs, including her, though she never let on and it was certainly never discussed in front of her – and after he died, she'd moved from the mainland to live in the castle, spending a large part of her fortune on restoring it to its former glory. She'd then turned it into one of the most successful hotels in the area, attracting the tourists with money to spend, hence the upmarket restaurant.

The hotel sat overlooking one of the most beautiful bays on the island, with a garden leading down to the cliff's edge and, below that, a rocky beach at the bottom. The beach could be reached by steps but only at low tide, revealing a half-moon-shaped patch of sand, but the rocks made it too precarious to swim. Still, when low tide coincided with Emily's downtime between shifts, she would walk down to the beach with Bertie, taking Margaret's dogs with her as her boss was now unable to manage the steps.

At first, Emily had been terrified of Margaret. In fact, everyone who worked there was a little terrified of Margaret. She always wore a tweed skirt and jacket, her silver-grey hair immaculately styled in a bun. Along with her long, glossy red nails and trade-mark red lipstick, she was easily the most glamourous octoge-narian on the island. Margaret ran a tight ship and didn't suffer fools. But, over time, Emily realised that underneath Margaret's very tough exterior was a woman who wanted the best out of the people who worked for her and, in return, wanted only the best *for* them. They'd had a few run-ins over the years, but their working relationship was based on respect and, for the most part, Emily loved it here.

As their friendship had grown over the years, Emily spent time with Margaret in her apartment in the castle, joining her for a dram every Sunday after service. They'd talk about the week they'd had, the week ahead, what food they could expect to get their hands on, who had booked to stay, how new recruits were doing. Very occasionally, Margaret would ask Emily about her personal life, specifically when she might go back to the mainland to visit her parents.

It was a sore point: Emily had left years before and rarely went home to visit. In Emily's mind, there were too many reasons not to go back. Too many questions, for a start. Her parents were both now in their seventies and they'd never understood why their daughter had chosen not to marry, let alone didn't have children. They were from a different generation, one where not doing either of those things just didn't make sense. All their friends had children and now grandchildren, many of whom still lived close enough for them to see them often. On the rare occasions Emily did return home, it was never long before the conversation turned from asking Emily how she was to whether she'd met anyone yet. She found it exhausting.

Not only that; they made her feel like she'd failed somehow. Even though she knew she loved what she did, had a sense of purpose in her life, that clearly wasn't enough for her parents. So, over time, the length between visits back home grew longer until it was just easier not to go. Her mother would write to her regularly with news of the garden or where they were next planning to go in their caravan. And there was always a mention of someone's daughter or son who'd just had another baby. She'd sign off 'love, always,' and Emily knew her mother meant it, but it made Emily feel sad that she couldn't ever expect them to really understand. She was happy on the island and she certainly didn't need anyone else to validate her happiness.

Margaret had, at times, tried to get Emily to talk about her life before she came to the castle, but Emily would simply change the subject. And, after a while, Margaret stopped asking. But she didn't give up on trying to persuade Emily to go back to see her parents more often. Margaret hadn't been particularly close to her own parents before they'd died (they'd detested Margaret's husband, as it turned out) and her advancing years gave her the benefit of hindsight. 'One day they won't be here any more, and you'll wish you could see them, even just one last time,' Margaret would say. Emily would nod, knowing she was right, but nevertheless not quite able to bring herself to book that ferry back over to see them.

Emily shut her cottage door behind her and turned on the light, gently stroking Bertie's head. 'Hello, boy. How are you?' He turned and padded back to his spot in front of the fire, the embers still warm. Settling in front of it, he looked up at her with his brown eyes. 'I know, long shift.' She flopped into the armchair next to him, sinking into the cushions. Reaching into her pocket, she took out her phone and tried to turn it on, but the battery was dead.

Heaving herself up again, she walked to the kitchen and turned on the light. The kitchen was small but cosy, with an old wooden table and six chairs around it. In the middle of the table sat a jam jar with a handful of wildflowers in it and, on either side, a wax-covered candle holder with just a thumb-sized candle left in each. The beamed ceiling was low and along the far wall was an old double sink with tall brass taps in front of a double window. Pots with herbs and plants lined the windowsill and open shelves groaned with crockery and glasses. At one end, an old range cooker warmed the room and, at the other, a small door led to a pantry stuffed with various bottles, jars, tins and packets of dried pasta, porcini, anchovies, olives and other ingredients she treasured like precious jewels.

Emily walked over to the wooden kitchen counter and plugged in her phone before switching on the kettle. As she waited for it to boil, she rinsed out her mug from the morning under the tap and popped a teabag in. She put away the clean plates she'd left to drain that morning while leaving her teabag to soak and, a moment later, noticed her phone screen light up. She typed in her pin and her screensaver lit up, a picture of Bertie on the beach taken last summer. Then the notifications came up. Three missed calls and a message from her mother.

Dad's had a fall. Can you call when you get this? X

Emily's heart began to pound. She immediately tapped on the screen and went to call her mother. The familiar voice answered on the second ring.

'Mum?'

'Oh Emily, I was worried you hadn't got my message.'

'I know, I'm sorry... how's Dad? What's happened?'

There was a small silence. 'He's OK, but it was quite the scare, I can tell you.'

'Where is he?'

'In hospital. Fell off the stepladder cleaning the bloody windows. He was lucky he didn't break anything, but he's a bit battered and bruised.'

Emily sighed with relief. She'd been expecting far worse. 'Oh, poor thing, when's he coming home?'

'Hopefully tomorrow, they're keeping him in tonight though.' Her mother's voice now sounded a little shaky.

'Shall I come over tomorrow?' Emily's mind whizzed ahead to how best to cover her shift for the next day.

'Actually, yes please. I'd love that and I know he would, too.'

'I'll text you and let you know when I'll be there, but I'll get an early ferry over, so assume I'll be with you by late morning.'

'OK, see you then.'

'Bye, Mum.'

Emily put down her phone and closed her eyes, leaning on the counter. She heard Bertie come into the kitchen and sit beside her. She looked down at him. 'Time to head home.'

21

Just as Emily had suspected, Margaret simply waved her hand the next morning, telling her to go and she'd see her the following day. 'And don't worry about cover, I can sort that out.'

'I've already messaged Lou; I spoke to her last night. It should be fine given it's one of our quieter nights, but I am sorry to leave you in the lurch, Margaret.'

'Please, dear girl, not another word. Leave Bertie with me, he can hang out with mine for the night. I'll send someone down to get him from the cottage later, leave it open. And if I need to ask you anything, I'll message you. Now, off you go.' She shooed Emily away with her long red nails.

'Thank you, I'll be back in time for service tomorrow, but I just need to go and see they're both all right.'

'I said not another word. Go!' Margaret scowled, then winked at her. 'We'll be fine.'

Emily went back to the cottage, gave Bertie a hug and told him to be good, then grabbed her bag and set off down the track to the ferry terminal at Craignure, the fastest sea route back to Oban. She'd booked a ticket online and, looking out at the relatively calm sea as she drove away from the castle, knew it would be a quick crossing. With luck, she'd be at her parents' house by lunchtime.

As the ferry moved away from the island, Emily looked back at the shore, the familiar sight of the pier and the pub sitting at the bottom of the tree-covered slope getting smaller and smaller as the boat made its way towards the mainland. She watched the sea below moving in circles behind the ferry, leaving an oddly flat stretch in its wake, with waves on either side. The water was dark and deep, holding secrets beneath.

Emily took in a long breath, filling her lungs with the fresh air. She felt safe on the island, free even. There was a time she'd loved the mainland too, but it held too many memories, painful ones, for her to ever feel free there now. Instead, the familiar knot in her stomach started to form and tighten as the island moved further away behind her.

Emily checked her phone for messages and let her mother know she was on her way. The reply came soon after: her father had been discharged and they'd both be at home by the time she got there. A sense of relief ran through her body, knowing her father was going to be all right. For a moment, Emily wondered whether she could turn back, but they knew she was on her way and no matter how much she didn't want to go, she knew she had to. She asked if she could pick up any food for them so that she could cook them lunch, but her mother replied she'd already got something, so not to worry.

Putting her phone back in her bag, Emily felt guilty at not wanting to see them. She knew they loved her; they just had a funny way of showing it. And if – or rather, when – they asked her if she'd met anyone, or started talking about other people's children, Emily resolved to tell them that she was very happy on her own. Perhaps then they'd think before asking her next time. The very thought of that conversation tightened that knot in her stomach a little more.

Emily drove south from Oban along the coast, through forests and across open moors, over the Crinan Canal and along the shores of Loch Sween to the village of Tayvallich, where her parents had lived since she was a little girl. The sheltered harbour came into view, dotted with white sailing boats and fishing boats, a sight so familiar, and yet living here seemed like another lifetime entirely. Her family lived in a small house overlooking the harbour, just next to the church. She'd spent her summers as a teenager working in the village pub, which is where she'd learned to cook. Emily had started as a waitress when she was fifteen and by eighteen had got herself a job in the kitchen. The owner, Jim, was a trained chef and after years working in London had moved to the village with his wife Pam, who'd also grown up nearby. Over the years, Jim taught Emily everything he knew, recognising her natural ability to put flavours together as soon as she'd set foot in the kitchen. The food at the pub was simple: fresh hand-dived scallops, crab, lobster, mussels and whatever else come in on the boats from the waters around them. There was always a pie of the day and, if the price was right, Scottish rib-eye too.

When she'd started in the kitchen, puddings were limited to locally made ice cream and bought-in cakes, so Emily had started to make her own, presenting them in turn to Jim and Pam to see if they might make it onto the menu. Before long, Emily's freshly made cakes, which ranged from orange polenta to pistachio, dense chocolate to the lightest lemon, became a hit with both tourists and locals alike.

It was in that first summer when she'd worked in the kitchen full time that she also met her first proper boyfriend, a boy she'd known since primary school. Not that she'd seen Jack for years, but suddenly here he was again, appearing at the back door of the pub with his catch of the day. Like his father before him, Jack was a fisherman and knew the waters of the Sound of Jura like the back of his hand. The sight of him walking up the path, his blond hair wild from the sea air, had made Emily's day. She'd tried very hard to concentrate on whatever she was supposed to be doing in the kitchen, prepping vegetables or making puddings, but it became increasingly difficult as Jack's visits became more frequent. They'd linger at the back door talking until she was called away, usually by Pam, who missed nothing.

Eventually, Jack had summoned up the courage to ask Emily out on a date and on her night off had taken her to a nearby cove that could only be reached by water. There, Jack had set up a small fire in the sand and together they'd cooked fresh scallops in butter and eaten them, alongside small drams of whisky, over-looking the setting sun as it disappeared behind the Jura, the iodine flavours filling their mouths. After that night, they'd returned to the cove as often as they could to sit and talk, eat and, by the end of the summer, make love. Emily had never been happier.

When Jack was offered a job on a bigger fishing boat, one that would take him away for weeks at a time, she was devastated. But she knew he had to take the job sooner or later and so, with her blessing, he left and life in Tayvallich seemed to lose its colour for Emily. She couldn't really talk to her parents about it – they didn't even know she had a boyfriend – but Pam took her aside soon after Jack had left and told her that no matter how impossible it might seem to Emily, she would one day feel better, and it wouldn't hurt quite this much forever.

To begin with, Emily didn't believe her. If anything, the pain got worse. But, one day, Jim came and found her in the kitchen, asking if he could have a word. He told her to go and sit at one of the tables in the empty restaurant and said he'd bring her a coffee. When he joined her at the table, he had a copy of a newspaper tucked under his arm. Jim set the coffee down in front of her, a double espresso with a dash of hot milk, just as he knew she liked it.

'Listen, I've got an idea,' said Jim, 'and before you interrupt me, just hear me out.'

Emily had nodded and sipped her coffee, wincing as the hot liquid hit her tongue.

Jim had put the paper on the table and pointed to an advert he'd circled in red pen. 'There's a job going at a hotel in Oban, and I think you should go for it.'

She'd looked at him, her eyes wide. 'But... don't you need me here?'

'Yes, we do. It will be awful without you. Pam and I will miss you terribly. But you're too good to stay here. You need to move on. Like Jack.'

Emily had felt her cheeks redden at the mention of his name. 'What did Pam tell you?'

'She didn't need to tell me anything. You knew he had to take that job and the same goes for you. You're too young to stay here forever if you really want to do what you love. And, Emily, you are a brilliant cook. Seriously, a natural. But I've taught you all I can. You need someone else to take you on now, help you get even better. Otherwise, you'll be stuck here with us. I know right now you think this job is enough for you, but it isn't. Which is why I want you to go for this one.' He had tapped the newspaper with his finger again, pointing to the advert. He turned it towards her.

Emily had craned her neck to read it. She recognised the name of the hotel, knowing some of the tourists who came to Tayvallich had stayed there. From what she knew, it was one of the largest in the town, set back on a hill to one side overlooking the harbour. 'But I haven't had any formal training, they'll never take me.'

Jim picked up his coffee cup. 'They will. I know the head chef there, worked with her years ago back when we were both making our way in the world. Anyway, I spoke to her and told her what you've been doing here. She's agreed to see you. Next week, actually.'

'But I'm not ready! What about my parents?'

'The job's not to start next week. Just go and see her for an interview.'

'Yes but...' Emily sighed. Her parents had always talked as if her going to university was a given, but she knew this was what she really wanted to do. She'd just never had the courage to tell them. But suddenly a door she hadn't anticipated had opened and, with Jack leaving, she knew, deep down, she needed to get out too. Staying here would feel like staying stuck and that wasn't going to help her, no matter how much she loved the place.

She'd moved to Oban the following month, having got the job and found a place to live all within a matter of days. Telling her parents had been much harder than she'd imagined, their faces falling when she admitted she didn't want to go to college or university or whatever it was they'd hoped she might do. They knew Emily loved working in the pub, but both had assumed it was just a summer job, not something she'd want to continue doing and certainly not as a career. But no matter how much she told them it was what she loved doing and that she had a real opportunity to get better at doing it, she could tell they thought it wouldn't last, or worse, that it wasn't a proper job.

Emily had left her parents under slightly strained circumstances, taking just a few small bags with her to start her new life in Oban. But it was what had happened just a few years afterwards that had really taken a toll on their relationship.

As Emily stood on the doorstep of her parents' house in the bright summer sun, a box of home-made brownies pinched from the hotel in her hand, she was instantly transported back through the years to her last summer there. The smell of the sea hung lightly in the air, the familiar cry of the gulls overhead rang in her ears. She knocked gently on the door, watching the shifting shape behind the frosted glass move slowly towards her.

'Hi, Mum.' Emily moved forward to hug her mother, a little shocked at how much older she looked than the last time she'd been home, a fleeting visit just before Christmas. It was as if her mother had aged five years in a matter of months. 'How's the patient?'

'He's through there. And driving me nuts already.' Her mother winked at her. 'Go on in, he'll be so pleased to see you.'

Emily popped her bag down on the floor and went through to the sitting room to find her father in his usual chair by the window, overlooking the harbour. He too looked much older than she remembered, not helped by the purple bruise on the side of his face. 'Oh Dad, you poor thing!' She bent down to hug him gently. 'What were you doing up a ladder, for heaven's sake?'

'Oh, stop it, you sound like your mother. It was just a fall. Could have happened to anyone.' Her father waved her concern away, his blue eyes glinting.

'Yes, but you shouldn't have been up there in the first place.' Emily took a seat next to him. 'So, why did they keep you in?'

'Oh, just a precaution. I think they have to be extra careful with old codgers like me.' Her father laughed his low laugh. 'So, come on, how are things at the hotel?'

Emily's mother came in with a tray with tea and sandwiches, setting it down on the small table in front of them. They sat and talked while taking in the view of the harbour in front of them. It took less than five minutes for them to ask if Emily had met anyone, but instead of feeling immediately cross as she normally did, she saw them differently in that moment; two people getting old who wanted her to be happy. The fact they equated that with her not being single was something she would just have to let go.

'Not yet, Mum. Maybe one day.' Emily shrugged and smiled, helping herself to another sandwich.

22

'Are you sure we can't persuade you to stay for some dinner with us? You've come a long way to see us.' The ruddy-faced man sitting opposite Stella smiled across the desk at her. They were in a small office in a business centre in Glasgow, the unremarkable headquarters of the wholesaler she'd been to visit. The meeting had gone well, enough for them to want to carry on the conversation and talk about plans for Star Pots once listed, but Stella shook her head, smiling back.

'Thank you, that's really kind, but I'm heading to Oban on the train now. I'm staying on Mull tonight.'

The man's face lit up. 'Really? Oh well, you'd better get going. Such a beautiful journey, one of the best in Scotland, I have to say.'

Stella went to put her laptop away in her bag. 'Yes, I've got a taxi back to the station and I'm hoping to make the last ferry to Mull. It leaves at eight o'clock tonight.'

The man looked at his watch again. 'You're cutting it fine, but you should be all right. Make sure you pick a seat on the left-hand side of the train, by the way. Best views are on that side.'

'Thank you so much for seeing me, I'll get the proposal over to you for in-store support as discussed and we can take it from there.'

'Great, I look forward to it.' He stretched out his hand and shook Stella's enthusiastically. 'Thanks again for making the journey up here, we really appreciate it. And it was great to meet you in person. You've built a fantastic business there with Star Pots.'

Stella's heart swelled a little. 'Thank you, we think so too.'

As the taxi took her back into the city centre over the Clyde towards the station, Stella glanced out of the window, taking in the grand Victorian architecture and the graffiti-lined boards surrounding building sites. She made her way to her train, picking up a sandwich on the way, and found herself a seat on the left-hand side as she'd been told. The train wasn't busy, so she was able to put her bag on the seat next to her and settle in. Stella opened her laptop, thinking she might start work on the wholesaler's proposal, given that it was fresh in her mind, but once the train started moving, she found herself leaning her head against the window, watching the unfamiliar landscape pass by.

The city's buildings soon gave way to the houses of the suburbs and then, before long, a landscape so beautiful Stella couldn't take her eyes away from it. The route took her alongside lochs, the waters so still they reflected the sky above and the mountains sloping down behind them almost perfectly. The train rattled on, passing through stations that seemed to belong to another time entirely, hugging the shores of lochs so enormous Stella couldn't make out where they ended. A huge mountain came into view, dwarfing everything around it. Then they passed through moors and, Stella noted, there wasn't a road in sight. She couldn't remember the last time she'd been so far away from anyone, anything. And instead of her mind rushing with the thoughts that normally took up all available space, she realised her head felt clear, as if given space to just be. To see and not have to do. She imagined staying on the train forever, just moving through the landscape, watching the sky change from clear to cloudy and back again as the hours passed by.

Stella's phone vibrated gently on the table in front of her and she turned it over to see a message from Max on the screen asking where his football boots were. She looked at the time, realising the children would be home from school now. She tapped out a reply, telling him where they were and asking if he was being good for Grandpa and Susie. He replied with a thumbs up and a sunglasses emoji. She said she'd call later when she had a better signal to say goodnight to everyone and signed off with a string of kisses.

As the train snaked its way towards its final destination, it stopped just outside the town. A voice informed the passengers they'd been held at a signal and should be on the move again soon, arriving in Oban ten minutes later than scheduled. Stella collected up her belongings and checked her ferry booking. Even if she missed the one she was hoping to catch, she would still make the last ferry of the day and be on Mull just before nine o'clock. Enough time, she hoped, to get to the hotel.

The train moved off again and slowly pulled into the station right on the waterfront, opposite the ferry terminal. By now, the sky had darkened, covered with thick grey clouds. She could see the ferry moving across the bay and out towards the islands beyond. She looked across the bay to the town, the seafront lined with imposing hotels. To the north sat another huge quay, the red roofs of the buildings on it stark against the grey sky. Behind, the hills were thick with trees interspersed with large grey stone villas and just above the town, a round stone mini Colosseum sat looking somehow out of place and quite at home all at the same time.

Stepping off the train, she made her way towards the terminal to check she could get on the next crossing and with that done decided to follow the road round to the south of the bay in search of somewhere to sit and take in the view for a while. Spotting a sign for a footpath to a viewing point, she followed the road and then a path, steep enough to have a handrail. The path led her, behind a row of houses and up to the top of the hill, where she came out, a little breathless, onto an open grassy space with benches dotted along the fence overlooking the bay. She looked down to her right to Oban below, the hills stretching into the distance behind the town. On the other side lay the islands, Mull rising up behind a smaller island in front.

Stella took a seat on an empty bench and looked towards Mull. She thought about what she was hoping to find, realising with a jolt of surprise that she hadn't thought about Simon all day. She'd been so consumed with the journey she'd taken, the meeting, the landscape that she'd passed through to get here, that she'd almost forgotten the reason she was here. Thinking about it now, realising that she might just come face to face with the woman who could perhaps tell her something she didn't know about her husband made her feel slightly sick.

The clouds started to slowly part, breaking up in the sky above her and letting the sunlight through onto the land and sea below. She watched the colours change from grey to shades of orange and pink as the sun slipped across the sky. She imagined what she might say if she did find Emily at the hotel, trying to run the conversation through in her head. But every time she thought about it, she realised how crazy it sounded.

She shook her head and smiled to herself. No wonder the girls from book club had looked at her like she was mad when she'd told them her plan. Still, looking at the view that lay below, she knew it had been worth the journey to see this alone.

Stella glanced at her watch and took one last look at the bay. Her mind felt clear up here.

Walking back down, she turned off the footpath a little way down the hill and took a different road back towards the town. The roads were quiet here, not a soul in sight. She passed a beautiful Georgian building, a small hotel with what she imagined must be some of the best views of the bay. It was nearly half past seven in the evening and, for a moment, Stella contemplated knocking on the door to ask if they had a room for the night. The idea of curling up on a bed with a view of the sea, perhaps after having a light supper in her room, before getting a good night's sleep was tempting. But she'd come too far, literally, not to see this through.

Following the road back towards the town, Stella walked into the ferry terminal and took a seat while she waited to board the ferry she'd watched come in. There were just a handful of other foot passengers waiting with her and they watched as passengers and cars disembarked from the ferry that would soon take them across the water. The waiting room emptied as people got up and made their way to the boat, but Stella stayed where she was. She closed her eyes and took a breath. She opened them to find the dipping sun had thrown an orange glow across the floor, flooding the room with light. *Remember to face the sunshine.* Lucy's words came to her as if she was saying them to her right there and then. Stella stood and turned her face to the light, following the other passengers onto the ferry.

23

Emily sat on one of the red plastic chairs on the top deck of the ferry, the blanket she always kept in her car for this journey wrapped around her body to keep warm against the sea breeze. The sun was yet to set, but there was a definite chill in the evening summer air. As ever, she sat on the right-hand side for the first part of the journey so she could see the Lismore Lighthouse as they passed, then swapped to the other side for views of Duart Castle. Standing high on a promontory above the sea, the castle looked magnificent despite the scaffolding. It had been undergoing restorations for as long as Emily could remember, but it was still one of her favourite sights on the island, especially from the water.

Her mind ran back over the day she'd had. It had been a relief to see her father on much better form than she'd feared. Despite the bruising to his face, his spirits had been surprisingly high. He'd even talked about getting back out to finish cleaning the windows before the end of the week, an idea that had been met with a cry of disbelief from her mother.

'You'll be doing no such thing,' she had snapped, before turning to her daughter asking for backup.

'Dad, perhaps stick to ground-level activities for a while.' Emily had lowered her voice. 'For your own safety,' she had said, winking at him.

After lunch, Emily and her mother had walked down to the shop together to pick up a few things. Seeing the harbour, the boats and houses she knew so well, Emily had felt a pang for her old life: growing up with her friends in the village, working in the pub, learning to cook, falling in love for the first time. Of course, her life back then had seemed terribly complicated, as is the teenage way. But now she could look back and see how lucky she'd been to grow up in such a beautiful place and she knew, no matter how much they sometimes drove her mad with their simplistic outlook on life, that her parents just wanted their daughter, their only child, to be happy.

Still, her father's fall had been a cruel reminder that they were getting older. Emily was grateful they had each other. The thought of either of them on their own was almost unthinkable. Which, inevitably, made her consider her own situation. If she was really honest with herself, she knew that as happy as she was – and she really was – there were times when she did wish there was someone to share her life with. But it had been so long, she wasn't sure she could remember how to do that. Part of her loved being able to do what she liked when she liked. But the truth was, she kept herself busy, working all the hours she could, so that she didn't have a chance to feel lonely. As much as she loved her work, her long walks, her island friendships, Emily was starting to realise that maybe, just maybe, she was ready to fall in love again.

* * *

There was still plenty of light – it was at least an hour until sunset – when the ferry approached the dock. Emily was already back in her car and she checked her phone as she waited. There was a message from her mother asking Emily to let her know when she was home safely and another from Lou asking if she could pick up some tobacco before heading back to the hotel. Emily replied with a thumbs up, knowing the convenience store in Tobermory would be open until late at this time of year.

As she drove off the ferry, turning right and heading north along the island's main road towards Tobermory, she passed a woman waiting at the bus stop. She looked a little younger, Emily thought, and was fairly smartly dressed in a light mac and wide-leg trousers, a deep blue scarf hanging loosely around her neck. Emily couldn't help but feel a little sorry for her, knowing the woman would likely spend the rest of her evening trying to find a taxi, once she'd worked out there were no buses, to take her wherever she wanted to go.

The road stretched out ahead of her, running alongside the coastline like a tarmac canal. She glanced in her rear-view mirror at the woman at the bus stop, watching as she looked first one way, then the other, before dropping her bag to the floor. There was something about her that made Emily pull in by the side of the road. She stepped out of the car, leaving the engine running.

She called back to the woman. 'Hey, I'm sorry to tell you this, but there are no more buses tonight. Have you booked a taxi?'

The woman glanced up at her, brushing her dark hair back from her face. 'Shit, really? God, sorry. Didn't mean to swear.' She looked at her phone, swiping at the screen. 'I thought I'd booked a taxi, but they're not here and apparently there isn't another one free until much later.'

'Where are you going? I might be able to help.'

The woman looked at Emily.

'Are you OK? You look like you've seen a ghost.'

'I... er... I'm going to The Glengower Hotel...'

'No way! That's where I'm going. I work there, but I've had a day off. I've got to go via Tobermory to pick up something from the shop, but if you don't mind the small detour, I'm probably your best bet. Want a lift?'

'Yes please. If you really don't mind. I'm not sure I'll get there otherwise.'

'Come on, hop in. I've had to hitch my way back up to the hotel enough times. Taxis round here are rarer than hen's teeth, even at this time of year. Just shove your bag on the back seat. Please excuse the mess.' Emily nodded at the dog blanket on the back seat. 'I'm Emily, by the way.' She held up her hand.

'Stella.' Stella climbed into the passenger seat.

Emily looked at her again. 'All good?'

'Yes, thank you.' She smiled but kept her eyes on the road ahead.

'Great, let's go. Tobermory is about half an hour from here, but then it takes a while to reach the hotel, even though it's not that far as the crow flies. The road is terrible.'

There was a brief silence.

'So, what brings you to Mull?'

'I had a meeting in Glasgow and then thought I'd, you know, make a trip of it. I came up from London this morning, then, after the meeting, I took the train from Glasgow to Oban.'

'Oh, it's such a gorgeous route, isn't it? I love that journey, not that I make it very often.'

'So... you live, I mean... Do you work at the hotel?' The woman seemed nervous despite her best efforts.

'Yes, I'm a chef there. Have been for a while, actually. I used to work on the mainland, in fact, I worked in Oban for years, but then came out here for the job at the hotel and, well, I'm yet to make it back.' Emily noticed the woman's hands in her lap, her fingers wrapped so tightly together, her fingertips were white.

'You must love it here, it's so beautiful.'

'It is, which is why it's hard to leave. Like a parallel universe. How long are you staying?'

'Just the night. I go back to London tomorrow.'

'What? You've come all this way just for one night?' Emily looked across at her passenger again. 'That's insane!' She laughed.

They carried on along the straight road, the sea flashing in and out of view in between gaps in the trees. Streaks of orange and pink coloured the sky as the sun moved further towards the sea.

Emily turned on the radio, the familiar voice of Joni Mitchell filling the air.

The woman took a breath and turned to Emily. 'I'm really sorry, please can you stop the car?'

Emily looked across. 'Sure, hang on. Do you feel OK?' She pulled the car into a layby overlooking a small bay. Up ahead sat the ruins of the castle and, beyond that, a white house overlooking the bay from the other side. She turned the radio down.

The woman turned to Emily. 'I'm sorry, I didn't want to say this while you were driving in case... Actually, it's definitely going to... Sorry. I'll just say it.' She took another deep breath. 'My name is Stella and I'm married to Simon.'

Emily looked at the woman. 'Simon who?'

'Simon Forest.' She watched Emily's face fall as the name registered.

Emily stared at Stella, an unmistakable look of shock on her face.

Stella forced herself to keep going, trying to keep her voice steady. 'He's gone and I don't know where.' Her shoulders dropped. 'I don't know why.'

Emily shook her head, trying to make sense of what she was hearing. 'But... what do you think this has got to do with me? Is this why you've come here? You don't think he's here, do you?'

Stella realised in that instant the thought that he might be here hadn't even crossed her mind. 'No, really I didn't. It's not that. I just...' Stella put her head in her hands, then looked at Emily. 'I'm so sorry, I didn't know what else to do. I didn't see it coming. I just thought that maybe you could help me...'

Emily felt panic and anger all at once. 'What the hell has it got to do with me? I haven't seen him for years and I hope, *really* hope, I never see him again.' Emily gripped the steering wheel. 'I need some air.' She opened the car door with some force and walked to the front of the car. She leaned against the bonnet, looking out towards the castle ruins ahead, then across to the mainland on the other side, the hills now dark against the indigo sky.

After a moment, Stella opened the car door and walked round to stand beside Emily. 'I'm so sorry, I should have said as soon as you offered me a lift. But I panicked. In my head, this trip had become something much bigger than it should have been. This was the part when you'd tell me he's done this disappearing act in the past and it's not just me he's abandoned. I think that's what I was hoping for. That there was no way I could have known and perhaps then I'll be able to forgive myself for marrying him in the first place. Forgive myself for what I've put my kids and my family through. Because at the moment I can't ever imagine forgiving myself for loving him.' Stella bit her lip to stop the tears from falling. 'I'm so sorry, this really isn't your problem and now I'm here...' Stella shrugged, laughing nervously, 'I can see this was a very stupid thing to do.'

There was a long pause.

Emily sighed and turned to Stella. 'You're not stupid, Stella. But if we're going to talk about this, we need to do it properly. Come on, let's go.' Emily motioned for Stella to get back in the car.

24

They drove on towards Tobermory, strangers bound together by a man they both knew. Joni sang about the hissing of summer lawns as each of them wondered what the other might say. The silence wasn't uncomfortable; rather it was as if they both realised the conversation ahead of them had to happen, just not yet.

Emily turned the car down a road leading to the seafront and parked by a small clock tower, opposite a shop. 'Stay here, I won't be a moment.'

Stella looked out across the water at the fishing boats swaying gently, tethered to their buoys, and up ahead, a row of picture-perfect houses painted in primary colours sat overlooking the harbour. She thought about following Emily to ask if she could at least buy whatever it was she was getting by way of saying thank you – or sorry – but she heard Emily's voice, talking to someone just outside the shop. Stella looked back to see Emily hug a woman, waving back at her as she crossed the street.

The car door opened and the sound of glass bottles clanking together came from the tote bag Emily put on the floor on the seat behind Stella.

'Right, home.' Emily waved to the woman again as they drove off.

'Who's that?'

'Jeanie runs the post office here, I've known her for years. I was just asking about her husband, he's not been well. He's the local taxi driver, as well as running the post office with her. That's how I knew your chances of getting a taxi tonight were slim to none. He's been ill for a while, poor thing. They're such a lovely couple.'

Emily turned left just before the bright red house and then climbed the hill out of Tobermory. Soon, they were back on a single-track road taking them away from the coast and across open moors towards the northern tip of the island. The road swept up and down steep hills, through woods and alongside streams, the landscape open and wild. Then, after taking a sharp right turn on the road, a drive marked with white gates came into view, a sign for the hotel to one side.

Emily turned to Stella. 'I can take you straight up to the castle, or, if we're really going to talk this out, we can go to my cottage instead. I can call and let them know you're here. Up to you.'

Stella looked straight ahead, music still drifting out of the car stereo. 'Can we go to yours?'

'We can.' Emily drove on up the drive and as they rounded the corner, the land dropped away to reveal the castle set against the dark sky. Below, the sea stretched to the mainland and yet more islands in the distance.

Stella gasped. 'Oh wow, it's so beautiful.'

'My house isn't quite so grand, just to warn you.' Emily turned off the track, down a smaller one to her cottage, the sight of which never failed to lift Emily's heart. 'But it's home.' Emily parked the car and turned off the engine. 'Come on in.' She got out and went on ahead towards the front door. 'Beware of the dog,' she called back to Stella, who'd followed her up the path. 'He gets terribly overexcited when he meets new people.' She called out to him, and as soon as the door opened, Bertie was dancing around Emily's legs, wagging his tail so fast, Stella thought he might topple over. 'Hello, boy,' said Emily, rubbing his head with her free hand.

'He's lovely, what's his name?'

Bertie shifted his attention to Stella, tail still wagging furiously.

'Bertie. I left him with Margaret and her dogs.'

'Margaret?'

'The owner of the castle. I'm sure you'll meet her. She's amazing and has run this place as a hotel since her husband died. Come on in, sit down.' Emily turned on some sidelights and closed the curtains, then gestured to the armchair by the fire. 'I'll light that in a minute, let me just ring up to the hotel.' She went through to the kitchen, leaving Stella in the sitting room.

Stella looked around the room, clocking some of her favourite books on the packed bookshelves. Photo frames jostled for position: one of Emily with whom Stella assumed to be her parents, another of Emily beaming into the camera on top of a hill with Bertie by her side. It was that same wide smile Stella had seen in the photo on the beach.

'Shift over, I'll light the fire. Here you go.' Emily handed Stella a tumbler with amber liquid inside.

'Thank you.' Stella took the glass and sniffed it, the scent of smoke and brine hitting her nose. 'What is that?'

'Whisky. Single malt from the island.'

'I've never really drunk whisky.'

'To be honest, I don't drink it that often, but tonight, I think we need it.' Emily bent down and lit the kindling in the fireplace. Whoever had brought Bertie back down to the cottage had set the fire, too. The small flame flickered and jumped and soon the wood crackled as the flames took hold, the smell of woodsmoke mingling with that of the whisky. 'Here, there's some water in there if you want to add a drop to your dram. I would if I were you, it helps bring out the flavours.'

Stella splashed in a dash of water to her glass and took another sniff. The aromas softened, smelling like peat and heather. She let the liquid roll around her mouth a little, feeling a gentle burn as the flavours took hold of her taste buds. She shook off her coat and put it next to her on the floor, then took a seat.

Emily sat down on the sofa opposite her, Bertie curling up at her feet. 'OK, so I think you should go first. Then I'll tell you what I know.' She took a sip of her whisky and set the glass down on a small wooden side table on top of a pile of books.

Stella sat up and took a deep breath. 'So, as I said, I'm married to Simon. We met years ago, I'd just come out of quite a long relationship and definitely wasn't looking to get married or have kids. I was still too young, or so I thought anyway. But then I met him at work, and he was much older, well not that much, but at the time it seemed like a big deal. We were friends for a while, but then as soon as we got together, that was it. We moved in together, he wanted to get married, have children pretty much straight away.' Stella took a sip of her drink, wincing a little as she swallowed. 'Woah, that's strong.'

'I promise, it gets more delicious.' Emily took a sip of hers. 'Go on.'

Stella sat back in the armchair, resting her glass in her lap. 'Well, we had three children, again pretty quickly. Max is ten, the girls – twins, Millie and Isla – are nearly eight. I left my job when I had the kids and started my own company a few years later and when it started to do well enough, Simon joined to run the finances. And up until a few months ago, I thought our life was...

well, perfect.' Stella looked up at Emily. 'Sorry, I'm sure that sounds really smug, but honestly, that's how it felt. We had the usual rows that I assumed all married people do, but nothing out of the ordinary.'

'Then what?' Emily took another sip of her whisky.

'Then, everything just imploded. Out of nowhere, or seemingly out of nowhere. I found a tie. One that I hadn't bought him. I remember thinking, when I first saw it, it was the kind of tie he wouldn't really buy himself. So, I asked him, and he was cagey about it, tried to brush it off. It was the first time I'd ever even thought about the fact that he might have been unfaithful. And then,' Stella sighed, 'he told me he didn't love me any more and he left. No warning, no explanation. He just left. And he didn't just leave me, he left his kids. That's the bit,' Stella swallowed hard, 'that I just can't understand.'

'Did you ask him if he'd had an affair?'

'I didn't get a chance. He'd packed a bag before telling me he was leaving me. He just came downstairs and told me he was going. I've not heard from him since.'

'And there's no one you know who might know what or why or where, I guess?'

'Exactly, which is why I'm here. None of his old work colleagues have heard from him, none of our friends, or even his old friends. Not that he had that many, as it turns out. I'd always thought that was because he moved away from here when he was quite young. Anyway, he's gone. Disappeared, basically.'

Emily shifted her feet, tucking them under her. 'So, what led you to me?'

'I found an old wallet of his in a suitcase, one that I remembered he'd used when we first got together. I found your name on a piece of paper tucked inside.' Stella looked at Emily, waiting for her reaction.

'What else was on it?'

'Just your name and an old phone number. Not a mobile number, though. I assumed it must have been a landline or something.'

Emily closed her eyes and shook her head. 'It wasn't a phone number.' She opened them and looked at Stella. 'It was my bank account number. The one he emptied before he disappeared.' Her eyes were glistening.

'He what?' Stella sat bolt upright.

'I know. It gets worse.' Emily stood up. 'I need a top-up for this bit.' She poured another dram for them both, putting the bottle down by the side of the fireplace.

'So, what happened?' It was Stella's turn to ask the questions.

'Simon and I met when I was a still a teenager, the first summer I moved away from home. I was working in a hotel in Oban, he was a waiter there. He was a bit older than me. I assumed I'd be the last person he'd be interested in back then. I'd had my heart broken for the first time the previous summer so didn't want to rush into anything, but he was very... persistent. In the end, I said yes and we started going out. He was quite full on, talked about marriage, having kids from the beginning. But I was just a baby myself. Anyway, we were together for a few years, it all got very serious. He moved into my flat in Oban and we agreed to start looking for a house. I'd been left some money by my grandparents, not exactly a fortune but enough back then to put towards a deposit. We got engaged; my parents were furious. They thought I was way too young. And then Simon said we should start trying for a baby. I assumed I'd get pregnant quickly given that I'd spent the last few years terrified of getting pregnant. But, as it turned out, I didn't and after having loads of tests to work out why, I found out I was infertile at twenty-one. Cysts on my ovaries.' Emily stared at her glass.

'I'm so sorry, that must have been awful for you,' said Stella.

Emily nodded slowly. 'It was. He'd always said he loved me more than anything, but soon after that he just... checked out. I tried everything, said we could get treatment, surrogacy, adopt. We argued about it for a few months, tried to patch it up, but it always came back to that. And eventually he left. I remember him standing by the door in the kitchen. I just couldn't believe what was happening. I was in shock. Not that I wanted children then, but to be told it's not an option, it's a lot for anyone to take in, let alone a twenty-one-year-old only child who's already all too aware that her parents dream of having grandchildren one day. I was their only hope. And instead of offering any help or support coming to terms with it, he just eased himself out of it. It was like I wasn't part of the plan any more. His plan, anyway. His parting shot was to clear out my bank account.'

Stella sat in silence for a moment, slowly shaking her head. 'I'm so sorry. I can't believe he did that to you.'

'The next time I went to pay my rent, I got a message from the bank saying the payment hadn't gone through. I went in to see them and it turned out he'd taken pretty much everything in there, including the money we'd saved for the deposit. After he'd gone, I went to his mother's house...'

'Wait, I thought his mother died when he was little?'

Emily looked confused. 'What did he tell you?'

'That she died when he was small and that his father was an alcoholic; he said he hadn't seen him for years. In fact, he always said he had no family apart from his father.'

Emily laughed dryly. 'Wow. His mother died last year. Went into hospital for a routine operation, but sadly didn't ever come home. She was pretty old, though. She hadn't seen him since he left Oban, when he left me. She adored him; he was her only son. He had a sister too, well, half-sister, but we lost touch not long after he left. I think she was done with him too. But I stayed in contact with his mother, she was lovely. She lived just outside Oban, was born and raised there.'

Stella couldn't believe what she was hearing. Everything she thought she knew about her husband's life before they'd met was based on lies. 'And what about his father?'

'I don't think he'd ever been in Simon's life, his mother told me he'd left when she was pregnant. She raised him on her own until she married his stepfather.'

Stella swirled her glass, watching the liquid move around inside. 'Jesus, he told me such a different story.'

Emily stood up and threw another log on the fire. She sat back down and patted the side of the sofa next to her. Bertie curled up beside her, his head on her lap. 'I think, when I knew him, Simon wanted to create a life completely unlike his own. He wanted to be the perfect father, the perfect family man and when he found out he couldn't do that with me, he moved on, taking my money on his way out.'

'But we have three children. Three!' Stella threw her hands up in despair, then suddenly caught herself. 'God, Emily, I'm so sorry, that was really insensitive.'

Emily smiled gently. 'I knew what you meant.' She took a sip of her whisky, then poured a little more water from the jug into the tumbler. 'I made my peace with the fact I might never be a mother a while ago. It's fine… most of the time, anyway.' She sighed. 'When he first left, I tried to find out if he'd met someone else. More than anything, I think it would have helped me knowing there was a reason. It's the not knowing that was so hard.'

'But why would he walk away from a family, the thing he said he wanted most of all?' Stella grabbed the bottle and topped up her glass.

Emily thought for a moment, weighing up whether to say what she was thinking. 'Obviously we don't know, but I think he won't have left you unless there's something better out there for him, whether that's money or meeting someone else. He's lied to us both. He's stolen from me—'

Stella cut in. 'And from me.'

'Seriously?'

'Yes, I found out just recently. He's been taking money out of the business, skimming it so no one would notice.'

'Do you know why?'

Stella shook her head. 'Well, I guess so that he could spend it on things I wouldn't know about. We have a joint account for everything else.'

Emily shook her head in disbelief. 'What an arsehole.' She looked up at Stella. 'How much?'

'Thousands over time.'

They both sat in silence for a moment, staring at the flames in the fire.

'You know,' said Emily, 'I wasted so much time after Simon left. I didn't want to see my friends, I was too embarrassed to see my family for a while, couldn't face anyone saying "told you so". Turns out no one had been that keen on him. My parents certainly weren't. So I threw myself into work instead and closed myself off from people, relationships of any kind, really. I didn't trust my own judgement. I really loved him, or at least whoever he was when we got together. But, after that, I didn't let myself get close to anyone.'

'Have you had any relationships since?' Stella said, immediately worrying she was prying too much.

'A few, but nothing that went anywhere. I fell in love with another chef about five years later, but that was a disaster. It was a relief when he moved on to another job, to be honest. Then I did have an on-and-off relationship with a hotel guest for years; he was a writer and used to come and stay at the hotel when he was doing his research. But he clearly had no intention of ever settling for one person, so I ended that for the sake of my own dignity. My friend Lou, she works at the hotel, forced me onto a dating app, but the problem is island life doesn't really lend itself to finding someone you don't already know.' Emily grimaced, making Stella laugh. 'So, what will you do?'

'I'm not sure yet. I'm getting my head around the fact that he's not coming back, and even if he did, I know I can't be with him any more. The damage is done. But he is the father of my children, so I guess when – if – he does pitch up in our lives again, I have to be prepared to have some sort of civil relationship with him for their sakes.'

'It must have been really hard, I'm sorry.'

'I've had to tell the children a version of the truth, there's no point in lying. He's been gone too long for me to be able to cover it up for him. But, obviously, I can't tell them why he left because I still don't know the answer. Sometimes I wonder if I married a psychopath, but to be honest, I think I married a very damaged, dishonest man. He's just very good at hiding it. Until now, that is.'

The women let that thought sit between them for a moment. Bertie yawned, loudly.

'What time is it?' asked Stella.

Emily looked at her watch. 'Just past eleven.'

'Really? I'm so sorry, I didn't realise it was so late. I should leave you, get up to the hotel.'

'I'll walk up with you, see you in. I asked them to leave a key for you, so I can show you where to go.' Emily stood up and offered Stella her hand, pulling her up from the armchair.

Stella looked at Emily. In that moment, she felt like they'd known each other for years. 'Thank you so much.' She gently squeezed Emily's hands.

Emily nodded. 'It's been good for me too. Not that I wish any of this had happened to you, of course. But I haven't talked about him for years and I hate the fact he stopped me living my life for so long. Not any more, though.' Emily hugged Stella. 'You must make sure he doesn't do that to you either.'

They stepped out into the moonlight; it was so bright, it looked like a security light was on. 'Is it always like this at night?' Stella asked.

'It's a Strawberry Moon,' said Emily, looking up at the sky. 'It symbolises new directions.'

Together, they walked towards the castle, the sound of the sea below reaching them like a low whisper.

25

Stella woke to hear a gentle knocking at the door. She opened her eyes and looked around, waiting for them to adjust to the darkness. The room was large, with an open fireplace at one end, an old antique dresser to one side and a tall, dark wooden wardrobe on the other. To her right was a huge window, thick curtains pulled shut.

Moving slowly, Stella got out of bed and made her way over to the window, pulling at the heavy fabric with both hands and hooking them back with the rope ties on either side. The blue sky was completely clear of clouds. Lush green grass sloped down to a ledge with the sea beyond and the long shadow of the castle lay at an angle across the manicured lawn below.

The knocking started again. 'Stella, are you awake?'

It was Emily's voice.

Stella went to the door. Her head ached. She remembered the whisky, wondering quite how much they'd had. It had been going down like water by the time she left. She opened the door to find Emily standing there, dressed in leggings and a hoodie, holding out a bag, head tilted slightly to one side, a now familiar wide smile on her face.

'What's this?' asked Stella.

'Swimming stuff. I've only got a couple of hours until I'm back in the kitchen, so we've got to get going.'

Stella rubbed her head. 'What time is it?'

'Just gone eight.'

'You're kidding.' Stella looked slightly bewildered. She turned to grab her watch from the side of the bed, squinting at it to read the time. 'I've got to head off soon! I have to get back to London tonight.'

'As long as I stick you on the ferry by eleven, you'll be in London by tonight, no problem. You can't come all this way and not have a swim in the sea. And before you ask, I've got breakfast. I snaffled some bacon rolls for us from the kitchen.'

'Coffee?' Stella winced, hoping she didn't sound too high maintenance.

'Flask in the car. I'm the same.' Emily grinned. 'Now, chuck your clothes on. I'll wait for you downstairs.'

Stella nodded, too bewildered to argue. She closed the door and headed into the bathroom. She held the side of the sink with one hand, splashing her face with cold water with the other. She caught a taste of it in her mouth, crisp and clean. Throwing on her clothes, she headed downstairs.

A woman stood at the bottom of the stairs, immaculately dressed in a tweed suit with a heavy string of pearls around her neck. She smiled kindly at Stella and held out her hand.

'You must be Stella. I'm Margaret. Emily told me you got here late last night. I do hope you slept well?'

Stella eyed the woman, wondering how much Emily had told her. She smiled back and shook her hand. 'Lovely to meet you, Margaret. And yes, thank you. It's so quiet and peaceful here.' Her mind hadn't stopped whirring when she'd first got into bed but before long she'd fallen into a deep sleep.

'Emily said you're heading to the old castle ruins for a swim in the bathing pool. It's quite the most beautiful morning for it.' Margaret's eyes sparkled as she spoke. 'And given you're not staying long, at least you'll get to see some of the place before you go.'

'I know, I'm so sorry it's such a fleeting visit. I'd love to stay longer, but I have to get back to my family.' She looked around the castle hall, the walls heaving with paintings of landscapes, ancestors, and animals. 'What an amazing place.'

'Thank you. Next time, I'll show you round properly, but for now, someone's waiting.' Margaret nodded towards the open front door. Emily stood at the bottom of the stone steps, beckoning Stella. She took Stella's hand, patting it gently. 'Off you go, the swim will do you good.'

'I'm not sure about that, but I don't think I've got a choice.' Stella laughed. 'I'll be back to pick up my bags. And pay the bill, obviously.'

'It's done.' Margaret waved her hand at Stella. 'I'm happy you had a good night's sleep. Now, go.'

'No really, you don't have to do that.'

Margaret raised her hand to silence Stella.

'Well, then thank you very much, that's so kind of you. See you in a bit.' She turned and went down the steps to join Emily.

'You have no idea how lucky we are to have weather like this,' she said, picking up the rucksack by her feet and slinging it over one shoulder.

They set off down a path leading away from the castle through a small wood, which soon gave way to open land with gentle hills sweeping away to the sea. The fields were dotted with sheep and Highland cattle, their comic faces watching the women closely as they walked past.

'Which island is that?' Stella pointed up ahead.

'That's Coll.' Emily looked towards the island in the distance, then turned to her right. 'And over there is the Ardnamurchan Peninsula. If you ever get the chance, you must go. It's so beautiful, like a fairy tale.'

Stella laughed. 'I'm slightly over fairy tales.'

'Ha, yes. Sorry.' Emily nudged Stella. 'Right, up here. You've got to see these.'

They walked just off the track and along a small path to three seemingly random stones standing up on their sides like soldiers, a circle of small boulders around them.

'What are they?' asked Stella.

'Standing stones. Some kind of Stone Age meeting place, apparently. I rather like their randomness, the fact that no one really knows how long they've been here or even why they're here in the first place. Not everything has an explanation.' Emily checked her watch. 'Perfect timing. It's low tide about now, so the pools will be ready and waiting for us. Up here.'

Stella put her hand gently on one of the stones. It felt cool to the touch. A small shiver ran down her arm.

She turned to follow Emily and they headed back to the path and continued towards the sea, past the ruins of an old fort and down to the shore, where, just as Emily had said, a series of small natural bathing pools sat with water so clear Stella could make out the rocks and stones underneath. They picked their way down through the rough grass and Emily laid the bag down a few steps away from the edge of the water.

'So, the trick is to not think about it for too long. Just keep walking and get in the water as quickly as you can.' Emily was stripping off down to her swimming costume as she talked. She pointed to the bag. 'There's a costume in there for you. I'm getting in.' With that, Emily turned and walked straight into the water, launching herself with a delighted yelp.

Stella riffled around in the bag and quickly stripped off behind a small rock, almost toppling over in her hurry to get the costume on. She walked to the edge of the pool, the stones pressing hard beneath her feet. She took a deep breath and started walking, one foot in front of the other until the water was up to her waist, not daring to stop in case she couldn't start again. The sun sprinkled the surface of the sea with glittering light.

'After three!' shouted Emily. 'One, two...'

Before she could get to three, Stella moved swiftly forward, swimming underwater before coming up for air in the middle of the pool.

'Look at you! You're like a fish!' Emily laughed.

Stella let out a shout of glee, the energy coursing round her body. 'It's bloody FREEZING!'

'I know, keep moving. Follow me.'

Stella swam on across the pool towards Emily, then spun round, treading water for a moment to take in the mountains in the distance, forests covering the gently undulating hills and the rocky outcrops on either side of her.

'Bit further?'

Stella nodded.

She swam on beside Emily, strong strokes carrying her forward. And with a smile, Stella realised it was the first time since Simon had gone that she felt like she was swimming towards something rather than away from it. More than that, she felt alive. Present. Hopeful.

* * *

After their swim, they sat wrapped in towels on a small grassy patch just up from the shoreline, eating the bacon rolls and drinking hot, milky coffee from tin cups. The gulls argued loudly overhead and Stella and Emily watched as an otter sniffed its way through the rocks just below them, its sleek brown fur the same colour as the seaweed it was foraging through. A little further out, a second otter swam on the surface of the sea, disappearing every now and again before coming up to have another look around.

'No wonder you hardly leave this place.' Stella took a mouthful of her roll.

'I know, it's not easy to leave.' Emily sighed. 'But there are times when I do wonder if I'm just hiding away. Like, I know what my life holds up here. No surprises. Well, usually.'

They exchanged a look, making them laugh.

'I am sorry for just turning up. I'm not really sure I explained my thinking.'

'You don't have to. But I'm hoping it's helped in some way, so you can move on or whatever. Not that I'm one to really talk about moving on.' Emily cradled her coffee cup, looking out across the sea.

'How about we both agree to stop giving ourselves a hard time over Simon?' Stella stretched her legs out in front of her. 'I've spent so long thinking about him, about what happened. Seriously, it's been like a full-time occupation since he left. And I don't want to do that any more. I'm exhausted by it. Talking to you has made me realise we were on a hiding to nothing. This is Simon's doing. So instead of spending any more time wondering what I should have done differently, or what I did wrong, or what I didn't do...' Stella looked across at Emily, 'I'm going to leave here remembering how I feel right now. And that is ready to live again. Happily, without him. If I can do that, you have to promise me that you'll not just hide away here forever. In fact, I want you to come and visit us in London. Not that it's a patch on this place, but we could go to some lovely restaurants, see some sights. I'll definitely have to take you to some of the food markets, I think you'd love it.'

Emily smiled at her new friend. She held her tin mug up. 'To moving on.'

Stella raised hers to meet it. 'To moving on.'

They sat for a few moments, then Emily stood up and held out her hand to take Stella's now empty mug. 'Right, we'd better get going, I don't want you to miss that ferry.'

As they walked back up towards the castle, Emily told Stella a potted version of Margaret's story and Stella vowed to come back again one day with the children, thinking how much they'd love it.

Driving back along the road to Tobermory, they talked easily. Stella asked about the boy Emily had mentioned the night before, the one who first broke her heart. Emily told her about the fisherman, how she'd tasted her first malt whisky on that beach. In turn, Emily asked about Stella's life back in London, listening with interest as Stella talked about her father, step-mother and sister and her friends. Emily loved the sound of Stella's book club; the fact that they'd only ever managed to all finish the same book at the same time once had made her laugh.

The women pulled up at the ferry terminal just in time to watch the ferry dispatch its latest batch of day trippers on to the island. Emily got out of the car and grabbed Stella's bag from the back seat. Bertie sat up as Stella gave him one last rub behind the ears.

Emily handed Stella her belongings.

'Thank you so much. I can't even... I don't know what to say, other than thank you.' Stella dropped her bag at her feet and hugged Emily.

'Well, for what it's worth, you've helped me too. And I'm really glad you came, even if it was a little bonkers.' Emily hugged her back just as hard.

Stella laughed. 'I'm sorry, it was a little left-field but...' she sighed, 'I'm so glad I found you.'

'I'm glad you found me too.' Emily smiled. 'Now go or you'll miss your ride.'

Stella waved from the top deck of the ferry before Emily got into her car and swept the car round back onto the road, waving out of the window as she drove away.

Stella took a seat on one of the red plastic chairs at the back of the boat, watching the island recede in the distance. After a while, she picked up her bag and moved to a seat at the front, facing forwards. She thought about the previous evening, silently thanking the universe for making hers and Emily's paths cross as they had done. Of course, she wished she'd known about what had happened with Simon and Emily before now, but she knew that wasn't how life worked. It was time to stop waiting for him to come back, saying he'd made a terrible mistake. In fact, the mistake had been falling in love with him in the first place. And now she knew she wasn't the only one.

26

'Well, how did it go?' Caroline's voice crackled down the phone as Stella watched the passing landscape through the train window.

Stella lowered her voice, despite having the carriage to herself. 'Really well. Although,' she closed her eyes for a moment, 'I still can't believe I went.'

'So, what happened?'

'I found Emily before I even got to the island, turns out we were on the same ferry. She'd been back to see her parents on the mainland.'

'Wait, you didn't just go up to her?'

'No, she saw me at the bus stop. Knew I'd be there until morning unless she gave me a lift.'

'Seriously?'

'I know. Weird. I couldn't bring myself to say anything at first, then I blurted it all out and thought she might leave me at the roadside. Thankfully, she didn't. In fact, we sat up until late talking and, honestly, Caroline, it felt like talking to an old friend rather than a complete stranger.'

'What did she have to say about Simon?'

'Quite a lot, as it turns out. I'll fill you in properly when I see you, but basically, it's not the first time he's done this. Which, even though it doesn't fix anything, makes me feel like I know more about what I'm dealing with here. Or rather, who I'm dealing with. It just makes me wonder why I didn't see him for what he is.'

'Listen, Stella, none of this mess is your fault. And, anyway, you are clearly far better off without him.'

'I know that now, but it doesn't make it that much easier. I'm worried about the children, about coping on my own – even though I know how lucky I am to have you all. It's going to be hard and that's before I've even thought about what happens when he does finally resurface.'

'Let's worry about that when it happens.' Caroline's voice was calm, reassuring. 'Listen, I'll let you go, but just to say, I spoke to Susie this morning and everything's fine at home. I'm not sure your children have eaten anything but pizza for three days though.'

'I left them loads of stuff in the fridge...'

'I know, but Dad's clearly a soft touch. Safe journey and text me when you get home.'

'I will. Love you.'

'Love you, too.'

Stella sat for a moment, familiar worries starting to crowd her mind. She took herself back to how she felt in the sea that morning, remembering how her head had felt clear. There had been no sense of panic or overwhelm. But like a slow rising tide, she could feel the fear creeping back in.

She took out her laptop, deciding that work would at least take her mind off thinking about what lay ahead. The home screen greeted her with the familiar picture again, the one on the Greek beach. She still hadn't been able to bring herself to change it. Stella looked at the photo more closely, studying Simon's face. *Who are you?* she thought. She'd looked into those eyes so many times and yet, now, it was like looking at somebody that she used to know, or perhaps had never known at all.

She typed in her password and set up a connection, then went to look at her emails. Scanning down the names, she saw one from her solicitor. Opening it, she read it and hit reply. Yes, she would like another meeting and, in the meantime, please could they start divorce proceedings. She hit send, shut down her laptop, plugged in her headphones and watched the world fly past her window.

* * *

Later that night, Stella sat at her kitchen table with her father and Susie. An open bottle of red wine sat between them, almost empty. Tea lights gently flickered in their holders. They listened as she told them about her trip and, slowly, the whole story came out. About the missing money, the family she'd known nothing of and Simon's history of leaving, seemingly without so much as a backward glance.

'I've been honest with the children; told them I don't know when their father is coming home. But what I now know is that I have to move on without him.'

'So, if he were to turn up on the doorstep right now...?' asked her father.

'I'd tell him to leave.' Stella looked determined. 'I've spent so long thinking there must be an explanation, that we can fix it – whatever it is – but I don't think that any more. It's not just that he left me. He left our family. He stole money from us.'

'I'm so sorry, Stella.' Susie reached across the table and squeezed Stella's hand.

'Divorce is the only option now. I'm seeing my lawyer next week to discuss it.'

'Well, if there's anything you need us to do, just say.' Her father spoke softly. As awful as it was to see her like this, he felt a small pang of relief to see that determination back in his daughter's eyes. Much as everyone thought Caroline was the stronger of the two, it was Stella who'd had the same inner strength as her mother.

'I will, thank you. Now, you should go. You must be tired.'

Her father laughed. 'Well, it'll be nice to have a lie-in in the morning, but honestly, the children have been so good. They've missed you.'

'I know, Dad. Thank you. I can't tell you how much I appreciate it. Talking of which, I bought you something to say thank you.' She went to fetch a bottle of whisky from her bag that she'd bought just before boarding the train at Glasgow. 'It's made at the distillery at Mull. Single malt, proper stuff.'

'Well, thank you, what a treat.' He took the bottle and studied the label.

'And, Susie, this is for you.' Stella handed her a book she'd picked from the bestsellers shelf in the bookshop at the station. 'It's had a good write-up.'

'Oh, thank you! You didn't have to do that, but I'm glad you did. I've been dying to read it.'

'I mean it, I don't know what I'd do without you both.'

Stella waved them off at the door, then returned to her kitchen. She was exhausted but happy to be back home. She blew out the candles on the table, noticing that the broken light bulbs she'd been meaning to replace for weeks had been changed. Smiling to herself, she put the glasses in the dishwasher and turned out the lights. The children's packed lunches could wait until morning.

She let Percy out into the garden for a moment and checked her phone as she waited by the open back door. A new message from Liz flashed up on the screen, asking Stella if she could give her a ring when she had a moment. Her daughter was in the same class as the girls, so Stella hoped there wasn't anything going on at school she needed to worry about. Seeing Liz was still online, Stella called her back. The phone rang a few times before she answered.

'Hi, Stella, thanks for calling me back.'

'Hey, Liz. I'm sorry it's so late, but I saw that you were still up, is everything OK?'

There was a pause.

'Stella, I didn't know whether to say anything or not because I'd heard... I didn't want to get involved.'

Stella's stomach dropped. 'Liz, what is it?'

'It's just that I was at a meeting today at an office in St James's.'

Stella remembered as she said it, Liz worked for an accountancy firm.

Liz lowered her voice. 'I shouldn't really be telling you this.'

'Please, Liz...'

'OK, but you didn't hear this from me. There was a woman in the meeting, we do her accounts. She's an investor in various businesses, including yours. Annabel Collins.'

Stella tried to keep her voice as calm as she could. 'What about her?'

'She took a call while we were in the meeting. I saw the name flash up on her phone. Simon's full name. Maybe it's just a coincidence but the way she spoke to him was... well, they clearly know each other pretty well.'

Stella leaned against the door frame. She felt winded.

'Stella?'

'Yes, sorry, Liz. I'm here.'

'Like I said, I could lose my job telling you this, but I'd heard what happened and I just thought you should know. Please, please don't say I told you.' Her voice shook a little.

'No, of course I won't. Thank you. You didn't have to do this, I understand that.' Stella let out a long sigh. Just when she thought an end to the pain was in sight, she realised this might just be the beginning. 'Thank you, Liz. And I really appreciate you telling me.'

Stella hung up and called Percy in. She closed the door and turned off the lights before heading upstairs, looking in on her children as she passed their rooms, all fast asleep.

Exhausted, she climbed into bed and lay in darkness listening to the sounds of the city until it was light outside.

27

'And you're sure this is what you want to do?'

Stella sat opposite her solicitor, desperately trying to keep her composure. She wanted to scream, *Of course this isn't what I want to do! I want my life to not have been completely screwed up by someone who, as it turns out, has betrayed me in more ways that I ever thought possible.* Instead, Stella nodded slowly. 'Yes, it really is.' She'd gone to the office that morning for their usual Monday morning planning meeting, delivered the news about the potential new account to her team and then said she needed to be out for a couple of hours as she had an appointment with her lawyer.

Since finding out about Simon being in what she assumed was close contact with Annabel Collins, she'd not told anyone. Her instinct had been to go straight on to the book club group chat for some instant moral support or to her father or Caroline for advice, but in this case, she already knew what she had to do. She needed to divorce Simon. And she needed a plan. The night after she'd spoken to Liz, when all the kids were in bed, Stella had sat at the kitchen table and started writing that plan. Having spent so many months wondering about everything – where he was, who he might be with, even – she didn't want to waste a second more waiting for answers that might never come.

The plan covered everything she wanted from the divorce, from the financials – the house to the business – and, most importantly, how she wanted them to manage parenting between them. Pages and pages of scribbles were slowly condensed down until she had just one page, with a Post-it note covering each area listing her wishes.

It was a brutal process; she went from feeling absolute rage to sheer sadness as she wrote, but by the time the clock on the wall struck midnight, Stella had it all down on paper. She had then opened her laptop and typed out a list of questions for her solicitor, emailed them over ready to be discussed further at their next meeting.

By the time had Stella closed her laptop, her head was pounding, her fingers weak but she had also felt surer about it than anything she'd done for months. She had gone upstairs, splashed cold water on her face, undressed and fell into bed. She had slept until dawn.

Now, here she was, in her solicitor's office, the piece of paper on the desk between them. Her solicitor leaned over to study it more closely. She was similar in age to Stella, smartly dressed in a dark sleeveless dress, her blonde hair cut into an immaculate short bob, a slick of red lipstick on her lips. She pointed at the paper. 'And you say you haven't spoken to him yet, but you'd like me to contact him with notice of divorce papers. Do you have grounds for divorce? When we last met, he'd recently left, but if I remember correctly,' she looked at the screen in front of her, 'you didn't know if or when he was coming back.'

'Yes, that's right. He left, he didn't make contact, still hasn't, but now I have reason to believe he's with someone else. But I don't want to divorce him on those grounds. Not unreasonable behaviour or adultery.' Stella sat up and looked straight at her solicitor. 'I'd like a no-fault divorce.'

The solicitor sat back and looked at Stella. 'But from what you're saying, you could have any number of reasons to divorce him. Are you sure?'

'Yes. I don't want to have to cite the reasons. We were fine, or so I thought.' Stella clenched her fist. She'd run over this so many times in her head before coming today. She knew she had to see it through. 'The point is I want this marriage to be over and I really don't want to fight about it. However, I do want to see him to discuss this,' Stella tapped the piece of paper, 'so that I can tell him what I want.'

Her solicitor sat forward again, looking at Stella's wish list. 'And you think he'll go for this. Put the business back in your name, put the house back in your name.' She moved her finger further down the page as she spoke. 'Agree to have the children every other weekend if that's what they want too.'

'Yes, I haven't spoken to the children about that yet. I won't until I've got an agreement with him.' Stella dug her nails into her palm, reminding herself that as much as she might never want to see him again, the children would want to see their father. And that, Stella reminded herself, his reasons for leaving were for him to explain, not her.

'And even though you haven't heard from him for, how long is it exactly?'

'Four months.' Stella blinked. 'And three days.'

'But you think he'll respond when he receives the divorce application?'

'Yes, I'm sure of it. I want you to tell Simon he needs to contact me to have a meeting once he's seen our requests. He needs to text me so that we can set up a time and it must be just us.' Stella took a breath. 'And could you also say that Emily says hello?'

The solicitor looked at Stella, one eyebrow raised.

'Stella, is there anything else you want to tell me? Anything I should know?'

Stella held her solicitor's gaze. 'No.' She felt her cheeks redden. She'd always been a terrible liar, but she didn't want to share Simon's secrets, not until she'd had a chance to look him in the eye and ask him about them herself.

'OK then, I'll prepare the papers and send them to the email and address you've given me.' She looked at the address Stella had written down. 'This is a business address in St James's.'

'Yes,' said Stella. 'I have a feeling if we send the papers there, they'll get to him.'

'In that case, I'll get on to it as soon as I can.'

As Stella stepped out of the office into the bright London light, she looked at her watch. She had an hour before it was time to collect the children from school so she decided to walk some of the way home, crossing the river over her favourite bridge and heading through the park. She found an empty bench and sat for a few moments; the air warm on her face. The meeting had been harder than she'd imagined, but Stella knew the really tough one was yet to come.

She took out her phone and typed a message to the book club group, asking if anyone was free for a chat over a glass of wine at hers later that evening. They all answered immediately. Sarah said she'd bring wine, Lucy said she'd bring snacks. Bridget sent a string of excited face emojis. Stella sent them a message back saying she'd see them later, then turned her face back to the sun.

* * *

'What's for tea, Mum?' said Max, dropping his school bag just inside the front door.

'Excuse me, that doesn't live there, does it? Pick it up and hang it where it belongs. Have you got homework?'

'Didn't get any today,' Max called over his shoulder as he took the stairs two at a time.

'Do not even think about turning the TV on until your room doesn't look like it's been burgled, Max!' Stella called up after him.

'Mum, where's my gymnastics stuff?' Millie looked at Stella, eyebrows raised.

'Shit! Gymnastics. I totally forgot,' Stella cried.

'You said shit.' Isla loved an excuse to repeat any bad language she heard.

'I did, Isla. But I didn't mean it. What time does it start, can you remember?' Stella looked from Isla to Millie, hoping for an answer. They both stared back. 'Right, hold on. Let me check.'

Stella went into the kitchen to find Percy asleep in his basket.

'Hey, why didn't you come and say hello?' She walked over to his bed and he looked up at her, not even bothering to raise his head. 'Oh no, what's wrong with you?' She bent down and gave his head a stroke. 'Please don't be ill, not now.'

She looked at the fridge, hoping to find the piece of paper with all the gymnastics class timings on it.

'There are five hundred bits of paper stuck to this fridge, but the one I'm looking for isn't here. Obviously,' she said, to no one in particular.

She scrolled through her phone to find the email, only for her phone to ring while looking at it. It was the dog walker, a part-time luxury she'd afforded herself not long after Simon had left.

'Hey, Jen, I was just about to call actually. Was Percy all right today?' Stella looked at Percy lying in his basket.

'Hi Stella, I wasn't sure if you'd seen my message. Percy got his nose into a discarded bin bag on the common today, it was on the floor by one of the bins so I've no idea what he might have eaten. He got there before I could stop him, I'm so sorry.'

'Don't worry, it's not your fault. I'll keep an eye on him.' Stella caught Percy's eye. He looked guilty as charged. 'I'm sure he'll be fine but thanks for letting me know. Bye, Jen.' Stella hung up and went back to riffling through the papers to find out what time she needed to be at the community centre with Millie.

'Got it! We've got half an hour.' She held a piece of paper above her head triumphantly. Her phone rang again. She reached for it and looked at the screen. It was her sister. She decided to leave it ringing, instead putting her phone down on the side and taking a pot of pasta sauce out of the freezer for later. Picking up the overflowing laundry basket, she riffled through it to find Millie's leotard and tracksuit. Holding them up, she called out to Millie to let her know she'd found them.

Just then, Max came into the kitchen in his football kit. 'Mum, can you walk me over the road, I've got practice in half an hour.'

'I thought it was tomorrow?'

'No, Mum, it's today.'

Stella could almost hear the plates crash as they stopped spinning one by one, smashing to the floor. She took a deep breath. 'Go and tell your sisters and we'll walk over together.' She stepped over the washing basket, then kicked it into the storage cupboard by the side of the back door so she could pretend it wasn't there for at least another day.

Just then, the dog got up, made a hideous retching sound and promptly threw up on the kitchen floor.

'You have got to be kidding me,' said Stella, exasperated.

The twins ran into the kitchen, fascinated to know what was going on.

'Percy's been sick!' Millie cried, pointing at the floor.

'Ugh, gross,' added Isla, unhelpfully.

'Yes, thank you, girls. Millie, open the door so he can go outside.' Stella went back into the cupboard to get the mop and bucket. 'And, Isla, can you get some kitchen roll for me.'

Percy looked at her apologetically as he passed her on his way outside.

Stella felt guilty. 'Sorry for shouting.'

'That's OK,' said Isla, handing her the kitchen roll as instructed.

'I was talking to the dog, but thank you.' She sighed heavily.

'Are you all right, Mama?' asked Millie, quietly.

Stella looked at her daughter, her little worried face peering up at her. She stroked Millie's cheek softly. 'I will be. Now, let's get this mess cleared up.'

28

'Where did you get these?' Sarah held up a crisp before popping one into her mouth.

'No idea, I found them in the cupboard at home. Al must have bought them the last time he went to the supermarket. Not that he goes very often, but the best thing is, when he does, he buys all the things I'd like to buy but don't. It's like I'm pre-programmed to pick up only the boring stuff. Pasta. Tins of tomatoes. Washing powder. Loo roll,' said Lucy, picking up her glass. 'But when he goes, he comes back with absolutely nothing essential, or useful. Only things like that.' She nodded at the bowl of crisps. 'Which is annoying, but actually quite good.'

Sarah laughed, pushing the bowl across the table to Stella. 'Here, try them, they're so delicious.' They sat round Stella's kitchen table, an open bottle of chilled Albariño in the middle.

'I'm on the olives,' said Stella, 'and the taste is taking me straight back to Florence. Do you remember the really fat ones we ate in that bar on the first night?'

'I remember the negronis,' said Bridget.

'Remember those insanely good sandwich things in the market?' said Sarah, closing her eyes at the memory.

Lucy nodded. 'So good.' She topped up everyone's glasses, then stole a quick glance at Sarah and Bridget while Stella's back was turned as she grabbed something from the oven. 'Ask her,' she mouthed at them.

Bridget cleared her throat. 'So, come on, Stella. What's going on?'

Stella came back to the table and put a plate piled with warm cheese straws between them. She sat down and put her hand on the stem of her glass, turning it slowly. 'I've asked Simon for a divorce.'

'Wait, you know where he is?' gasped Lucy.

'Not exactly. But I've got a pretty good idea who he might be with. I got a phone call last week from...' she remembered Liz begging her not to say she'd told Stella anything, 'someone. Please don't ask me who, it doesn't matter. Anyway, they were at a meeting with a client, someone they work for who also happens to be one of the investors in Star Pots. And when they were in the meeting, she saw Simon's name flash up on the screen of this woman's phone. From what she said, they sounded like they were a lot more than friends.'

'Oh Stella, I'm so sorry.' Sarah reached across the table for Stella's hand.

'Sorry, Stella, I know he's your husband, but, man, I want to throttle him,' said Bridget, matter-of-factly.

'I think we all do,' agreed Stella. 'But that's not going to help anyone, least of all me. So, I've thought about this a lot. As you know,' she looked at Bridget, 'he's stolen money from the business. And it looks like he's shacked up with someone with a lot more money than me. But that's the least of it.'

'Oh god, what?' whispered Lucy.

Stella took a sip of her wine and then put the glass back down, swallowing hard. She looked up at her friends. 'I found out something in Mull that goes some way to explain what I'm dealing with here. It's not pretty.'

She told them about Emily, how they'd sat in front of the fire in her cottage as Emily had recounted her story from meeting Simon to him disappearing pretty much as soon as he'd found out she couldn't have children. How devastating that must have been to find something like that out so young, only to be swiftly dumped by the man she thought loved her, was engaged to.

'Knowing that helps me understand why he pitched up in my life and wanted to get on with having a family so fast. I always thought it a bit sad that he seemed to come without any attachments – no family, no real friends, other than work colleagues – he explained everything away so convincingly. Turns out his mother died only a few years ago. He told me she'd died when he was small. And he'd never even known his father, so the whole thing about him being an alcoholic was just another story.'

'Oh Stella, I'm so sorry.' Bridget's eyes pooled with tears.

Stella took a sip of her wine. 'Simon wiped out Emily's bank account before he left.'

There was a silence as they digested what Stella had just said.

'Bloody hell. He really does have form,' said Lucy.

'Sadly, he does. But as awful as this sounds, and I can only say this to you, it helps me to know that. Because now I know I'm dealing with someone who lies, someone who doesn't care about other people's feelings and who will do whatever they need to do to make themselves feel better. Although I'm not sure better is the right word. I'll have to ask him that.' Stella picked up a cheese straw and took a bite.

'Wait, what do you mean? When are you seeing him?' asked Sarah.

'I'm not sure yet, but soon, hopefully. I saw my lawyer today. She's sending him divorce papers via the investor's office. Annabel Collins.' Stella paused for a few seconds, took a sip of her wine. 'I've asked for a meeting, just me and Simon, so I can talk to him. I've written down the conditions of our divorce, and when I see him, I'll then give him a chance to either agree or not. And if he doesn't...' Stella trailed off.

'What will you do?' Bridget asked, quietly.

Stella looked at the flame of the candle flickering in the middle of the table. 'I'm sure I'll think of something.' She looked up at them, her eyes steady.

'Oh Stella, I can't believe he's done this to you. Will you be all right seeing him on your own? Don't you want someone with you?' asked Lucy.

'To be honest, the thought of seeing him makes me stomach turn, but yes, I'm sure. I need to do this bit on my own.'

'We're all here, you know that,' said Sarah, quietly.

'Of course, I know that, thank you.' Stella raised her glass to them.

'So, what happens now?' Bridget chinked Stella's glass.

'I wait for his message.'

'What if he doesn't respond?' asked Lucy, reaching for a cheese straw.

'I'm pretty sure he will.' Stella smiled. Once he realised Stella knew about Emily, she suspected that would be enough to bring him to the surface, if only to find out what she knew. 'Who wants a top-up?'

* * *

The sound of a far-off siren reached Stella's ears and for a moment she stayed where she was, lost in a dream. But then she opened her eyes to find Max standing by the bed, gently shaking her.

'What time is it?' She looked at Max in his school uniform, then at the clock on the table beside her. Seeing the time started with an eight, she sprang out of bed. Throwing on some clothes, she told Max to go and wake the girls.

'They're having breakfast.'

'Really? Are they dressed?'

'Yes, I woke them up. We decided to leave you asleep.'

She'd gone upstairs just after eleven, not long after Lucy, Bridget and Sarah had left, but hadn't fallen asleep until well after four o'clock; she remembered looking at the time as she desperately tried to stop her mind from running through all the possible scenarios of the meeting that lay ahead. 'I must have fallen back to sleep... OK, you go down and ask them to get their bags ready, I'll be down in a minute. Thank you, darling.'

Max nodded and went back downstairs, deciding not to tell her she'd been crying out in her sleep.

Ten minutes later, they were all out of the door and on their way to school. Stella couldn't help but suspect that the children had all made a pact to behave that morning. There were no lost bags and not a single argument on the way to school. She dropped them off at the gates and headed back home to walk Percy before going to the office. Even he'd seemed to have got the memo about being good as gold, trotting behind her on the walk and showing no sign of having eaten anything he shouldn't have done the day before.

As Stella made her way around her usual loop of the park, past the playground and round the bandstand, she found herself thinking about the early days of their marriage. It had been so long since she'd dared to think about them, as if Simon had taken any happy memories with him when he left. But Stella thought right back to the beginning, to their honeymoon; how happy and fearless she'd felt. She remembered the small hospital room where Max had been born, how Simon had held her hand throughout. And when the twins arrived, how her world had been so totally turned upside down and yet, at the same time, how she'd felt this was always meant to happen. Simon was so proud of the children. As Stella ran through the milestones in their time together, she realised the happy memories all belonged to her too. They weren't Simon's to keep.

Her phone buzzed in her back pocket. She reached for it, calling Percy, who'd gone to sniff around a bench before looking at the screen and seeing a message from an unfamiliar number. She stopped dead in her tracks, staring at it. Taking a seat on the empty bench, she moved her other hand to the screen and tapped it to open the message. It took her a few seconds to focus on the words.

Where do you want to meet?

Stella couldn't believe her eyes. After all this time, with no idea why or where he'd gone, here he was. It was as if he was making an arrangement for after-work drinks, not a meeting with his wife who he'd not spoken to since the day he'd walked out. The message actually made her laugh out loud. How could he be so casual? Then she remembered. This was the real Simon, not the person she thought she'd married.

Stella looked at Percy sitting beside her, gazing up at her. She stroked his head. If Simon was where she thought he might be, at Annabel Collins' flat in town, it would take him about half an hour to get to the park. She checked her watch, then typed in a reply.

10 a.m. today. The bench opposite the house.

Stella had waited long enough. She wasn't going to waste a single day more.

29

Walking back across the park, Stella felt elated and nauseous all at the same time. It felt good to take control of the situation, finally. That and the fact that she knew if she left this confrontation any longer, she might lose her nerve. She let herself back into the house and dashed upstairs to have a shower and change out of the leggings and hoodie she'd thrown on in such a hurry that morning.

But instead of opening her own cupboard, she found herself opening Simon's and taking out the clothes in bundles, throwing them on to the bed. Soon, the pile of clothes, including suits and shirts, jeans and jumpers, covered the bed. She took out his shoes and made another pile on the floor.

Stella ran down into the kitchen to grab some bin liners and took the roll back upstairs. She started putting the clothes in, taking them off their hangers and stuffing them in as fast as she could. Shoes went in too.

Next, she opened the drawers in his cupboard, taking out T-shirts and gym kit, socks and boxers, stuffing them straight into more bags. She threw in ties, noticing the only one he'd taken was the one he'd been wearing that day, the one that had started this all off. She opened the huge sash window in their bedroom and, one by one, dropped the bags out onto the small lawn in the front garden below. By the time she'd finished, she was breathless.

Stella checked her watch. Fifteen minutes to go. She went back downstairs, deciding to forgo the shower, and sent an email to the office instead. She let Lily know she had a meeting with Simon and would be in later that afternoon. Catching sight of herself in the mirror in the hall as she passed on her way to the front door, she stopped for a moment and looked at her reflection. Her face was flushed, her hair escaping from the ponytail she'd put it in that morning. She looked into her own eyes, a sense of determination running through her.

Stella went to the sitting-room window and looked out to the bench on the other side of the road between two sweet chestnut trees. It was empty. She glanced at her watch, it was still five minutes before they were due to meet. Just then, a man came into view. Her heart lurched; she knew that walk. She watched as Simon took a seat in the middle of the bench, taking his trench coat off (since when did he wear a trench coat? she wondered) and folding it up next to him on the bench. She watched him from the window for a few moments, then went to the front door.

Stella reached for the latch and opened it. Percy appeared at the sound of the door, tail wagging gently. 'I'll be back soon.' The dog looked up at her, then sat down by the bottom of the stairs, sighing as he lay his head heavily on his paws. 'I promise.'

Crossing the road and walking towards the bench, Stella watched Simon shift position on the bench. She walked up and took a seat next to him, without looking at him.

'Hello, Stella.'

She turned her head to see Simon looking at her, wearing

sunglasses she'd never seen before. He took them off and smiled, the creases at the corners of his eyes as familiar to her as ever.

Stella took a deep breath. Much as she wanted to keep looking at him, she found herself turning her face away after a few seconds. He looked the same, but different. His clothes were different. And, she noticed he wore trainers. Simon never wore trainers, at least not that she knew.

'So, how have you been?'

Stella almost laughed. Instead, she pressed her lips together for a moment. 'Fine, you?'

'Yes, well. A bit stressed, obviously.'

Stella couldn't believe his choice of words, but if this was going to go her way, she knew she needed to stay as calm as she possibly could. She'd run through the conversation so many times in her head since deciding she wanted to meet him. Now she just had to stick to the script. She fixed her gaze on a spot on the grass in between the goalposts on the football pitch up ahead and took a deep breath. 'Simon, you left us with no warning. You walked out on your children.'

'Stella, I—'

'Simon, please let me say what I need to say. Then I'll listen to what you have to say.' She looked at him and their eyes met properly for a few seconds before he turned his face away. 'I don't know if you left me for someone else and, to be honest, I'm not sure I care any more. But I do know that you have lied to me, for years. That you are not who you say you are. Your mother didn't die when you were young. You didn't know your father, who may or may not have been an alcoholic. You left Emily when you discovered she couldn't have children. You came to London, you met me, got married, had children. All pretty quickly, at your insistence, if you remember.'

'Stella, it's not what you think.' He turned to her, putting a hand on her shoulder.

'Please don't do that,' snapped Stella. She took another deep breath. 'You stole money. From the business – our business. I've seen the statements.'

Simon stared at the ground, shaking his head. 'It wasn't like that...'

'You took money from your own family! And you cleared out Emily's bank account too, all those years ago.'

Simon didn't move. 'Who told you that?' His voice was cold.

'Emily did.'

Simon let out a small laugh. "She would say that.' He paused for a moment. 'How do you know Emily?'

Stella ignored his question. 'We both have proof of what you've done.' Stella took out her phone and held it up. 'It's all here.' She looked straight at him.

'What's all there?' His voice was steady, but she could see he was struggling to keep his composure.

'Statements from her bank showing you took all her savings. And as for Star Pots, it's taken a while, but we've got all the evidence we need to show how you took money from the business account without the proper authority. It's my business.' She put her phone back in her pocket.

'Half your business.' Simon shot back.

'Fifty-one per cent is mine, so I think you'll find it's more mine than yours.' Stella calmed her voice as much as she could. 'Now, I want a divorce and I have some very simple terms. I want the house and business back in my name. You will see the children every other weekend, once I know where you are living and I'm happy it's a good environment for them to be in. We'll agree on the financials. And...'

He went to speak, then closed his mouth again.

'And as long as everything is done in a civil manner as quickly as possible, we won't take the evidence to the police.'

Simon looked at her, his eyes blazed. 'We?'

Stella didn't flinch. 'Me and Emily.'

'You wouldn't dare!' His voice rose. 'Do you really want to put the children through that?'

'Of course not. But I would if it meant protecting them from you doing any more damage to this family.' Stella's eyes were steady.

'You can't threaten me.' Simon's face reddened, his voice now slow and deep and angry. She'd never heard him sound so menacing.

'No, Simon, you can't threaten *me*. This is how it's going to be unless you want everyone, including your children, to know the truth about you. About your lying, deceitful behaviour. Your choice. You can either turn up and be a good father to them and I won't tell them what you've done, or you disappear for good. I don't want you hurting them any more than you already have. This isn't about you, for god's sake, Simon. You can't just pick and choose where and when you show up in life when it comes to your own children. Technically, you shouldn't do that to the person you marry either, but clearly it's too late for that.' She delivered the words calmly and deliberately, much to her own surprise.

Simon started laughing, slow-clapping Stella. 'Wow, look at you.'

Stella's eyes flashed with anger, but she continued in the same measured tone. 'No, Simon. Look at *you*. You left me for another woman, who, as we both know, is ridiculously wealthy, not to mention ridiculously married. I'm not sure when you were planning to tell me that part...'

'Now, you listen to me.' Simon stood up from the bench and turned to face her.

'Please, go ahead. I've been waiting to hear this for a long time.' She sat back and re-crossed her legs.

'Like I said, it's not what you think. In fact, I'd been unhappy for some time.'

'Really? Then why didn't you tell me?'

He shook his head again. 'You wouldn't understand.'

'Try me.' Stella tilted her head to one side, looking at him.

Simon opened and closed his mouth like a goldfish for a few seconds, then shut it.

Stella waited for him to say something.

He sat back down again. 'I didn't mean for this to happen.' Simon shifted uncomfortably, leaning forwards, then back. He still couldn't look at Stella.

'Where the hell have you been all this time? You left everything behind!'

'It all happened so fast. At first, I thought it was just... Annabel was, is, very determined.'

'Please don't tell me you're going to blame her for what's happened. Simon, take some bloody responsibility!' Stella couldn't hide the exasperation from her voice. It was like dealing with a toddler who'd grown bored with his toys. 'Just tell me why, Simon. I really want to know.'

Again, Simon said nothing.

Stella steeled herself, taking a breath. 'OK, if you can't answer that, tell me how the hell you can leave your children like that? Have you thought how they might feel in all of this?'

'Of course I have! Every day I think about that, Stella. I know you think I'm a terrible father for doing what I've done...'

'It's doesn't matter what I think now! It's how they feel, Simon. You've left them, they're wondering what they did wrong. And I'm the one left trying to reassure them that you'll be back, or maybe not, but that they mustn't worry. But I don't have any idea what you're thinking or what you're doing, let alone why you've done what you've done.'

Simon slumped over, his head in his hands.

'The truth is, Simon, I think something better came along. At least, to you it seemed like something better. And then you got found out. Or rather, you knew it was only a matter of time before I found you out. All this time I've been searching for reasons, but I'm not sure it's any more complicated than that, not really. It's just that most people know that when the whole grass is greener thing happens in life, it doesn't mean to say you act on it. You did it to Emily and now you've done it again with me.'

She looked at him, his shoulders shaking slightly. He spoke, head down. 'I'm sorry, Stella.'

A moment passed, then Stella spoke, her voice quieter. 'Simon, I just want you to tell me why. And if you can't tell me now, then go ahead and figure that out in your own time, but in the meantime I've got our children to think about. That's all that matters to me right now. So, putting them first, I think you need to work out what you want: to live in her flat, which is where I presume you are, and not see your kids properly or find somewhere to live and build yourself a life where there's room for them too. Your call.'

Simon still wouldn't – or couldn't, Stella wondered – look at her.

When it was clear he wasn't going to say anything more, she slowly stood up from the bench. 'I guess, knowing you as I do now, you're weighing up your options to figure out what suits you best. I wasn't given that choice when you left, but I'm making up for it now. You've had the papers. I want a divorce and you will agree to it. You'll also pay back the money you took from the business, no matter how long it takes. I really hope I don't have to see you in court.'

With that, she made her way around the bench and started back towards the house. After a few steps, she stopped and turned to face Simon.

'By the way, your clothes are in bags outside the house. I suggest you come and remove them before they get nicked.'

As she walked away, she felt her legs shaking. In fact, her whole body trembled. But with every step she took, she knew it was time to leave the past – and Simon – behind.

Stella let herself into the house to be met with Percy by the door, tail wagging as usual. She grabbed her bag from the kitchen. 'Right, you're coming with me to the office today. We've got work to do.' She grabbed his lead from the hook by the door and together they set off to the office.

'And so, what that means for us is that if we're going to plug this hole here,' Lily squinted at the screen in front of her in Stella's office, pointing to a spreadsheet, 'then we have to make up this number in additional business.' She moved her finger and tapped the screen.

Stella looked closely. 'Well, that's achievable.' In fact, the number terrified her a little, but she didn't want to let Lily know she was panicking.

Lily looked back at Stella. 'In the next six months, really.'

Stella swallowed. 'OK, that's... a challenge.' She shifted in her seat. 'But if we all know what we've got to do, we'll be fine.'

'There is another option, as you know.' Lily held Stella's gaze.

'Yes, I know. But we're not going to let that happen.'

'Stella, it would fix our cash flow in one go.'

'Lily, I'm not going to sell any more of this business to anyone else. In fact, I want to buy it back from the investors. As soon as possible.'

'But the offer from—'

Stella put her hand up. The last thing she wanted to hear was Annabel Collins' name again. 'Please, Lily. I appreciate it's a big ask from the team, but I didn't start Star Pots to give it away to people who don't love it like we do. I mean, look at them.' She gestured to the office outside, a sea of familiar faces.

The receptionist put her head around Stella's door just then. 'I've got Caroline for you.'

'On the phone?' Stella went to pick up the handset on her desk, slightly confused.

'No, she's here. In reception. Shall I send her through?'

'She's here?' Stella couldn't hide her surprise. It wasn't like her sister to turn up unannounced like this. 'OK, yes. In fact, no. Tell her I'll be out in a minute. I'm really sorry, Lily, I've got to go.' She stood up and gathered her things from her desk, shoving them into her bag.

'No problem.' Lily nodded. 'Let's catch up later.'

'Thanks.' Stella went to shut down her laptop. She looked at the screensaver, now a picture of just her and her three children. She'd changed it just a few days ago and even though it was a relief to not have to look at Simon's face on the screen every time she opened it, at the same time it was a terrible reminder that he just wasn't around any more. Snapping the laptop shut, Stella put it into her rucksack and woke Percy up from his slumber under the desk. She turned off the light in her office and walked through the main office, Percy close behind her, calling out her 'goodbyes' as she left.

Caroline gave her one of her classic functional hugs, then looked her sister up and down. 'Wow, so casual.'

Stella looked down at her leopard-print leggings. 'We're very casual here.' She smiled at her sister, teasing her.

'Well, let's hope you're allowed into the restaurant dressed like that. I've booked us a table for lunch.'

'Where? I've got the dog!'

'The usual, I've asked for a table outside.' She looked at Percy. 'You've lucked out, my friend. It's a lovely day,' Caroline nodded towards the window, 'we can walk.'

'But where's your car?'

'I came up by train so I could have a glass of wine or three.' Caroline grinned. 'Might even go shopping afterwards.'

'OK, what's happened to you? Where's my sister, what have you done with her?' Stella laughed.

Caroline nodded. 'Yes, very funny. Come on or we'll be late.'

30

They strolled along the river to the restaurant, arm in arm, Percy in front. The sky had clouded over a little since the morning, but the sun was still warm. They caught up on the essential stuff, running through each of the children in turn, discussing how their father and Susie were. Stella asked Caroline about Philip and got the usual answer. According to Caroline, Philip was fine. Philip was always fine, thought Stella, but Caroline had a way of changing the conversation so that it never went any further when it came to discussing her and Philip's relationship.

They reached the restaurant just before two o'clock and were shown to a table outside overlooking the river. Within minutes, a waiter brought two glasses of sparkling Italian wine to the table and, soon after that, a small plate of bruschetta. They lifted their glasses and looked at one another.

'To my sister,' said Caroline.

'To mine.' Stella smiled.

They took a sip.

Stella put her glass down. 'So, what made you come all this

way, really. Come on, I know you. You've either got something to tell me or you're worried about me. Which one is it?'

It was Caroline's turn to smile. 'Both.'

Stella's eyes widened. 'Really?' She couldn't help but laugh.

'You go first. I want to hear all about Mull. How was it? How was the mystery woman?'

Stella sat up and coughed. 'Well, there's been a development. Quite a big one.'

'You've finally heard from him?' Caroline nearly choked on her wine.

'More than that, I've seen him.'

'Seriously?!'

'Yes, I saw him this morning.'

Caroline's mouth hung open. She was, for once, speechless.

'I know. It's a bit of a shock, but it all happened so quickly. I found some things out and, well, basically it left me with no option but to ask him for a divorce. I met him today to tell him what I want.'

'Wait, back up. What's happened? How did you find him?'

'One of the mums at school. Long story short, she was in a meeting and the woman Simon's now with took a call from him. She saw his name flash up on the screen and said from the way they spoke, they're clearly more than friends.'

'Oh, Stella, I'm so sorry. What a cliché.'

'She's one of the investors in the business. Annabel Collins.' Stella still found it strange to say her name out loud. 'Although, weirdly, knowing that he's left me for someone really wealthy makes it a little bit easier.'

'Really? Why?'

'I know it sounds ridiculous, but in Mull I found out stuff from Emily, the woman I met, about his past and his behaviour. He lied about his family. He left her because he found out she couldn't have children. He cleared out her life savings as a parting shot. It was the deposit she'd saved to put towards the house they were hoping to buy together.'

Caroline shook her head in disbelief. 'I cannot believe we're talking about the same man I've known for more than a decade. I mean, you know how I felt about him but still...'

'I know, it's terrible. But knowing he's done all these things sort of helps me understand what he's done to me. It's nothing he hasn't done before. Somehow, for whatever reason, he's able to move on from one life to another when he sees something better on the horizon. With Emily, it was children. With me, it was, I think, money.'

'But you had money!'

'I know, that's what Emily said. But he met someone who had more, a lot more, and who, I imagine, in his eyes probably seems to offer him more.' Stella shrugged. 'I think he saw himself in that life, which, to him, was more exciting than the one he had with us. And so, we were dumped.'

'But how can he just do that? How can he leave his children?' Caroline's voice rose again.

Stella shook her head. 'Honestly, it's something that I ask myself at least a thousand times a day. But at the start, it was ten thousand times a day. And in time, I'm hoping he will see them...'

'But he can't just walk back into the children's lives, surely.'

'Well, he can if he wants to. He is their father and I know the children still love him; they'll want to see him. I can't stand in the way of that, it's not fair on them, no matter how much I might hate the fact that he gets to do that. Caro, I've had time to think about this. And, believe me, this is not where I was even a few months ago. I was so angry at him. I still am at times, but I've been able to get used to life without him. I know we'll be OK. And now I know what I do about him, I don't want him in my life any more than he has to be.'

'So, what did you tell him today?'

'That I want the house in my name, the business fully back in my name. An agreement on when he sees the children. Proper financial agreements I'm happy with.'

'And what on earth makes you think he's just going to say yes to all that?'

Stella picked up her glass and leaned across towards Caroline, lowering her voice. 'Because if he doesn't, Emily and I will go to the police and tell them that he stole from us both. Simon knows he risks losing his new life if Annabel Collins finds out what he's done in the past. And that's the very last thing he wants to lose.'

'But what evidence do you have that he actually stole the money? I mean, I might not like him, but Simon's a smart man. Surely, he'll try to wriggle out of it by saying it was money from the business, so it was his anyway, don't you think?'

'You're right, he could. But he won't want anyone knowing what he's done. Not just to me, but to Emily too. Quite rightly, it's awful.' Stella closed her eyes for a moment. 'Although,' Stella held up her phone, 'I might have pretended to him that I had evidence on here about the stolen money from Emily, too. Just to be on the safe side. I mean, I'm sure we could find it if we really needed it, but it was so long ago.'

Caroline stared at Stella. 'You didn't!'

Stella smiled. 'I bloody well did.'

'OK, so what happens now?'

'I know it'll take some time, but if he agrees to a no-fault divorce, which I hope he does for all our sakes, it takes months rather than years.'

Caroline sat back in her chair and looked at her sister. 'You're sounding very calm about this. Are you sure you're all right?'

Stella sighed. 'Not really, no. I'm heartbroken. But at the same time, I know I can't change what's happened. He's not begging to come back. I don't even know whether he will step up and be a good father again. But I have to give him that chance, knowing I tried my best to make our family, fractured as it is, work. And to be honest, Caro, he's left me with no choice. At least I'm giving him one.' She smiled at her sister. 'Right, please can we order? I'm starving.'

Caroline smiled. 'I don't know how you've done it. You're amazing.'

They ordered their dishes: calamari with red chilli and rocket, followed by seafood risotto for Stella, and for Caroline, roasted red peppers, anchovies and borlotti beans, followed by ravioli stuffed with ricotta, covered with marjoram butter. Two glasses of chilled white wine replaced the empty flutes in front of them, a pear-scented Arneis from Piedmont recommended by Joseph when he'd come by the table to say hello.

As Stella squeezed her wedge of lemon over her chilli-flecked calamari, she remembered Caroline had said she too had some news. 'So, enough about me and my disastrous marriage... what did you have to tell me.'

Caroline laughed. 'Well, it's about me and Philip.'

Stella's face fell. 'Please don't tell me you're splitting up...'

'No, don't be silly. Philip and I will be married forever. I know it's perhaps not the most exciting marriage on earth, but he is kind to me, even if he is a bit of an old bore sometimes.'

Stella tried to interrupt through a mouthful. 'Oh, he's not...'

Caroline shook her head. 'Yes, he is, I know he is. I know you and Dad think he is too.'

'We don't!'

'You do. And, to be honest, so do I sometimes. But he does love me, Stella. And the boys. He's just not very good at showing it. It's the way he was brought up. You know, packed off to boarding school at eight years old. Never saw his parents. Anyway, that's not the point.' Caroline took a large sip of her wine. 'I realised, partly helped by coming to London to look after the girls when you went to Florence, that I totally love being here. I've been stuck out in the country for so long, surrounded by dogs and mud and fields and farm shops and fucking coffee mornings.' She looked at Stella, who was laughing despite having a mouthful. 'And as much as I love most of it, I really, really miss being in a city. I know it was only *Matilda* we went to see, but the whole thrill of being back in a theatre, with crowds and cheering and singing and whooping, well, it made me remember that I used to love all of that too.'

Stella eyed her sister, her glass to her lips. 'Caro, where is this going? And why do I feel worried. Are you going to join a West End show or something?'

Caroline burst out laughing. 'Of course not! I think I've left that a bit late. But I do have something to ask you.'

Stella put down her fork. 'What is it?'

'I've been trying to find a job where we live, but no one wants someone who's not worked, properly, that is, for years. I was out of the game for so long bringing up the boys. I watched you do what you did, with Star Pots, and I was so full of admiration, but at the same time, just a little bit terrified. It left me thinking, what am I going to do? And I think the reason I've been so horrible to Philip for years now – no, don't say I haven't, because I know I have – is because I'm unhappy. I'm bored. Like, really bored.'

'You're not going to go back to the civil service, are you?' Stella asked, clearly worried at the idea. She remembered how much Caroline hated it by the end.

'First you think I'm going on the stage, now you think I'm heading back there!' Caroline chuckled. 'No, I'm not sure they'd want me now. But what if I knew someone who could do with an extra pair of hands around the house one day a week in return for a bed for the night, as long as she doesn't mind me going off to the theatre or whatever else I might fancy doing in the evening?'

Stella's mind went straight to the overflowing laundry basket, the constant beeping from the dishwasher that she'd been meaning to get seen to for months and the list of chores that needed doing that just seemed to get longer every time she looked at it. 'Really, you would do that?' The thought of another pair of hands once a week, especially ones as capable as her sister's, was enough to make her laugh and cry at the same time.

'Yes, and it means I can drop in on Dad and Susie more too; I miss seeing them.' Caroline moved her roasted peppers around the plate, rolling them in the herby butter. 'Plus, as well as giving me a change of scene while hopefully being helpful, it'll give Philip a break too. It's quite intense, just the two of us at home. The boys are both fully grown adults and completely self-sufficient nowadays... well, almost. They're not around much and I think that might be because the atmosphere at home isn't great. Maybe by spending a little bit of time apart, we'll appreciate the time we have together a bit more.'

'You've really thought about this, haven't you?'

'Yes, I have. Between you and me, a few months ago I was thinking of leaving Philip. But then I realised this isn't just about him. It's about me, too. I need to get happy again. Then perhaps I won't be such a pain in the arse.'

'You're not...!'

'Oh, come on, I can be. We know that. But maybe what's happened to you made me think. I wish, more than anything, that your marriage hadn't broken down, but as you rightly say, he left you with no choice. But I do have a choice, Stella. I must make an effort too. And I haven't been. So, let's give it a go and see what happens. What do you think?' Caroline looked at her sister hopefully. 'Please say something, do you think it's a terrible idea?'

Stella wiped the tears from her eyes. 'You daft thing, of course I don't think it's a terrible idea! I can't think of a better way to try to solve two problems at once. Are you sure? It wouldn't have to be the same day every week, we could work it so it suits you.'

'No, for this to work, I want to treat it like a job. Same hours once a week in return for a bed. I can then help you with the school run one afternoon and the following morning.'

'So then, if it's regular hours, I'll pay you as I would if I had someone in to help.'

'No, you absolutely will not. I'm doing this because I'm your sister and I want to help. And, to be honest, you're doing me a favour.'

'In that case, we have a deal.' Stella reached for Caroline's hand across the table. She squeezed it with both of hers. 'I don't know how to thank you.'

'I'll try not to be too bossy.' Caroline winked at her.

'If you're taking on our washing basket, you can be as bossy as you like.' Stella laughed. 'Thank you, I really mean it.'

'It's the least I can do.' Caroline checked her watch. 'Talking of bossy, we need to get going if we're going to be at the school gate in time to meet them when they come out.'

Stella looked at hers. 'Blimey, where did the last hour go? Fine, I'll get this.'

'No, this is my treat. Now, get their attention while I nip to the loo. Back in a mo.'

As Stella waited at the table, her phone buzzed in her bag. Reaching for it, she turned it over to see messages on the book club chat asking how everything went. She opened her phone and responded, telling them it went as well as she could have hoped and that she'd tell them more as soon as she heard. Then she went to check her emails. Scanning down, Stella saw one from her lawyer's office. Opening it, she read the first paragraph and, with a gasp, put her hand to her mouth. Not only had Simon responded, but he was prepared to agree to the terms, according to an email he'd sent to Stella's lawyer. She read it again, not daring to believe what she was seeing.

Caroline came back to the table and sat back down. 'Is everything all right?'

'Read that.' Stella handed her phone across the table.

Caroline read the email, scrolling down to the end. 'Well, there's a turn-up. Looks like you were right. He really doesn't want anyone knowing who he really is.' She handed the phone back to her sister. 'You win.'

Stella took the phone and put it back in her bag. 'I did what I had to do.'

31

ONE YEAR LATER

'Can someone please answer the door?' Stella yelled from the kitchen over the noise of the girls' birthday disco in the sitting room next door.

'Got it!' Bridget went to the door, paper cup filled with pink Prosecco in her hand. She opened the door to find Lucy and Sarah, both in sequinned catsuits. 'What the hell are you two wearing?'

'We were told it was a disco,' said Sarah, 'so we've come dressed for a disco.' She did a shimmy to show her outfit off to full effect. 'It's a bit tight, actually. Not worn it for a few years. Better not throw any dramatic moves.'

'Hello!' The twins appeared at the door, their cheeks flushed with sugar, dancing and total overexcitement.

'Well, look who's here! Anyone know if there are any birthday girls in the house?' Lucy looked at Millie and Isla. Both shot their hands in the air. 'Well, that's lucky because we've got presents in here.' She handed them a canvas tote bag each.

'Thank you!' they chorused before rushing into the kitchen to show Stella.

'All good?' asked Sarah, kissing Bridget on the cheek.

'All good,' said Bridget. 'Come in, we're hiding in the kitchen. Max and his friend are managing the decks in the sitting room. We're just setting up tea.'

The three friends went through to join Stella.

'Oh, it looks amazing in here!' Lucy cried, looking at the balloons and bunting decorating the kitchen.

'You're here!' Stella cried, thrilled to see them. 'You really didn't have to come.' She hugged Lucy and Sarah in turn. 'Bridge, pour them a paper cup of something, will you? I've just got to throw some decorations on this cake.' She gestured to an enormous triple layer chocolate cake sitting on a cake stand on the island.

'We wouldn't miss our god-daughters' birthday party for the world!' Sarah laughed. She took the cups from Bridget and took a seat on the sofa in the kitchen. 'Jesus, how many have you got in there?'

'There's about twenty of them, I think. Told the parents to drop and run.'

'Best way,' said Lucy. 'And who made that amazing cake? Please don't tell me you did, or I'll have to hate you.'

Stella laughed. 'No, I did not. Susie dropped it over this morning; she made it for them.'

'Seriously?' Bridget eyed it longingly. 'It looks incredible.'

'Right, who wants to brave going in there with these?' Stella held up some packets of glow sticks.

'I'll go.' Sarah jumped up from the sofa and shimmied her way across the kitchen. 'Back in a mo.'

As soon as Sarah had left the room, Stella turned to Lucy. 'Is it me or is there something different about Sarah today?'

Lucy grinned. 'She had another date with the not-weird guy from work last night.'

'The sound man?' Stella looked hopeful.

'Exactly, the sound man.' Lucy smiled, then took a sip from her cup.

'No wonder she's glowing,' said Stella, laughing. 'He sounds lovely, no pun intended.'

'That's about date six, so he must be doing something right,' said Lucy, nodding. She turned to Bridget. 'And so, come on, how's it going with...' Lucy struggled to find the name.

Bridget topped up her glass. 'Sadly, that's not happening any more.'

'Oh no, why? I rather liked that one!' Stella seemed genuinely sad to hear the news.

'Look, it's not been that long since Neil moved out. I'm just not sure I'm ready for this whole dating thing quite yet. I've sort of forgotten how to do it. The last one just felt a bit forced, you know?'

Stella picked from a bowl of smoky bacon crisps snaffled from the children. 'It'll come back, I promise.'

'Oh, listen to you.' Lucy laughed. 'Such a pro, now.'

'Very funny. Look, I know it took me a while to get back on the horse, but I'm just making up for a bit of lost time, that's all.' Stella shrugged her shoulders at her friends, knowing they were as thrilled for her as she was.

The doorbell went again. 'I'll go,' said Bridget, sprinting to the door. The sound of shrieks and music came from the sitting room as Max came into the kitchen.

'Mum, can me and Ollie have a packet of crisps?'

'Yes, help yourself.'

'Thanks.' Max grabbed a couple of packets from the cupboard and went back out.

'So,' Lucy turned to Stella, 'what was Simon's excuse today?'

Stella sighed. 'Work, apparently. I don't know, I'm done

trying to make him see the children. I think he's so wrapped up in his new life...' Stella waved the thought away. 'Honestly, it's so boring now. It's hard for the children because they never really know when they're going to see him, he cancels so often. There's always some excuse. Maybe one day he'll get his act together, but I'm not going to hold my breath waiting for that to happen.'

Sarah came back into the kitchen. 'What did I miss?'

'Nothing, I was just saying I don't think Simon is coming today. He texted to say he's got caught up at work.'

Sarah raised her eyebrows. 'On a Saturday afternoon?'

'I know, it's pathetic.' Stella sighed. 'Anyway, boring. Who was that at the door?'

Just then, Bridget came back in with Caroline to a chorus of hellos. Stella hugged her sister. 'Where's Philip?'

'He's meeting me at the theatre later.'

Stella couldn't believe what she was hearing. 'Are you being serious? Philip, the same man you're married to? The one who absolutely hates going to the theatre?'

Caroline laughed as she shrugged off her coat, putting it over the side of the sofa. 'I know, I can't believe it either. And not only that, thank you,' she took a paper cup from Bridget, 'he booked the tickets himself and we're going for dinner afterwards and staying in town.' She looked at her sister and grinned.

'Are you sure it's the same Philip?' Stella laughed.

'I know, it is a bit of a turnaround, but what can I say?' Caroline laughed too. 'Ooh, I meant to say, look at this.' She reached for her phone and tapped at it a few times, then turned it round to show them the screen. 'Can you see that?'

Stella took the phone and looked closely. It was a photo of the front of the bookshop in Caroline's local town. 'It's your book, in the window!'

'Ah, look at that!' The Star Pots recipe book had been a great success, with another already commissioned.

'Let me see,' said Sarah, reaching for the phone.

Bridget, Sarah and Lucy all cooed at the picture of Stella's book in the window of a bookshop as if it were a new-born baby.

Lucy looked up at Stella. 'So bloody proud of you.'

Stella felt a rush of love, looking at her friends and sister in her kitchen. She couldn't imagine how she would have made it through the past year without them. After the shock and turmoil of those first few months, life had settled down, but it was still incredibly hard at times. She often had to remind herself that life might not have gone to plan, but at least she was now in charge of what happened next. And that was definitely something to be excited about. 'Thank you. And actually, I've been meaning to tell you. I had a card from Emily the other day.'

'Mull Emily?' asked Lucy.

'Exactly, and she's suggested something. How do you feel about another book club trip? Apparently we could stay in a cottage on the estate where the hotel is. Emily said it gets booked up, but if we're quick, she could get it for us for a long weekend or a midweek break.'

'Are you kidding? Definitely!' said Sarah.

'That sounds amazing!' added Bridget.

'I'm in,' said Lucy.

'You too, Caro,' said Stella.

'You don't want me crashing your book club...'

'Yes, we do!' They all chorused.

'Brilliant, I'll let Emily know, get some dates sorted,' said Stella.

The doorbell went again. She glanced up at the clock and said she'd go, leaving them chatting in the kitchen. She passed the sitting-room disco, popping her head around the door to see the twins and their friends twirling round the makeshift dance floor, glow sticks waving in the air. Max and Ollie sat on the stairs eating their crisps.

'I think that might be your dad, Ollie.'

Stella opened the door to see Charlie standing there, his dog sitting at his side.

'Hello.' He smiled at Stella. 'How's it going?'

She motioned to the room where the noise was coming from. 'Carnage, actually. Have you got time to come in for a quick drink? We're about to give them some cake. I'm sure Ollie might like some?'

Ollie looked at his father hopefully. 'Please?'

Charlie looked at Stella. 'Well, if you're sure I'm not imposing. I was just walking the dog. I'm happy to wait out here if easier.'

'Don't be so ridiculous, come on in.' Stella beckoned him in.

Percy came to the door to say hello to his new canine companion, tail wagging.

'What are we doing tonight, Dad?' asked Ollie.

Charlie scratched his head. 'No plans, Ol. It's just us tonight.'

'Can we go to the cinema? Max can come too?'

Max looked at Stella, his eyes lighting up. 'Please?'

'He's very welcome to. I mean, it would just be the three of us...' Charlie looked at Stella. 'Unless, of course, you might like to join us?'

Stella laughed. 'You're very kind, but I think I'm going to be clearing up here for a while.' Laughter came from the kitchen. 'And I've got a few friends that might be hanging around.' She looked at Charlie. 'But I'd love to another time. Now, come and have a piece of cake and some Prosecco from a paper cup.'

'Well, I can't refuse an offer like that,' he said, following her into the kitchen. He really hadn't planned to stay, but then again when did life ever go to plan?

ACKNOWLEDGMENTS

When I started writing my wine blog back in 2009, I never dreamt it would lead me to writing fiction books. I'm so grateful that it did and my first thank you is to you, lovely reader, for picking up this book and reading it. I couldn't do this without you!

Writing a book is a real team effort and I'm lucky to be surrounded by incredibly supportive people, not least my very special agent Heather Holden Brown and Elly James at HHB Agency. Thank you to Amanda Ridout and her brilliant team at Boldwood, especially my wonderful editor Sarah Ritherdon and to Nia Benyon, Claire Fenby and Megan Townsend. Huge thanks also to Sue Lamprell, Jade Craddock and Sandra Ferguson for their insight and expertise and to Alice Moore for yet another beautiful cover design.

Enormous thanks to my beautiful (and very funny) friend Helen Thorn for helping me better understand heartbreak and healing, she is a true inspiration. My thanks also to Louise Avery for her invaluable insights into life on Mull and to my friends and fellow professional winos Victoria Moore and Emily O'Hare for sharing their experiences of life in Florence. Thank you to Alie Plumstead and Charlotte Russell for reading early drafts of the book and telling me what they really thought and to my dear friend Bella Eccles for being brilliant, always.

Finally, thank you to my family for their constant encouragement along the way. Above all, I couldn't write the way I do without the love and support of my husband Ross and for that I am eternally grateful. Thank you, darling. Only love.

MORE FROM HELEN MCGINN

We hope you enjoyed reading *This Is Us*. If you did, please leave a review.

If you'd like to gift a copy, this book is also available as an ebook, digital audio download and audiobook CD.

Sign up to Helen McGinn's mailing list for news, competitions and updates on future books.

https://bit.ly/HelenMcGinnNewsletter

This Changes Everything, another wonderful read from Helen McGinn is available to order now.

ABOUT THE AUTHOR

Helen McGinn is a much-loved wine expert on TV and in print and an international wine judge. She spent ten years as a supermarket buyer sourcing wines around the world before setting up her award-winning blog (and best-selling wine book) *The Knackered Mother's Wine Club*. She is the drinks writer for the Daily Mail and regularly appears on TV's Saturday Kitchen and This Morning. Helen lives in the New Forest.

Visit Helen's website: www.knackeredmotherswineclub.com

Follow Helen on social media:

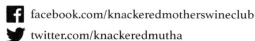

facebook.com/knackeredmotherswineclub

twitter.com/knackeredmutha

instagram.com/knackeredmother

Boldwd

Boldwood Books is an award-winning fiction publishing company seeking out the best stories from around the world.

Find out more at www.boldwoodbooks.com

Join our reader community for brilliant books, competitions and offers!

Follow us
@BoldwoodBooks
@BookandTonic

Sign up to our weekly deals newsletter

https://bit.ly/BoldwoodBNewsletter

Printed in Great Britain
by Amazon